SHATTERED TRUST

Tonya Hance

ISBN-13: 978-0-6927-4051-4
ISBN-10: 0-6927-4051-1

ABOUT THE AUTHOR

Tonya Hance is a Christian speaker, photographer, and writer who shares her love for God through spiritual analogies. She is passionate about hiking, caving, canyoneering, and exploring God's awesome world. She has a strong interest in discovering and photographing historical and archaeological remnants such as ghost towns, mining camps, and ancient Anasazi ruins.

Tonya also travels to various churches and events presenting a program entitled, "Step Into the Light", in which she incorporates caving analogies to help lead people to Christ by operating on the premise that without Jesus one lives in a spiritual cave of darkness. By combining caving techniques and Biblical references as analogies, she shows the audience their need for Christ's light in their lives.

This presentation is a result of her own spiritual journey of being stuck in a dark, hopeless place to experiencing the light and freedom of God's love. Tonya spent many years of her life as a painfully shy and withdrawn social recluse trapped behind strongholds and walls she had erected. She is a living example of how God can change people from the inside out, make beauty from ashes, and totally transform lives. Her favorite Bible verse is Philippians 4:13, "I can do all things through Christ who gives me strength."

To sign up for Tonya's blog and view her photography, please visit her website at www.tonyascapturedinspirations.com. Her blog is located on her website under the heading, "Adventures with Tonya". She may be contacted via e-mail at tonya@tonyascapturedinspirations.com

Shattered Trust

Tonya Hance

PROLOGUE:

Tara panted for breath as she hid among the boulders. She stared in fascination at the droplets of blood dripping from the ragged cuts in her skin. The thorn bushes she had frantically ran through sliced her like knives. As she sought to regain her breath, she gripped her throbbing side. The vicious punch was sure to leave a nasty bruise. She trembled as she heard Stewart's angry voice and heavy footsteps come closer. Heart pounding, she begged God to make her invisible. "Hide me among the clefts of these rocks," she prayed in desperation as she realized that she no longer had the strength to run. Catching sight of Stewart's leering face, she curled herself into a ball and waited for the beating to come as she thought to herself: *Why is my trust always shattered?*

Tonya Hance

~PART ONE~

~ CHAPTER 1~

"I am not going!" Tara exclaimed to her college roommate, Wendy.

"Why not? Don't you think it is time for you to get over this aversion to church? I don't understand why you hate God anyway." Wendy was volunteering at a popular Christian band's concert at her church that evening.

Tara sighed. Wendy was always inviting her to events at her church. Wendy knew nothing of her past and couldn't understand why Tara wanted nothing to do with God, church, or pastors. She was a great roommate, but if she knew Tara's secrets, she wouldn't be. She would make a big deal out of it and tell her to go see a counselor. It was much easier to pretend that her life was perfect like Wendy's.

Wendy was beautiful and popular with long, blonde hair that glistened in the sun and green eyes that sparkled with life. She came from a respectable family in Savannah, Georgia. Wendy had been a debutante and was part of the Junior League of Savannah. Her mom, a former Georgia Peach, had been a debutante in her day as well. She called

Wendy once a day to chat and sent her homemade goodies once a week. She even sent extra treats sometimes for Tara too!

Tara had no family and was close to no one. She had learned not to trust anyone because they always let her down. Wendy seemed great, but Tara was not about to let her walls down around her. Every friendship and relationship had ended poorly in Tara's life. It didn't pay to get close to anyone because eventually somebody would get upset with her and abandon her for not meeting their expectations.

Wendy paused in front of Tara. "Please come with me to the concert at church tonight! It is going to be so much fun! You will love it! I really want us to hang out and get to know each other more."

Tara responded, "I don't want to spend my evening with a bunch of goody two-shoes who don't live in the real world. I don't want to praise a God who doesn't even care about His people. That's why!"

Wendy looked hurt and disappointed as she left. Thoughts ran through Tara's mind. *I'm always disappointing people. Why couldn't I have just gone to the church with Wendy tonight? Instead, I hurt her feelings – again.* Tears welled in Tara's eyes as she fought them back. *I'm a horrible person to treat Wendy that way.*

Wendy was the nicest person Tara had ever met. She actually seemed to genuinely care about people. She was beautiful, outgoing, and popular. Wendy had never met a stranger and was a friend to everyone she met. Wendy was everything Tara was not but secretly wished she could be.

Tara didn't have any friends. Wendy was the closest thing to a friend that Tara had ever had. But, Tara told herself, *That is only because Wendy is my roommate. She is too nice not to speak to me.*

Most people ignored Tara. She wore baggy clothes to hide her figure and to avoid attention being drawn to her. Her stringy blonde hair was always messy, seldom brushed, and she wore no make-up. She was quiet and withdrawn but highly intelligent and had no problem maintaining a 4.0 G.P.A. She spent a lot of time reading and hiding from the world around her. She did not date at all. She knew all too well what men were like. *Poor Wendy must be disappointed to have me as a roommate,* she thought. *Wendy deserves someone who would laugh and hang out with her, not an antisocial roommate like me.*

Tara sighed as she laid on her bed and retreated into a book. Only in her books could she be safe. Tara was deep into a historical fiction story about a cowboy desperately in love with a school teacher when Wendy returned practically bouncing in excitement.

"Oh, how I wish you could have been there tonight! We had such a good turnout, and somebody actually gave their life to the Lord. You should totally come sometime!"

Tara ignored Wendy's chatter and returned to her book. Wendy missed the cue and continued.

"The band was talking tonight about joy – about finding joy in all circumstances just like Paul did. He was in prison, yet he was praising God! I want to have a faith like that!"

Tara looked up from her book and frowned. "A faith like that?" she questioned. "Why would you want to have a faith in a God that would allow you to go to prison in the first place for serving Him? Paul was beaten in prison! Beaten! He was a fool for praising God. God didn't care about him. If so, He sure had a funny way of showing it."

Wendy sat down surprised that Tara even knew those details about Paul as much as she was against God. Tara must have had some religious upbringing. She softened her voice as she explained, "Tara, the truth about God's love is not that He allows bad things to happen.

Rather, when they do happen because we live in a fallen world, He is right there beside us, walking with us. He cries when we cry. He hurts when we hurt. God was there with Paul in prison. That is why Paul was able to find joy. Paul's joy came from knowing God and having a relationship with Him. His joy was not based on his circumstances. Take Philippians 4:11-13 for example."

Wendy opened up her Bible and began to read. Tara rolled her eyes. The last thing she wanted was a Bible study.

"Not that I was ever in need, for I have learned how to be content with whatever I have. I know how to live on almost nothing or with everything. I have learned the secret of living in every situation whether it be with a full stomach or empty, with plenty or little. For I can do everything through Christ who gives me strength." (Philippians 4:11-13)

"See, Tara. Paul found the secret to life! No matter what he was facing, no matter what he went though, he was sustained by his relationship with Jesus. He had joy because of that relationship. Even in prison, even during the hardest times imaginable, Paul had joy because of Jesus. God used his imprisonment to spread the Good News that salvation is found in Jesus Christ alone."

Tara rolled her eyes yet again. "So, you are telling me that Paul had joy because God used him? God put Paul in prison and allowed him to be beaten in order to *use* him to spread the *good* news? Wendy, you are an intelligent person. How can you buy this crap? If God *uses* people in that way, that is just one more sign that He does not care. Would you want Him to use you in that way? Would you want Him to allow you to be beaten or worse so that his message can spread?"

Wendy smiled, "I would be honored for God to use me in a mighty way, and I hope and pray that my faith is strong enough to stand in the most adverse circumstances."

"Then, you are stupider than I thought," Tara angrily said.

Tears filled Wendy's eyes, "Tara, why are you so down on God? What happened?"

"None of your business. Now leave me alone". Tara pointedly looked at her book and began ignoring Wendy. She knew she had hurt her feelings as she could hear Wendy sniffling as she made her way to the bathroom they shared. Knowing Wendy, she was probably in there praying for her.

~CHAPTER 2~

Tara could hear Wendy stirring the next morning making breakfast in the kitchen. Recalling how she had hurt her feelings the night before, Tara pretended to be asleep to avoid confrontation. As Wendy left for class at Bridger College - a private college in the heart of Savannah that they both attended, Tara hurriedly got ready for the day. She skipped breakfast as she always did. She ate once a day, if that. She felt so ugly and huge when, in reality, she was quite petite.

She did not realize that she had rushed out the door without grabbing her wallet until lunch time when she had no money to purchase food. She sat alone at a small table in the cafeteria sipping water in her plastic bottle when Wendy approached with a tray overflowing with fries and a large, juicy burger.

"I noticed you weren't eating. I thought you might be hungry," she said softly.

Tara did not understand Wendy. She had hurt Wendy's feelings and made her cry last night. Yet, Wendy had bought her lunch! *Why is she being so nice to me despite how rude I was to her?* She frowned in confusion.

"Thank you," Tara muttered.

Wendy awkwardly stood in front of Tara. "Do you mind if I sit with you? I already ate, but I thought you might like some company."

"It's a free world," Tara said as she cleared her books from the small table. Wendy was not discouraged by Tara's standoffish attitude and sat down.

"Tara, I had hoped to talk with you this morning, but you were asleep. I'm sorry for pushing my beliefs on you last night. I don't know why you are so down on church and God, but you were right. It is none of my business. I just wanted to say sorry. I want so bad to be friends with you, but it seems like you don't like me at all."

Wendy paused. Tara stared down at her food and did not reply.

"If you ever want to talk, or if there is ever anything I can do for you, please let me know. I do want us to be friends, and I'm sorry for being so pushy. I just know what God has done for me and can't wait to share Him with others. Have a good rest of the day. I'll see ya later." Wendy stood up and walked away leaving Tara in deep thought. *Why was Wendy so nice to me? What does she want?*

Tara came home late that night after Wendy was in bed to avoid her. Wendy seemed like a nice person and like she wanted to be good friends, but if she only knew the truth about Tara, she would walk away in disgust. It was better to keep Wendy at arm's length. She wouldn't understand Tara's issues.

A few days later, Tara was approached by four jocks as she walked across the campus. They immediately began mocking her for her appearance.

"When is the last time you brushed your hair? You so ugly your momma took one look at you when you popped out, and she popped you right back in!" The guys surrounded her as they began hurling insults. Tara froze and began to shake in fear. She felt tears welling up in her eyes and immediately pushed them back. She had not cried since she was a young child. Jack had taught her not to cry; the punishment was always worse when she cried. Tara tried to walk away, but one of the guys stuck his foot out and tripped her. As she fell on the ground, she covered her face and cringed. Curling herself into a ball, she anticipated the blows with dread while the guys roared in laughter.

Just then, she heard a familiar voice scream, "Stop it! Back off now!" It was Wendy.

"Aww, Wendy. We're just having a little fun with the weirdo," one of the guys, named Jake, explained.

"Don't call her that and back off now!" Wendy demanded. She leaned down and helped Tara up into a sitting position as she put her arms around her. "It's okay, Tara. It's okay," she said over and over. Tara was visibly shaking as Wendy led her home.

Wendy enveloped Tara in another hug as they sat on their couch together. "Tara, don't let their words get to you. Don't internalize them. God doesn't make mistakes! You are beautiful to Him!"

"No, I'm not." Tara sobbed as the tears she had been trying to control finally spilled down her face. "He hates me! God hates me! I am a mistake! I am so worthless and ugly!"

"God loves you," Wendy insisted. "And, He has given me a Christian love for you. I want to be your friend if you will let me."

"You'll just leave," Tara sobbed. "Everyone does. Nobody cares about me."

"I do," Wendy insisted. "And, God does too. He cares about you so much that He made us roommates. He wants me to be your friend."

Tara couldn't remember the last time anyone had given her a hug. It was comforting in a way. Yet, Tara couldn't stand to be touched. She pushed herself away from Wendy's embrace.

"Tara, please trust me," Wendy pleaded. "Those guys were being mean, but you were absolutely terrified of them. Please talk to me. Let me be your friend."

"I can't tell. I've never told anyone." Tara continued to violently shake.

"You can tell me. I think I have already guessed anyway." Wendy looked at her knowingly. "You have all the classic signs."

"What signs?" Tara asked defensively.

"Well, the baggy clothes you wear, for example. You have a great figure, but you do your best to hide it. Your lack of care with personal appearance. You do your best to avoid attention from men. But, I think the biggest sign was how scared you were a little while ago of those guys."

"Anyone would have been scared of them," Tara defensively said.

"Yes, anyone would have been scared. But, you were terrified. The way you were crumbling yourself into a ball and shielding your face. I could be wrong. But, were you abused or umm raped?"

Tara stared at Wendy in dismay. "Why do you ask that?"

"I've actually guessed it for a while and have been praying on how to approach you about it. I could tell you didn't want to talk."

Tears rolled down Tara's face as Wendy embraced her once more. "Will you please talk to me?" Wendy asked.

"I've never told anyone," Tara began.

"I know. Neither did I until a few years ago." Wendy said.

Tara stared at Wendy. She had been raped? Wendy, the most popular, beautiful girl on campus. Wendy seemed so confident and cheerful.

Wendy took a deep breath. "I have shared my story so many times in the past couple of years that it has gotten easier to talk about. But, it still hurts. My grandfather lived with us, and he began molesting me from an early age. I didn't like the way it felt, but I didn't really know it was wrong either. I mean, it was my grandfather. I trusted him. And, he broke that trust.

"It was really hard. I was very quiet and shy growing up. I felt like garbage. I didn't know what was wrong with me. My grandfather made me think it was how to show love, but he was sick. Very sick in the head. I struggled for years to forgive him. I had so much anger built up inside for what he had done. Then, I met a friend in my senior year of high school who introduced me to Jesus. I learned what real love is about.

"I understand your anger at God for not intervening in what happened with you. But, Tara, it is not God's fault. That was the work of the enemy. There is evil in this world. Even though God can choose to intervene, sometimes He chooses not to. And, that is hard to understand. It is hard to understand why God allows pedophiles to hurt little children. It is hard to understand why loved ones die from cancer. It is hard to understand why my fiancé was killed in a wreck two days before we were to be married.

"Yet, I believe with all my heart that God is love and that He is there with us through it all. He may not move the mountains before us, but He sure does equip us to climb them! God can make good come out of what was intended for evil. He can make good things out of bad things. I know because I have experienced it in my own life. I am a new person in Christ! He has used my story, my willingness to be vulnerable and share it, to help others who have been in the same situation. It was not a coincidence that we became roommates, Tara. It was God's doing. He wants to bring healing to your life. And, I believe He wants to use me to help with that process."

Tara stared at Wendy in shock. Wendy was so cheerful all the time. She never would have guessed that Wendy had a background like hers or had experienced so much hurt. Could she really trust her with her story?

~CHAPTER 3~

Tara let the moment pass. As much as she respected Wendy, she just couldn't share her secrets with her. She shuddered as a memory of a stained toilet bowl flashed through her mind. No, she would never tell. Wendy might have been raped, but she wasn't psychologically tortured too. She would never understand.

A long, awkward pause passed between them. Wendy nervously broke the silence.

"We are starting up a new Bible study this Friday night at Unplugged. Would you like to come with me? There will be lots of food!"

Unplugged was the new young adult ministry that Wendy was a part of. They met every Friday night at the church as an alternative to going to bars or clubs. Instead of drinking alcohol, they sipped on flavored water and lemonade as they listened to praise and worship bands that rivaled some of the talent in Christian music on the radio. They also divided up into small groups each week for a lively discussion about the Scripture they were studying.

Tara remembered Jack's fire and brimstone preaching and shivered as she imagined a sweaty, bald guy screaming "Choose God or burn!" at the young adults in the study. Thanks but no thanks! She'd pass.

"I'd rather not. I'm just not into church," she told Wendy.

On Friday evening, Tara attempted to concentrate on her philosophy book she was reading for class as Wendy got ready to go to Unplugged. Wendy glanced over at the page Tara was reading. Friedrich Nietzsche's famous controversial statement, "God is dead", was written in bold letters.

Nietzsche became known for that statement which occurred in several of his works, in particular "The Gay Science". Nietzsche stated, "God is dead. God remains dead. And we have killed him. How shall we comfort ourselves, the murderers of all murderers? What was holiest and mightiest of all that the world has yet owned has bled to death under our knives: who will wipe this blood off us? What water is there for us to clean ourselves? What festivals of atonement, what sacred games shall we have to invent? Is not the greatness of this deed too great for us? Must we ourselves not become gods simply to appear worthy of it?" The Gay Science (Section 125, The Madman)

Nietzsche's works expressed his fear that the world would be plunged into chaos by the decline of religion, the rise of atheism, and the absence of a higher moral authority. The world's dependency upon God for thousands of years had given order to society and meaning to life. Nietzsche warned that society would be plunged into nihilism – the belief that traditional morals, values, and beliefs have no value - without that dependency upon a higher power. Nietzsche believed that accepting nihilism would be dangerous because it advocates reform in the manner of extremism in its belief that a society's political and social institutions are so warped that they need to be destroyed. In nihilism, life lacks purpose and meaning. If God is dead, if there is no belief in a higher power to give order to society and meaning to life, the value human beings give to each other decreases and life becomes meaningless. Although Nietzsche was an atheist, he considered the belief in God an antidote to nihilism.

By saying "God is dead," Nietzsche did not mean that he believed that God was living and had died. Rather, he meant that God was no longer the one ruling factor in society's belief systems. The absolute moral Christian principles that the Western world was based on was falling apart as less attention was paid to God and more was being put upon churches and organizations in the name of Christianity. As people moved from faith to works, they grew apart from their relationship with God because more emphasis was put on self-achievement. Nietzsche believed the so-called death of God would move society more into the belief of nothing – nihilism. By breaking the faith in God, Nietzsche struggled with the question - how does society maintain any system of values in the absence of a divine moral authority?

Nietzsche believed that people had killed God through their own lack of morality and hypocrisy as Christians allowed their thinking and behavior to go against their own religious beliefs and instead reflect popular, modern beliefs and values. In Nietzsche's mind, God was dead, and it was His own people's fault. In his writings, Nietzsche searched for an absolute basis in morality that went deeper than the sinking Christian values he observed.

"God's not dead," Wendy declared.

Tara looked up, startled.

"Nietzsche was wrong. God's not dead. He's alive and at work in the world today."

"Yeah right. If He is alive, He is just a dictator waiting to strike down all who don't please him. He is sitting on his throne with a huge smile on his face gleefully anticipating who He is going to throw into an everlasting fire. I don't buy it! I believe Nietzsche was correct. God is dead! The concept of God is dead! The Christian values and beliefs that restrained people's thinking for thousands of years is over and replaced by a better system. Look how advanced we are! We don't need a belief in a higher power anymore. Life is what we make of it. You live and then you die! That's it! So, you might as well make the best of it and get all you can get out of it." Tara rolled her eyes as she emphatically added, "If your belief in God gives you peace, that's great. I'm all for it. But, it's just not for me."

Wendy stared at Tara. "I will give you one hundred dollars if you come with me to Unplugged tonight."

Tara placed her book on the nightstand. "One hundred dollars! Are you serious? What do I have to do?"

"Nothing, just come. I want to introduce you to God."

"I've been to church before. I've met your God." Tara sneered at Wendy. "And, He is as mean as they come."

"No, I don't think you have been truly introduced to God. I'm not sure what man-made false image of God you were introduced to as a child, but I want to introduce you to the real God – the God of love."

"Love, yeah right! Church is filled with a bunch of hypocrites who pretend to care but don't really. All they talk about is what a sinner you are and how you are going to burn forever in a fire for your sins. And, they can't wait to give you a taste of what hell is like. My foster dad, Jack, was a preacher. He used to pull branches off a tree and hit me with them - in the name of God. I had welts all over my back, butt, and legs all because the Bible says, 'spare the rod, spoil the child.' And nobody in that church cared enough to stop him! They saw the welts on me and looked the other way." Tara crossed her arms defiantly as she stood up.

"They had to know what else he was doing too, but the fact of the matter is nobody cared. God didn't care! Church members didn't care! Neighbors didn't care! I hate church, and I hate God! But, I will go with you tonight to Unplugged - for three hundred dollars that is. I need a new laptop. Mine is running slow." Tara expected Wendy to back down at the ridiculous amount of money.

Wendy shrugged her shoulders. "Ok, if that's what it takes to get you to come. I have some money in my savings that I can pull out."

Tara stared at Wendy in amazement. She was really going to pay her three hundred dollars just to go to one night of Unplugged? Tara thought she'd better make sure they were on the same page."

"Umm, just to be clear. This is just for tonight – one night. Don't expect me to go again."

~CHAPTER 4~

Tara stared in trepidation at the three crosses on the roof of New Life, a non-denominational church, as Wendy parked her SUV. She hadn't been to a church since she was a child. Her second foster family had tried to take her to their church, but Jack's preaching on hellfire and his abuse of her had caused her to be terrified of it. The preacher at their church spoke of love and not God's wrath, but fear was too ingrained in her at that point. Her anxiety was noticeable, and her foster parents weren't equipped to deal with it. She only stayed with them for a few months before being placed with another family. As Tara closed the passenger door and stared at the church building, waves of apprehension rushed over her. Was the promise of three hundred dollars worth facing her fear?

Wendy smiled at her as they entered the church. "You are going to love Pastor Jonathan! He is so awesome!"

Wendy led her to the sanctuary. Instead of hard, wooden pews lining the room, it was filled with chairs with soft, padded seats. In the front of the room were guitars, a keyboard, and a set of drums waiting to be played. Wendy greeted some people and introduced Tara to them as they made their way to a seat. Tara sat down nervously, ready to bolt as Pastor Jonathan made his way up the stage.

Pastor Jonathan, a handsome man in his mid 20's, was dressed casually in jeans and a black t-shirt with the word "Unplugged" written on it. The noise in the room silenced as he began to speak.

"Welcome! I'm glad you all were able to come tonight. Welcome to Unplugged!" The guitarist let out a rip as he finished.

The audience cheered and let out some whoops. Tara looked around in astonishment. She had never seen people this happy for church before.

"Now before our band starts, I want to explain what "Unplugged" is for those who are new here. A lot of times, we hear people in church talk about how they want to get plugged in, or we tell you ways that you can get plugged in throughout our different ministries. Well, I don't want you to get plugged in. I want you to get unplugged! I want you to get unplugged from everything you think you know about God! I want you to unplug from what you have been taught in school! I want you to unplug from what you have heard in church!

"I want you to unplug from what you have been taught about God in the past and open your mind to learning who He is right now through His Word. In the book of Acts, the people of Berea didn't just blindly believe Paul and Silas's message. Rather, they searched the Scriptures day after day to see if they were teaching the truth (Acts 17:11). That is what "Unplugged" is about. It is studying Scripture for yourself to learn who God is and who He isn't instead of taking somebody else's word for it. Many of us have been misled our entire lives about God through false teachings. As a result, we have put God in a box. We have an image of who He is based on our experiences instead of knowing who He truly is based on His Word.

"Now, those of you who have been here before know what to do. If you are new tonight this might seem strange, or even a bit painful. In order to truly be unplugged in our study tonight, we must unplug ourselves from technology first. So, everyone hold your cell phones and tablets in the air and turn them off. Don't just put them on vibrate or silent mode. They will still be a tempting distraction to you. Turn them off and place them under your chair. Trust me. You will survive for two hours without technology!"

Tara stared as fifty people in the room simultaneously turned their electronic devices off and placed them under their chairs. Wendy nudged her and pointed at her cell phone.

"It's only for two hours," Wendy whispered. The girl sitting next to Wendy noticed Tara's hesitation and began to loudly chant, "Unplug!" Soon the room erupted in people shouting, "Unplug! Unplug! Unplug!" Embarrassed, Tara turned her phone off and put it under her chair. *Three hundred dollars better be worth this,* she thought to herself.

The band began to play. Soon, everyone in the room was standing up singing along to the words on the screen. Tara noticed people tapping their feet and dancing in place to the music. This was sure unlike any church service she had ever experienced. People seemed happy here.

As the band finished, Pastor Jonathan made his way back on stage with a smile.

"It feels so good to praise God through music!" he exclaimed.

"Tonight, we are going to talk about the question, 'Is God dead?' There are a lot of people today who think just that. Every day, we see tragedies on the news. Earthquakes, floods, tsunamis, shootings. The world seems out of control. Atheists and people of other religions are quick to say our God is dead, but is He? Turn in your Bibles to Daniel, chapter 1. If you didn't bring a Bible, you can follow along with the words on the screen."

Pastor Jonathan paused at the sound of rustling pages as people searched for the book of Daniel. As the room became silent once more, he continued.

"During the third year of King Jehoiakim's reign in Judah, King Nebuchadnezzar of Babylon came to Jerusalem and besieged it. The Lord gave him victory over King Jehoiakim of Judah and permitted him to take some of the sacred objects from the Temple of God. So, Nebuchadnezzar took them back to the land of Babylonia and placed them in the treasure-house of his god. (Daniel 1:1-2)

"You see, in Nebuchadnezzar's day, people worshipped many gods. The Israelites were taken captive from Jerusalem and exiled to Babylon in 605 BC. Nebuchadnezzar not only wanted to take the people of Jerusalem captive, but he also wanted to take their god captive as well. This was a common practice in those days. By taking the sacred objects from the Temple of God, Nebuchadnezzar felt that he had conquered God, that he had taken Him captive. In Nebuchadnezzar's mind, God was dead. And, he had killed him."

As Pastor Jonathan paused to let that sink in, Tara reflected on her philosophy book she had been reading earlier in the day about Nietzsche. He too had believed that God was dead.

Pastor Jonathan took a sip of water as he continued.

"One night during the second year of his reign, Nebuchadnezzar had such disturbing dreams that he couldn't sleep. He called in his magicians, enchanters, sorcerers, and astrologers, and he demanded that they tell him what he had dreamed. As they stood before the king, he said, 'I have had a dream that deeply troubles me, and I must know what it means.'

"Then the astrologers answered the king in Aramaic, 'Long live the king! Tell us the dream, and we will tell you what it means.'

"But the king said to the astrologers, 'I am serious about this. If you don't tell me what my dream was and what it means, you will be torn limb from limb, and your houses will be turned into heaps of rubble! But if you tell me what I dreamed and what the dream means, I will give you many wonderful gifts and honors. Just tell me the dream and what it means!'

"They said again, 'Please, Your Majesty. Tell us the dream, and we will tell you what it means.'

"The king replied, 'I know what you are doing! You're stalling for time because you know I am serious when I say, 'If you don't tell me the dream, you are doomed.' So you have conspired to tell me lies, hoping that I will change my mind. But tell me the dream, and then I'll know that you can tell me what it means.'

"The astrologers replied to the king. 'No one on earth can tell the king his dream! And no king, however great and powerful, has ever asked such a thing of any magician, enchanter, or astrologer! The king's demand is impossible. No one except the gods can tell you your dream, and they do not live here among people.'

"The king was furious when he heard this, and he ordered that all the wise men of Babylon be executed. And because of the king's decree, men were sent to find and kill Daniel and his friends." (Daniel 2:1-12)

Pastor Jonathan paused again.

"Imagine how those wise men felt. The king asked the impossible from them – to tell him his dream, and their lives were at stake. They must have been afraid and wondered if this was a test on the king's part. If the king truly remembered his dream, then this was a test to prove their worthiness. They knew it was impossible to tell him his dream. They also knew that no matter how much they beseeched their gods, all they would hear is silence. Their gods did not speak to them."

Tara was becoming intrigued at the scenario that Pastor Jonathan described. Some people could tell what a dream meant after hearing the dream, but nobody could tell someone *what* they dreamed. That king was insane! Tara was on the edge of her seat as Pastor Jonathan continued to read.

"When Arioch, the commander of the king's guard, came to kill them, Daniel handled the situation with wisdom and discretion. He asked Arioch, 'Why has the king issued such a harsh decree?' So Arioch told him all that had happened. Daniel went at once to see the king and requested more time to tell the king what the dream meant.

"Then Daniel went home and told his friends Hananiah, Mishael, and Azariah what had happened. He urged them to ask the God of heaven to show them His mercy by telling them the secret, so they would not be executed along with the other wise men of Babylon. That night the secret was revealed to Daniel in a vision. Then Daniel praised the God of heaven." (Daniel 2: 14-19)

Pastor Jonathan smiled. "Daniel was placed in an impossible situation. His first reaction was to pray and ask his friends to pray. They didn't sit around moaning about how unfair the situation was, they prayed! They asked God to reveal the dream to them! They didn't know if He would choose to speak to them, but they did believe with absolute certainty that He could!"

Tara shook her head in astonishment. If she had been in Daniel's situation, she would have used that time to plan an escape, not pray. And, God cared enough to give them a response and tell Daniel what the dream was! Amazing! She listened intently as Pastor Jonathan continued reading.

"Then Daniel went in to see Arioch, whom the king had ordered to execute the wise men of Babylon. Daniel said to him, 'Don't kill the wise men. Take me to the king, and I will tell him the meaning of his dream.'

"Arioch quickly took Daniel to the king and said, 'I have found one of the captives from Judah who will tell the king the meaning of his dream!'

"The king said to Daniel, 'Is this true? Can you tell me what my dream was and what it means?'

"Daniel replied, 'There are no wise men, enchanters, magicians, or fortune-tellers who can reveal the king's secret. But, there is a God in heaven who reveals secrets, and He has shown King Nebuchadnezzar what will happen in the future. Now I will tell you your dream and the visions you saw as you lay in your bed.'

'While your Majesty was sleeping, you dreamed about coming events. He who reveals secrets has shown you what is going to happen. And it is not because I am wiser than anyone else that I know the secret of your dream, but because God wants you to understand what was in your heart." (Daniel 2:24-29)

Pastor Jonathan cleared his throat as he looked slowly around the room.

"Daniel goes on to explain what the dream was and what it meant. We will study that another night. But, let's take a quick look ahead in verse 46 at King Nebuchadnezzar's response after the dream was revealed to him."

"Then King Nebuchadnezzar threw himself down before Daniel and worshipped him, and he commanded his people to offer sacrifices and burn sweet incense before him. The king said to Daniel, 'Truly, your God is the greatest of gods, the Lord over kings, a revealer of mysteries, for you have been able to reveal this secret." (Daniel 2:46-47)

"In essence, what King Nebuchadnezzar was saying was, 'Your God is not dead!' Nebuchadnezzar's gods did not speak. They were silent. They did not live among the people. Yet, Daniel's God had revealed the dream to him! That was huge in Nebuchadnezzar's mind. There was no way that Daniel could have known what the dream was on his own. He showed that he served a living God that dwells among us. Daniel served a God that was still in control although Nebuchadnezzar thought he had taken Him captive when he put the sacred objects from the Temple of God in his own treasure-house. Daniel proved to Nebuchadnezzar that you can't contain God. You can't put Him in a box and take Him captive! God is living and in control even when He seems silent for a while.

"Many people in the world today think that God is dead just because He seems silent. They think that God must no longer be in control just because He doesn't stop the tragedies we see on the news. They mock us for believing in God and for our faith. 'Where was your God?' they cry out every time there is a tragedy. They laugh in our faces for believing that God's not dead."

There was a murmur of agreement around the room. What was once a Christian nation was now being belittled for its faith in God.

Pastor Jonathan smiled as he took a sip of water.

"You all have heard me speak long enough. Now, it's your turn. Divide up into groups of seven or eight and discuss how we can know that God's not dead in our world today."

The room became noisy with the sounds of shuffling chairs as everyone gathered into groups.

~CHAPTER 5~

Tara followed Wendy as they made their way to a small group gathered in the corner. Several people smiled at her as the others looked at her with open curiosity. Wendy introduced her.

"This is Tara, and it's her first night here at Unplugged."

Quick introductions were made. The leader of the group, Travis, quickly got down to business. Travis was lanky with wire-rimmed glasses that accentuated his face. His curly brown hair hung over his eyebrows giving him the appearance of a shaggy poodle. The name-brand clothing he wore spoke of money. Tara instantly disliked him.

"Wow! Jonathan had a really good message tonight from the book of Daniel. I never thought of that story that way before. I think there a lot of similarities that we can draw for our own time period. In what ways do you feel our culture treats God as if He is dead or no longer as powerful as He once was?"

Hannah, a thin girl with long, auburn hair, spoke up.

"Well, look at all the changes that have happened in our lives alone. Prayer is no longer allowed in school. Christmas is no longer called Christmas for fear of offending someone. We used to, as a society, be afraid of offending God. Now, we are more concerned with not offending people."

Another voice piped in.

"Society is so politically correct these days that it's hard to stand up for the religious beliefs we have for fear of being sued or ostracized."

The guy sitting next to Tara joined in.

"Our country was founded on Christian principles, but we are becoming less and less a Christian nation. Murders are at an all-time high. Drugs, alcohol, and sexual immorality are rampant. Face it, God has taken His hand of protection off our country and is letting us have our own way."

Travis interjected. "Those are all good points. Just like in Daniel's time, God seems silent, doesn't He? We wonder why He doesn't swoop in and save us from this chaos. We wonder why He has let our country go so far from the Christian principles it was founded on. We wonder why He has allowed our Christian brothers and sisters to be persecuted for standing up for their religious beliefs. We are mocked for our beliefs while God seems silent."

Wendy cut in. "But, He's not silent. He is still there with each and every one of us."

Travis interrupted, "How do you know?"

"Because that is what a relationship with God is like! You just know that He is there, and that He hasn't abandoned you. He is there in the good times and in the bad times. Even when He seems silent and doesn't act, He is still there. That is where faith comes in. Daniel had that faith in God! He believed without a doubt that God wasn't captured just because He was silent. He knew that God couldn't be put in a box."

"So it all comes down to faith!" Travis exclaimed. "We know that God is still alive and powerful even when He is silent because that is what the Bible says. Faith is believing it. And, God does speak to us on a daily basis – in the sunrise and the sunset. In the mountains and the scenery all around us. We just have to open our eyes."

The members of the group nodded their heads in agreement.

"We need to pray that we can have the faith of Daniel to believe in God even when He seems silent," Hannah exclaimed.

Travis looked directly at Tara.

"Do you have any thoughts on our discussion tonight, Tara?"

Tara's face got red as the group focused their attention on her.

"I umm, well, umm, I'm not sure I believe in God - at least not a personal God."

The guy seated next to Tara who smelled a little too strongly of cologne asked, "A personal God?"

"Well, umm, you know a God that cares about individuals. Like I think that there is a God that created the world who sits on His throne watching everything that is going on. I'm just not sure He cares about us as individuals though."

"If He doesn't care about individuals, how do you explain what He did for Daniel by answering his prayer about the dream?" Travis asked.

Tara shifted uncomfortably as her face turned bright red. "I can't. I'm not sure that we can believe everything in the Bible. It was an intriguing story tonight though."

Travis smiled, "There's more where that came from! Like we concluded, it all comes down to faith and seeing God for who He is and not what our image of Him is."

The group closed in prayer. Travis pulled Tara aside as she was getting up to leave.

"I didn't mean to put you on the spot. I'm sorry. I hope you will come back to Unplugged next week."

Tara just shrugged her shoulders at him as she walked away. She wasn't sure she would go back. Yet, Unplugged was kind of fun. The music was great and Pastor Jonathan was an excellent speaker. He knew how to hold an audience's attention.

She followed Wendy to her vehicle. Wendy was chattering nonstop.

"I'm so glad you came tonight, Tara! What did you think?"

"It was a good discussion," Tara replied. Wendy looked at her quizzically but left the topic alone.

As Wendy lay reading in bed later that evening, she heard the familiar sound of retching coming from the bathroom the two of them shared. Tara was purging again. It seemed she was doing it more frequently these days. Wendy knew she would find several junk food wrappers in the garbage can under the kitchen sink if she looked. She also knew that Tara would deny having a problem if confronted.

The sounds of the retching continued as Wendy debated what to do – ignore it or confront Tara in the bathroom. After saying a quick prayer for direction, Wendy decided to take action and headed to the bathroom.

"Tara," she called as she gently knocked. "Are you okay in there?"

There was no response. Wendy opened the door slightly and stepped in. Tara sat on the floor in front of the toilet staring at the contents inside. A large empty bag of potato chips lay on the floor beside her. She looked up, eyes slightly dazed, as Wendy entered.

"Tara," Wendy said once again as she put her arm around Tara's shoulder. Tara screamed and jumped as if she were being attacked.

"DON'T TOUCH ME!" she cried as she rocked herself back and forth. "Don't touch me!"

"I'm sorry," Wendy apologized. "I just wanted to see if you were okay. I heard you vomiting."

"I'm fine!" Tara exclaimed harshly. "Now leave me alone."

"Did you eat that entire bag of chips just now?" Wendy questioned as she sat down on the floor next to Tara.

Tara was once again staring dazedly at the toilet bowl. She shuddered as an image of Jack stuffing her head in a similar bowl popped in her mind. Shaking the image off, she took her anger out on Wendy.

"It's none of your business what I did!" Tara exclaimed. "You are just my roommate; you aren't a friend! Believe me, the last person I want as a friend is a Christian goody-two shoes like you! Now leave me alone!" she demanded.

"I'm just worried," Wendy began as Tara cut her off.

"Well, don't be! I'm not your concern. Don't think that just because I went with you to Unplugged tonight that we are suddenly joined at the hip. I went for the money,

Wendy, not for any other reason. I don't care about your God, and, to be honest, I don't care about you. I know what you rich people are like. You're all alike. You think you are so much better than me just because you have money and come from a respectable family."

Wendy tried to interject. "That's not true."

"True?" Tara questioned. "Weren't you all too happy to show me off tonight at church wanting applause for bringing in your poor, messed up roommate? I can just picture your conversations with your friends there."

Wendy's eyes filled with tears as she stood up. "Tara, I asked you to go tonight because I wanted to spend time with you. I wanted you to come to know the Lord in the same way I do. And, I wanted you to meet some new people who could possibly become your friends. I care about you."

Tara's eyes hardened. Wendy didn't care about her. She only cared about showing off her new *project*.

"Make sure to leave me the cash on my nightstand before you turn in," she said in return.

~CHAPTER 6~

Tara smiled as she finally sank into her bed. That was the easiest three hundred dollars she had ever made! Even though she had to go to a church event for it, the money was worth it. Her eight year old laptop was on its last legs. As she closed her eyes to prepare for the sleep to come, she reflected on how ironic it was that she had just been reading about Nietzsche believing that the concept of God was dead while the subject at Unplugged was about how God was not dead. Who was right? A great philosopher or the church folks? It had to be Nietzsche. If God existed, He sure didn't care.

Tara shivered as a memory of Jack's angry face came to mind once more. No, she wouldn't be fooled by the wolves in sheeps' clothing at that church. Christians couldn't be trusted. They were two-faced and hypocritical. Well, that is, except for Wendy. She actually seems like the real deal. Tara was confused by that. How could someone as sweet as Wendy believe in the same God that Jack did? It just didn't make sense. She had never once seen Wendy raise her voice or point out her sins. Wendy seemed to genuinely care.

Tara thought of the people she had met that night at Unplugged. Jonathan was obviously well liked. And, Travis didn't demean her when she said that she didn't believe even though he was obviously well-off. He actually apologized for putting her on the spot! The people there at Unplugged were very different from the church she had experienced under Jack's leadership. Tara's eyelids became heavy as she fought sleep while seeking to comprehend the differences in the churches.

She enjoyed a weekend delving deep into her historical fiction novels in between continuing her study on Nietzsche. She hardly crossed paths with Wendy at all. She was probably off saving the world somewhere on Saturday and at church showing off her halo on Sunday.

On Monday morning, Tara awoke to the sounds of birds chirping outside of her window. She rolled her eyes as she thought of what Wendy would say: "God is singing you good morning!" She couldn't resist a smile as she got dressed and headed to class.

The full scholarship was difficult to maintain, but Tara was thankful that it covered everything but her apartment. She worked part-time at the college in the office to pay for her living expenses. She loved her job at the office. She didn't have to interact with anyone. All she had to do was type and input data into the computer. It was the perfect job for an antisocial introvert like herself. Yet, oddly enough, she found herself wishing for company that afternoon while sitting alone in her cubicle.

Ever since the incident with the jocks, Jack's face occupied her thoughts constantly. His shouting demands of "Repent!" tormented her at night. She either woke up in a cold sweat from the nightmares, or the flashbacks were so bad that she couldn't sleep at all. His words echoed in her mind. "Worthless! You are worthless!" She focused her attention back to the computer to drown the memories out.

She arrived home before Wendy and opened the utensils drawer to pull out a knife to cut the steak she had broiled in the oven. Suddenly, she was hit with a wave of violent flashbacks: Jack's voice screaming "worthless" at her as the water in the stained toilet bowl swirled. She flinched at the memory of a timer as the thought of slitting her wrists entered her mind. She stared at the knife. Suicide was wrong, but what did she have to live for? No family, no friends, nothing. The knife shook in her hands.

Her cell phone suddenly vibrated with a text message, startling her. It was a number she didn't recognize. Tara's brows creased as she read the message. *"Just wanted you to know that you are beautiful in God's eyes!"* She was certain that someone had accidentally texted the wrong number. She was anything but beautiful. Still, the message made her smile. She hesitantly put the knife back in the drawer and ate her steak like a hamburger instead of cutting it.

Memories suddenly flooded her mind of being bullied in school. She cringed as she remembered her classmates, led by the popular kids, shouting "Ugly! Fat! Reject! Trash!" She ran to the bathroom and stuck her finger down her throat and waited for the relief to come.

~CHAPTER 7~

Tara hadn't seen much of Wendy the past few days, but on Thursday night, Wendy hesitantly approached her.

"Do you want to go to Unplugged again tomorrow night?" she asked.

Tara crossed her arms. So this was how it was going to be. Wendy was going to hold the three hundred dollars over her head. Well, she would put a stop to that right now.

"I only agreed to go there for one night," she defensively said.

"I know. I was just hoping that you would come back is all."

"Are you going to pay me more money to go?" Tara demanded. "Three hundred dollars isn't enough to get a good laptop. I need another two hundred."

Wendy hesitated. She hadn't been completely forthright with Tara the last time. She didn't really have that three hundred dollars in savings. She had to sell her DSLR camera to get the money. Times were hard. With her father recently disabled in an accident, her family was financially struggling despite the appearance that they were wealthy. Wendy didn't have a scholarship like Tara. With a full course load, she was only able to work part-time, and she sent part of the income she made home to her family to help them out. They had never struggled with money before, but now suddenly they were counting pennies to make ends meet. Could she really afford to give Tara two hundred dollars more? Tara was obviously taking advantage of the situation. Yet, Wendy believed that God wanted Tara at Unplugged. She decided to trust God to provide the money somehow. After all, she could sell her laptop and use the computers at the library instead.

"Okay," Wendy agreed. "I will give you two hundred dollars to attend Unplugged with me again."

Tara smiled. Wendy was a pushover! Unplugged wasn't that bad. She was actually looking forward to hearing Pastor Jonathan share another story. He was a very good speaker and quite easy on the eyes.

~CHAPTER 8~

Jonathan smiled as he looked out at the audience gathered for Unplugged. He never dreamed the ministry would have taken off the way it had. The number of attendees grew every week. It had started off as an outreach ministry with five people meeting once a week in his small apartment on the north side of town and blossomed dramatically.

He grimaced as he remembered his first efforts at explaining his vision for Unplugged. The five people had looked at him like he lost his marbles when he asked them to turn their cell phones off and told them that he wanted them to unplug from distractions and everything they had ever been taught about God. It was a new concept – even for himself. He had been raised in a very legalistic church that believed salvation could be earned by works. The concept of grace seemed foreign to him when he first read in Scripture in Ephesians 2:8-9 that one is saved by grace and not by works. Yet, as he looked out over the audience gathered for tonight's session, he grinned because he knew that God had prepared him for such a time as this.

All of his years of futilely trying to earn points with God through his actions and buy his salvation had proved fruitless once he realized the truth about grace. The Bible became more than a manual of do's and do not's. It became his lifeline and his cherished connection with the living God who spoke to him through it. Yes, Unplugged seemed like a radical idea at first that people wouldn't buy into in an age where they are spoon fed the doctrine at every turn. With the advance of technology and computer screens put up in churches, people no longer brought their Bibles to follow along and read for themselves. Unplugging from everything one has been taught about God did indeed seem radical, yet it was absolutely necessary to teach people to search the Scriptures for themselves instead of blindly taking someone's word for the truth. There were many people who professed to be Christians wandering in confusion due to being misled and uninformed of the truths of God's Word and love.

He cleared his throat as he began. "I'm so excited to see y'all here tonight at Unplugged. Let's bow our heads and pray."

The shuffling of feet and the conversations in the room suddenly stilled as each person reverently closed their eyes.

"Father, I thank You for the works that You have done and are doing through Unplugged. I thank You for revealing Your truths to us, and I praise You that Your mercies are new every morning. You know every one of us by name. You know every hair on our heads and what we are going to say before we even say it. It is no accident that we are gathered here tonight. We ask that You open our hearts, minds, and ears to the truth tonight. Let us not be biased on what we think we know about You, but let us instead come to truly know the real You – not the image that we have built up in our heads. Give us ears to listen, and a heart to receive. In Jesus's name, Amen."

Jonathan glanced around the room as he began his sermon. There was the usual mix of people in the audience – some middle aged but a large majority were young adults. They seemed to be drawn by the simplicity of Unplugged. Instead of going to Unplugged to simply be entertained, they seemed to truly want to grow in their relationship and knowledge of God. He said a quick prayer in his head that God would steal the show and speak through him this evening.

He cleared his throat as he began.

"The title of tonight's message is 'For such a time as this.' You have probably heard the story from the book of Esther where that phrase came from. Esther, the young orphan drawn into the king's court, had a choice to make, and it wasn't an easy choice. In fact, it was a choice that could have cost her life.

"The story begins in Susa which was an important city in the Persian Empire and the winter palace of the king. King Xerxes reigned over one hundred twenty-seven provinces that stretched from India to Ethiopia. That's a large distance with a lot of people to keep happy. Perhaps fearing revolt, he sought to impress all of his nobles and officials by giving a banquet that lasted one hundred eighty days as he presented a stunning display of opulence.

"When that banquet was over, he gave another banquet – this one for all the regular folks in his kingdom. People from the least to the greatest came to this seven day banquet which was held in the courtyard of the palace garden. The courtyard was decorated magnificently. Gold and silver couches sat on a mosaic pavement of precious stones waiting to be enjoyed by the guests. Meanwhile, drinks were served in gold goblets, and, by the king's instructions, the guests were allowed to have as much as they wanted. This was a party fit for a king!

"The only downside is that this was only a party for men. King Xerxes's wife, Queen Vashti, was having her own party for the women in the royal palace. I wonder how happy the men were with that. They could have as much as they wanted to eat or drink while sipping out of gold goblets and sitting on gold and silver couches, but the only company they had was other men. I'm not sure I could have endured a seven day party like that."

The audience chuckled as Jonathan continued.

"Imagine a seven day party with unlimited alcohol – and not the cheap stuff. They were served royal wine. The guests were drunk. King Xerxes was drunk and maybe even a little nervous. King Xerxes needed to keep his kingdom happy to prevent revolt. This party was a way of keeping him popular and well-loved with his people. He had a lot of expectations on him – the present one being to entertain. It had been seven days since these drunken men had seen a woman, and they were tired of looking at each other.

"King Xerxes knew his wife was stunningly beautiful, and he summoned her to come to him wearing nothing but her royal crown. She refused. Not only was she hosting her own party and expected to entertain there for her guests, but she was offended because it would not be suitable behavior for a queen to parade naked in a room full of drunken men. It took courage on her part to respond to the king's drunken demands with dignity and refuse his request, yet she paid the price. The king was humiliated, divorced her, and banished her from his presence by issuing a public decree.

"After King Xerxes had sobered up and calmed down, he regretted what he had done, but he couldn't take his decree back. He had acted in anger, haste, and embarrassment and later regretted it. Have you ever acted upon your emotions and later regretted what you had done?"

Heads in the audience nodded. Many could identify all too well with King Xerxes.

Jonathan took a drink of water and continued.

"King Xerxes was now lonely and in need of female companionship. So, his personal attendants suggested a beauty contest. Beautiful young women across the empire would be gathered. The one who pleased the king the most would be made queen. A search for the new queen began. This was the first recorded beauty contest in the world although the women were not all willing participants.

"Among the candidates, a young, orphan Jewish girl named Esther was chosen. She was raised by her cousin Mordecai. She didn't have a voice in being chosen. Nobody said 'no' to the king's men. Mordecai warned her to not tell anyone that she was a Jew. There was a lot of racial tension going on in those days, and she must have wondered and questioned God about why she was there at the palace when she clearly did not belong.

"Esther was an orphan living in exile in a foreign land, torn from her home and the only family stability she had without a choice. Yet, she was not bitter. In fact, she found favor among all. She made the most of her circumstances and composed herself in a caring, compassionate manner and was admired by everyone who saw her.

"Esther won the contest. The king was so delighted in her that he declared her to be the queen. This poor orphan girl now suddenly had wealth and power at her disposal. Yet, she still maintained the secret of her nationality. Even though she no longer lived under Mordecai's care, she still respected and followed his directions."

Jonathan glanced around the room and asked, "How many of you are still following your parents' directions now that you are no longer living with them? How many of you respect your parents enough to obey them at your age even when it might not make sense to you? I have to be honest. I rebelled against my parents the moment I left home and became a party guy and a player. I thought my parents were ancient, set in their ways, out of touch with the world, and I ignored their advice. As a result, I made a lot of choices that I regret. One of them being that I can't give my future wife the gift of my virginity. I didn't keep myself pure, and I regret that every day. We can learn a lot from Esther."

Tara stared in surprise at Pastor Jonathan. He seemed so – perfect. She couldn't believe that he had once been rebellious and slept around. He seemed so tight with God, yet how could God accept him when he was so obviously a sinner? Jack would have yelled "Repent, you sinner!" at him while telling him how God was going to punish him for his actions by throwing him into an everlasting fire. Yet, Jonathan acted like God loved him despite his past mistakes. She wondered how that could be. It was like Jonathan and Jack preached about two different gods. Who was correct? She turned her attention back to Jonathan as he continued his message.

"Esther became queen. As queen, she had an expectation to please the king. But, that expectation came with limits. She couldn't come to him whenever she wanted. She had to wait to be summoned into his royal presence. To appear before him without being summoned was breaking the law, an infraction that would be punishable by immediate death.

"Haman was King Xerxes's top advisor, and he became angry at Mordecai because he noticed that Mordecai refused to bow down in front of him. You see, Mordecai was determined to serve God and knew that he wasn't supposed to bow down before people, yet Haman only served himself. He wanted to be worshipped, and Mordecai's refusal to do so angered and humiliated him. So, he sought revenge. Rather than only seeking revenge on Mordecai though, he sought to absolve his hate of Jews by devising a plan to destroy all of them in King Xerxes's empire. They were different than he was. He didn't like or understand them, and he wanted to wipe them out. He wanted to perform genocide.

"So, he lied to the king. He told him that the Jewish people refused to obey the laws of the king and that it was not in the king's interests to let them live. The king trusted Haman's judgment and gave him permission to do as he pleased against the Jews.

"A royal decree was issued in the name of King Xerxes and sealed with the king's signet ring which made it binding and irrevocable. The decree declared that all Jews – young and old, women and children must be killed on March 7 of the following year. There was already racial tension against the Jewish nation. Now, Haman stirred it up even more by giving the people a year to plan the annihilation of the Jews. The city of Susa fell into confusion because of the ripple effect: evil spreads quickly.

"Queen Esther was understandably troubled by this decree and even more concerned when Mordecai sent a message to her asking her to go to the king and beg for mercy for her people. King Xerxes had not summoned her in thirty days. She knew she could die if she approached him without being summoned. Her life would be on the line if she followed Mordecai's wishes. She sent a message back to Mordecai explaining just that.

"Mordecai sent back the following reply to Esther that we can find in Esther 4:13-14. 'Don't think for a moment that because you're in the palace you will escape when all other Jews are killed. If you keep quiet at a time like this, deliverance and relief for the Jews will arise from some other place, but you and your relatives will die. Who knows if perhaps you were made queen for such a time as this?'

"Mordecai knew and had faith that God's timing was perfect and that everything He did was for a purpose. He believed that God had placed Esther in a position of authority and urged her to act quickly on behalf of her people.

"Esther could have been concerned only with saving herself, but she realized the wisdom of Mordecai's words. Maybe she was in the palace for 'such a time as this.' She sent a reply back to Mordecai asking him to gather all of the Jews to fast and pray for three days. She also asked them to pray for her as she broke the law and approached the king after she too fasted and prayed for three days. She understood the risks she was taking, and she wanted prayer support."

Jonathan paused for a sip of water and looked intently around the room. "How many times is our very first reaction to a situation to pray and to ask others to pray for and with us? Too often we try to fix the situation on our own or complain about the unfairness of it. Yet, Esther did neither. She believed Mordecai's words that she was placed in the palace for 'such a time as this.' How else could a despised Jew become a queen in a Persian court except by divine intervention? That is why she was willing to risk it all in the hope that God would save her people."

Tara glanced around at the people sitting near her. Wendy, who sat beside her, seemed totally engrossed in the message. Travis looked the same. She pondered the words 'for such a time as this' as she tried to understand the faith and courage of the young Jewish girl Pastor Jonathan was describing. She focused her attention back to him. She didn't want to miss what happened next. She was glad Wendy had taken her to Unplugged again and felt a small sense of shame for accepting the two hundred dollars. In truth, she would have gone back here for free. Pastor Jonathan had a way of making the dusty, dry, Bible stories come to life in a way she had never expected.

"With enormous personal risk and her life at stake, Esther broke the law and entered the throne room. King Xerxes seemed to be in good humor and was amused by her unexpected appearance. He welcomed her as she sighed in relief. The king seemed so amused in fact that he acted as if he would practically grant any request she had. In return, Esther asked the king and Haman to come to a banquet she had prepared that day. They went to her banquet, and while they were drinking wine, the king asked her what she really wanted. He suspected she wanted more than just the pleasure of his company. So, Esther asked if the king and Haman would come once again the next day to another banquet that she would prepare and assured the king that she would explain her purpose then.

"They went once more to her banquet. While they were drinking wine again, the king asked what she really wanted and promised to grant it. This was the moment of truth for Esther! This was the moment for her to step out in faith! She didn't back down and responded in Esther 7:3-4 with the following.

'If I have found favor with the king, and if it pleases the king to grant my request, I ask that my life and the lives of my people will be spared. For my people and I have been sold to those who would kill, slaughter, and annihilate us. If we had merely been sold as slaves, I could remain quiet, for that would be too trivial a matter to warrant disturbing the king.'

'Who would do such a thing?' King Xerxes demanded in verse 5. 'Who would be so presumptuous as to touch you?'

"Esther replied in verse 6. 'This wicked Haman is our adversary and our enemy.'

"King Xerxes already knew of Haman's plot to kill the Jews and had even approved it. Yet, Esther was endearing to him. Seeing how Haman's plot affected her, he became upset, and in a rage, went out into the palace garden to think.

"Meanwhile, Haman who was frightened stayed behind to plead to Queen Esther for his life. In despair, he fell on the couch where she sat just as King Xerxes returned. The king thought he was assaulting her and demanded his immediate death. Haman got what he deserved, but the lives of the Jewish people were still at risk. Esther begged the king to issue a decree that reversed Haman's order to slaughter her people. According to Medo-Persian law, the king couldn't revoke the previous decree. It was binding. So, a new decree was written that gave the Jews authority to unite and fight back against anyone who attempted to attack them on March 7 of the following year. This new law allowing the Jews to defend themselves would go into effect the same day as the previous one.

"The Jews rejoiced and celebrated this new decree, and many people actually became Jews because they were afraid of what the Jews might do to them. God was in control! Many people converted to Judaism because of what was happening, and – don't miss this – the Jewish people welcomed them with open arms! God had a plan all along! Throughout the Bible we see example after example of how God works through His people so that those who don't know Him can come into His kingdom.

"Well, the day of the battle arrived, and many of the Jews' enemies were destroyed. The king even extended the decree to last for the following day, March 8, as well. This is why the Jewish people celebrate the Festival of Purim. God had not only preserved the Jewish people, but He had also destroyed their enemies. During the Festival of Purim, Jews celebrate the victory God gave them by exchanging gifts with one another and by giving presents to the poor as they remember when their sadness and mourning was turned into gladness and joy.

"Just as the Jews continue to celebrate their past victories that God has given them, we too can celebrate what God has done for us. Keeping a prayer journal is a great way to remind ourselves of what God has done and is doing in our lives.

"He doesn't always place us in a palace for 'such a time as this.' Those moments that God has called us for may not even be remarkable or memorable to others. Yet, God has a plan for each and every one of you. He has called you 'for such a time as this!' There is a time in our lives when we cannot be silent, a time when we must take a stand for what is right, a time when we have to act in faith despite our circumstances that – face it – don't look good.

"Esther had strikes against her. She was an orphan. Strike one! She was a woman. Women were considered insignificant in her time. Strike Two! She was a Jew in exile in a foreign land. Strike Three! Yet, God used her – despite everything she had going against her – to bring a nation back to God! Our circumstances are not mere coincidences. Esther is the story of God working unseen as He weaved together the circumstances of Esther's life to save a nation from genocide. Those circumstances were beyond Esther's control, yet God used those circumstances for His purposes which we know in Jeremiah 29:16 are plans for good, not for evil, to give us a future and a hope. We don't have the ability to see the big picture, but God does. He has a plan. He always has a plan!

"No matter what you have gone through, no matter what you may be going through, God has a plan. And, it's a good plan! Despite how tragic and horrible those circumstances may be, God has a plan to make something good come out of them. But, sometimes our willingness to be vulnerable is required.

"What would have happened if Esther wasn't willing to be vulnerable? What would have happened if she wasn't willing to swallow her fear and admit that she too was a Jew? We don't know. I believe that God would have used someone else to save His people. He would have raised up another person to be the voice for His people because God is bigger than mere mortals. He uses us, but He doesn't rely on us. God will still accomplish what His purposes are whether we are on board or not.

"Yet, He had a mission for Esther. Her mission, if she so chose to accept it, was to be the voice for His people. Was she afraid? Of course! The king could have had her killed instantly for just approaching him. Courage is not the absence of fear. Rather, it is the admission that something else is more important than fear. It is okay to be afraid as long as that fear doesn't inhibit you from acting.

"We all have times that we are afraid. It's hard to be vulnerable because we don't know how the other person is going to respond. It takes courage to be vulnerable. It takes courage to speak up. It takes courage to break the silence. Do you have courage? Do you have the courage to be vulnerable? Your vulnerability might not save a nation, but it just might save yourself."

Tara glanced at Wendy who was sitting beside her. If Pastor Jonathan was correct in his sermon, maybe Wendy was in her life for a reason. Did God care that her world was falling apart – that the flashbacks of Jack tormented her repeatedly? Did He care that she felt worthless and unloved? Did He care that her eyes were hollowed out from lack of sleep? If Jonathan was right and there truly was a time for a person to speak up, maybe it was now. Wendy had shared that she had been molested. She had been vulnerable and would understand to some degree. Maybe, she would help her.

Tara focused her attention back on Pastor Jonathan.

"The enemy wants us to think that we have to fight our battles alone. The enemy wants to keep us inhibited by pride. The enemy wants the walls around our hearts higher than Mt. Everest. You might be sitting here thinking, 'Jonathan, you just don't know what I've done. You don't know how ashamed I am about my past. You don't know what I am going through. It's deep stuff, Pastor. It's heavy, and I'm worried how people will treat me if they only knew. They would avoid me. They would make fun of me. They would mock me. Yes, I struggle with the guilt and with the heaviness of the burden, but I'm afraid of telling anyone.'

"Well, I haven't experienced every kind of situation that's out there. But, I can tell you one thing. Every single person in this room is struggling in some way. We have that in common. We all struggle! God doesn't call us to struggle by ourselves though. He tells us over and over in His words to pray together, to encourage one another, to intercede for one another. How can we do that unless we are truly vulnerable with one another? How can we do that unless we have the courage to no longer be silent?

"God has called us for such a time as this. For such a time as this! We are called for such a time as this to share the good news of the Gospel! We are called to give hope to a lost and dying world who have no idea what that hope even looks like. And, we are called to share our burdens with one another because God can use the messes of our lives to create masterpieces! He weaves together all of our brokenness, all of our struggles, and all of our tears into a beautiful tapestry. Our stories, no matter how bad, can encourage others who may be going through the same thing and need hope and encouragement that it gets better."

Tara felt the tears roll down her face as she glanced at Wendy once more. Wendy, who seemed to have it all together, had a painful and shameful past too, yet the life she lived was so much different than Tara's. Wendy had joy and peace. She stifled a sob as the realization hit her. Wendy didn't live as a victim. She lived as a survivor!

Wendy noticed Tara's tears and gently placed her hand on her arm.

"Do you want to talk?"

Tara nodded as the tears continued to flow.

"Do you want to talk to just me, or would you like to talk to several of us? I could ask Jonathan, Travis, and Hannah to talk with us during group discussion time. They are all prayer warriors."

Tara hesitated momentarily. Was she willing to share her story to more than just Wendy? Pastor Jonathan's words of "such a time as this" echoed in her head. She wanted to be courageous like Esther. Tara's voice shook as she replied, "I'd like that."

~CHAPTER 9~

Tara glanced nervously around at the group gathered in Pastor Jonathan's office. Wendy had rounded them up as soon as group discussion time began. Travis appointed another guy to take his place as the leader at his table as soon as Wendy told him there was a need for prayer warriors. Tara suddenly felt stupid for having called all this attention upon herself from people she had just met. She stared silently at the floor as Pastor Jonathan broke the ice.

"Tara, I know that we just met, but I want you to know that you can trust us. Whatever you tell us won't go any further than this room. What is on your heart?"

Tara continued to stare silently at the floor as the tears ran uncontrollably down her face. Wendy handed her a tissue as Hannah put her arms around her. Her body began to shake with sobs as she murmured, "I've never told anyone."

The group waited patiently. Wendy patted Tara on the back as she said, "It's time to be set free. God can do that. He will do that! He loves you, Tara."

"He hates me," Tara sobbed. "God hates me."

"Why do you feel that God hates you?" asked Travis.

"If He loved me, why did He make me so worthless? Why does He torment me?"

Jonathan asked, "Why do you feel He torments you?"

"Every time I close my eyes, I see his sweaty face and hear his angry voice."

"Whose face and voice do you hear?" asked Hannah as she handed Tara another tissue.

"Jack's," Tara sobbed.

Jonathan interjected. "Let's pray before we go any further." The group bowed their heads as he began to pray.

"Father, I don't know for sure what Tara has on her heart, but it sounds like a secret burden she has kept for many years. I ask that you will give her the strength and the courage to share that burden not only with You but with us also so that we may support her and encourage her. I pray that she will see You not as hate but as the true love You are. Amen."

Tara looked around the room and decided to take a leap of faith. What was the worst that could happen? Even if they all turned from her in disgust, she never had to see or talk to them again – except Wendy that is. And, she knew Wendy well enough to know that she would never mock her or put her down even if she was disgusted by Tara's story. Tara took a deep breath and began.

"When I was four years old, I was happy, truly happy. My parents loved me and showed it by spending time with me. They took me to the park and other fun activities in the small town where we lived in Georgia. I loved making cookies in the kitchen with mom and helping dad rake leaves in the fall. He always left a large pile for us to jump in.

"My world was wonderful until it suddenly shattered one summer night. My parents kissed me goodbye as they left me with a babysitter that afternoon. They were on their way to their tenth high school reunion. My dad gave me a huge hug as he said, 'Chin up! We will be back soon!' Only they didn't come back.

"I woke up to confusion early in the morning. Several police officers paced the living room floor as the babysitter rocked slowly back and forth with tears streaming down her face. I was scared. 'I want my mommy!' I cried. 'Where's my mommy and daddy?'

"An officer picked me up and roughly explained, 'Your mommy and daddy aren't coming back.' My parents had been killed in a car accident."

Wendy patted Tara on the shoulder. "I'm so sorry honey."

Tara took a deep breath before continuing.

"Since there were no close relatives, I was placed in foster care. My foster dad, Jack, was a short, fat preacher with a bald head that glistened in the sun. Jenny, my foster mom, was a timid home maker determined to obey Jack's every demand. At five foot six with dirty blond hair and a beanpole body, she seemed kind enough, but I missed my parents terribly. I did not like my foster dad, Jack, at all. He always stared at me disapprovingly and made me feel somewhat afraid.

"My foster parents took me to the small church where Jack was the pastor. He was particularly fond of fire-and-brimstone preaching. Sweat glistened on his face and spittle flew from his mouth as he shouted, "Choose God or burn in hell FOREVER!" I had never been to church before, and I was frightened. I did not want to burn in a fire. Jenny pinched my arm when I began to wiggle on the hard pew during Jack's sermons. Jack's eyes seemed to bore into me as he shouted, 'Do you want to experience the wrath of God? Repent! Repent now!'

"The congregation was silent as they each shook hands with Jack and exited the building. Church did not seem like a happy place - not like here. I had never heard of God before, and I did not like the image that Jack had portrayed of Him during his sermon. I pictured in my mind a stern person sitting on a throne gleefully ready to throw people in a fire for misbehaving.

"To me, God was the opposite of Santa Claus. I remembered my mom and dad taking me to meet him during our last Christmas together. He was a happy man with a long beard and kind eyes. He knew everything about me. He knew what I had done naughty and what I had done nice. Yet, Santa just patted me on the back and told me to try to be good as he gave me a candy cane and promised me a great present for Christmas. It seemed that God too knew everything about me, but, instead of giving me a candy cane, He was ready to throw me into a fire for misbehaving. I did not want to meet Him ever! I secretly hoped my foster parents wouldn't take me to meet Him.

"My foster parents brought me to the church every Sunday. Each week, Jack's face grew red and sweat glistened on his face as he shouted about the wrath of God from the pulpit. The message each time was the same, 'Repent or burn!' I was not sure what "repenting" meant, but I definitely did not want to be thrown into a fire. I was terrified of God!"

Tara nervously glanced around the room. Pastor Jonathan had tears in his eyes as he interjected, "I'm sorry that was your introduction to God. That is what Unplugged is all about – learning who God really is and not who we were taught He is. God is love! He really is!"

Tara smiled sadly as she bravely continued. The hard part was coming. She expected them all to lose their supportive smiles and leave the room in disgust in the next few minutes when they found out the truth about her.

"The parsonage was located across the street from the church. Jack spent many hours in his office at the church which was fine with me. When he was gone, Jenny and I had fun. Jenny was a whole different person when Jack was not around. She played board games and hide and seek with me. We laughed a lot when we were together. When Jack came home, though, Jenny changed. She became a quiet, withdrawn person. The atmosphere was tense in the home. I sensed that Jenny was afraid of Jack although I did not know why. Jack never interacted much with me at first. He just looked at me sternly and disapprovingly. I suppose it was because I was one of those sinners Jack preached about each week."

Tara glanced around the room once more. This was the moment of truth. This was the moment they would hear her most shameful secrets and lose their encouraging smiles. But, if it could possibly help her by sharing her story in some way, she was willing. She was spinning out of control, and she knew it. She was binging and puking quite frequently and the suicidal thoughts, although random, were present as well. If Wendy could be helped by sharing her story and become the person she was today, Tara was willing to try it for herself. She wanted more than what her life was currently like. She was tired of going through the motions and wanted true joy and peace like Wendy exhibited. Pastor Jonathan's words echoed in her head: "for such a time as this." She bravely plunged forward with her story as the tears rolled down her cheeks.

"I umm climbed a tree one day and hung upside down from a branch. My dress covered my face, exposing my panties, as I lightly swung my body from the tree branch like a monkey. Jack, who was returning home from the church across the street, saw me and stared in anger.

'Get in the house right now!' he demanded. I slowly came inside. I didn't understand why Jack was so angry.

"He grabbed me roughly by the arm and pulled me though the kitchen where Jenny was making dinner. 'What is going on?' Jenny asked.

'Stay out of it!' Jack said roughly as he told me to put my shoes on. He stomped down the hall and pulled a timer out from one of my board games. Jack gripped my hand tightly as he led me across the street to the church. We walked down the long hallway together until we came to a small utility closet. A light bulb with a pull string dangled from the ceiling and swung eerily in the closet as Jack turned it on. I looked at Jack questioningly. His eyes bugged out and looked crazy as he placed the timer on a shelf. He pointed at the timer and told me to repent. I was confused. Although I had heard Jack shout out the word, "repent" at his sermons each week, I still did not know what it meant. What had I done? Why was Jack so angry at me?

"Jack told me that I had three minutes. Three minutes until what? I wanted to go back home and be with Jenny. I was scared. But, Jack would not let me leave. 'Two minutes!' he shouted at me. 'Say it!'

"I didn't know what I was supposed to say. I began to cry. My tears seemed to make him angrier. 'Stop crying! Stop crying now!' he shouted as he shook me. I cried harder. I didn't know why was Jack yelling at me.

"Time's up!" he declared as the timer ran out. "I have to punish you now. This is your fault for being a tease. The Bible says in Romans 6:13, 'Do not let your body become an instrument of evil to serve sin!' Jack's normally round face was red and puffy as he angrily stretched out his arm. I thought Jack was going to hit me. Instead, his pants fell to the floor as his hand,"

Tara began to choke on the words as the tears flowed.

"As his hand slid up my underwear. I did not know what was going on – I was only four, but I didn't like it. It hurt. When he finished, his eyes stopped bugging out as the crazed look went away. Jack smiled sadly at me as he said, 'I wish I didn't have to punish you. If you had only repented, I wouldn't have had to. It's all your fault!'

Tara covered her eyes with her hands as her body shook with sobs. She was sure everyone was going to leave her now that they had heard. Instead, she felt many hands being placed on her shoulders and back and heard sniffling. She looked up, amazed at the support they were still offering her.

"When it was over, I backed away from Jack in fear. He picked me up and looked in my eyes. 'This is our little secret,' he said. 'You were a bad girl today, and I had to punish you. I need to make sure that you won't tell our secret for the Bible declares in Proverbs 21:23 that you will stay out of trouble if you keep your mouth shut.' We exited the closet, and he led me to a bathroom. As he flushed the toilet, he forced my head into the bowl. I was terrified as the water swirled around my face. He lifted me up from the toilet bowl and then forced me back in, again and again. 'I won't tell!' I cried. Jack smiled. He took a hairdryer from a drawer in the bathroom and dried my hair. Then, he walked me back across the street to the parsonage like nothing had happened.

"Jenny had dinner on the table when we returned. Jenny looked questioningly at Jack and could tell he was angry. I looked afraid. But, she decided not to push the issue. After all, Jack was a man of God. If he felt that I needed to be punished for something, it wasn't up to her to question his judgment or his actions. Dinner was a silent affair; nobody said a word.

"I felt dirty and ashamed, but I didn't really understand what had just happened. I was afraid of making Jack angry again, but I didn't know what I had done in the first place. Jenny looked sad as she gave me a hug and kissed me goodnight. I don't know what she thought Jack had done. I wanted to tell her, but I was afraid to. Jack had demonstrated with the toilet bowl what would happen to me if I told."

Tara was astonished that the group was still there with her. Jonathan looked at her with tears running unashamedly down his face as he said, "I'm so sorry, Tara. I'm so sorry. That's not a picture of God at all. I can't even imagine how you felt. I'm so sorry."

Wendy enveloped Tara in a warm hug as she hesitantly asked, "Was that the only time it happened, or was there more abuse?"

Tara's voice shook as she replied, "There was more. Jack ignored me for several days although he still cast disapproving looks at me. I was twirling around in my dress the following Sunday in the hallway when Jack happened to pass by. After the congregation left, Jack sent Jenny home as he gripped my hand tightly. As we passed by the bathroom, he shoved me inside and held me above the toilet while he shook me. 'You little tease!' he yelled. 'Apparently you didn't learn your lesson last time. Everyone could see your underwear. God's word says, 'Spare the rod, spoil the child!', he shouted in a booming voice. 'I have to punish you again. Remember what happens if you tell!' he exclaimed. To be certain that I understood, he turned me upside down and forced my face into the toilet bowl as he flushed it. 'I will flush you down the toilet next time!' he demanded. I gasped for breath as he pulled me out of the toilet and led me back to the utility closet.

"The same scenario was repeated. Jack's eyes looked crazy as he flipped the timer over and demanded for me to speak. But, once again I didn't know what he wanted me to say. His voice egged me on. 'Three minutes, two minutes, one minute, time's up!' he shouted as his pants fell to the floor. 'You are worthless,' he said when it was all over. 'You have been a bad girl!' I felt so dirty on the inside as he led me back to the parsonage.

"My personality changed as Jack repeatedly molested me during the next five years. I used to be vivacious, but I became quiet and withdrawn. I started sucking my thumb again and wetting my pants. I couldn't stand for anyone to hug me or touch me. I spent as much time as I could in my room. Whenever Jack was around, I always seemed to do something wrong to set him off. Each time he molested me, he made sure to ingrain in me that it was my fault."

"It wasn't your fault," Wendy softly said. "Tara, it wasn't your fault at all. He was a sick man, and he twisted Scripture for his sick purposes. He molested you and tried to justify it by using Scripture out of context."

"How long were you with this family?" Hannah asked with tears in her eyes.

"Jack passed away of a heart attack when I was in the fourth grade. I was placed with a new foster family, but the psychological damage was already done. I dressed like a tomboy and refused to wear a dress. I still sucked my thumb in class and when I felt nervous. My teacher thought I should have outgrown such childish behavior by that point and began putting iodine on my thumbs so that they would taste bitter. She encouraged the class to make fun of me for wetting myself and for the thumb-sucking, thinking that it would shame me into moving past those behaviors. The teacher repeatedly mocked me in front of the class. I felt worthless. I tried to stop the thumb-sucking and went so far as to wear gloves on my hands as I slept. But, my thumb was just so comforting.

"I was terrified of using bathrooms, so I would hold the urge as long as I could. I would rather wet myself in my desk in class versus go the bathroom. My teacher thought I was lazy and scolded me for it as the classroom erupted in laughter. The bullying began during that year and lasted throughout the rest of my school years.

"My new foster family tried to teach me that God is love, but I did not believe that. What kind of a loving God would have allowed what had happened to me in the past?

What kind of loving Father would have allowed His child to be psychologically tortured, raped, and bullied? As far as I am concerned, God is not love. He is torture!

"I didn't stay with that foster family long and soon was bounced to several other homes. By the time I turned eighteen, I had been placed in five different foster homes in the deep South – most of which were physically or verbally abusive. None of the families wanted to keep me. I was too antisocial, too shy, too insecure, too troubled. I longed for the love I once knew from my parents but never received it. I've always been less than."

Travis cleared his throat as he flicked his hair out of his face. "Tara, you are not less than. If you look for your identity in people, then you will think you are based on what you have shared. But, look for your identity in Christ. He thinks you are special, and He loves you so much." Travis wiped his eyes as he continued. "Do you have, well I'm sure you do because nobody could go through something like that and not have emotional scars, but do you have struggles because of what you went through? Like, you mentioned not liking being touched, and, well, we all have just been hugging on you. Does that make you feel uncomfortable?"

Tara reflected for a moment before answering.

"Yes, I know that I struggle with manifestations of shame. I am quiet, shy, and withdrawn. This is the longest conversation I have ever had with anybody and the most words I have ever spoken at once. Yeah, I struggle. I definitely struggle with commitments and relationships. I don't really have any friends, and I'm afraid to trust people and let down my guard. I'm afraid of being hurt. I also struggle with depression, and I think I have an eating disorder. I binge because it feels good and then I stick my finger down my mouth and puke it up because I feel so ashamed of binging. And touch, yeah I struggle with touch. I turn into a toy soldier most of the time when somebody touches me. But, it's odd because for some reason what y'all have been doing feels comforting and not threatening."

Jonathan smiled at her as he said, "Tara, I am so proud of you for breaking the silence today. Satan may have you in bondage in many ways because of your past, but I believe Jesus is going to set you free."

Tara quickly replied, "Jesus might love me, but God sure hates me."

~CHAPTER 10~

Jonathan cringed on the inside as Tara said those words. She wasn't the first person he had heard think of God in that way. How could he convince her that God truly loved her after what had happened to her? How could he convince her that God hadn't turned his back on her while she was being victimized repeatedly? How could he convince her that God was love when her image of God was based on that horrible preacher, Jack?

He smiled to himself as the thought hit him. It wasn't up to him to convince her. God would! God had drawn her to Unplugged even if she did not recognize that fact. God had spoken to her during tonight's message and gave her courage to share her secrets for the very first time. God was drawing her close and would reveal Himself to her. He silently prayed that she wouldn't turn away from God and would be open to discovering who He truly is before he addressed Tara.

"Tara, once again I want to tell you how proud I am of you for opening up tonight. That was true vulnerability! I know you must struggle with several questions. Does God even exist? If He does exist, how could He have let this happen to me? Why didn't He protect me? Doesn't He care about me?

"Those are all tough questions. We could ask more. Why does God put up with murderers? Why does He allow women to be raped? Why does He allow wildfires, earthquakes, and floods that kill thousands of people? Why doesn't He stop terrorists from carrying out their evil plans? If God is love, why does He allow us to go through such pain?"

Tara nodded. Those were her feelings exactly.

"Nobody truly understands evil except for God. Sin came into this world through Adam and Eve because God created humanity with the ability to choose. He gave us free will. We are not forced into having a relationship with Him. He gives us a choice. He could force us to be good and loving, but it wouldn't be a relationship at all. Instead, it would be a forced obedience. We would be like brain-washed robots obeying our programmer's every wish. Instead, God allows us the choice to reject Him and the choice to sin.

"The natural question is: Why does God allow sin to go this far? Why doesn't He stop sin at lying or theft? Why doesn't He prevent it from escalating to rape and murder? Yet, how would we want Him to act? If He controlled the actions of people to a degree, there is still no longer freedom to choose. People choose to ignore God, to defy Him, to go their own way, and sometimes to commit horrible acts against others just like you experienced.

"God created all of us with free will. Ideally, we would choose to follow God's will in all situations. Yet, we don't always choose to do so. God's will is not always followed, and people sometimes make very bad choices that impact others. Yet, God is not at the mercy of people. Rather, we are at His mercy. We may make mistakes. We may make wrong choices. Yet, God is still in control! Even though life may seem overwhelming at times, God reminds us in Jeremiah 32:27, 'I am the Lord, the God of all the peoples of the world. Is anything too hard for Me?'

"Why does God allow pain and suffering? If there truly is a loving and powerful God who is in control, then why does He allow illness, abuse, broken relationships, heartache, and injuries? I will be honest with you, Tara. I do not know the answer. I can tell you what Jesus promised, yes promised, in John 16:33. 'Here on earth, you will have many trials and sorrows. But, take heart because I have overcome the world.' He was being honest and truthful when He said that suffering is coming. It's a part of the world we live in.

"I don't have the ability to see things with God's mind or eyes to completely answer those questions. First Corinthians 13:12 says, 'Now we see things imperfectly, like puzzling reflections in a mirror, but then we will see everything with perfect clarity. All that I know now is partial and incomplete, but then I will know everything completely, just as God now knows me completely.'

"So, I can't give you a full answer. We can't understand everything from our perspective, but there are some biblical truths that can provide some answers for us. The first is: God is not the creator of evil and suffering. I say that because in Genesis 1:31 when God looked around at all that He had made, He said it was very good. God would not have called evil good."

Tara interjected. "Well, if God didn't create evil and tragedy, where did they come from?"

Travis, returning from refilling his coffee cup, sat down as he said, "That goes back to free will."

"Think about it this way, Tara," Wendy said as she accepted a glass of water from Travis. "In order to give us the ability to love, God gave us the free will to decide whether or not we wanted to because real love always involves a choice. God could have programmed us to say 'I love you', but it would just be empty words. It wouldn't truly be love because in order to experience love, we would have to choose whether or not we wanted to.

"God gave us free will so that we could experience love. However, people have abused that free will by rejecting God and walking away from Him. As a result, evil has been introduced to the world."

"I don't understand," Tara said. "Why does evil exist just because people chose not to accept God?"

Travis adjusted his glasses as he said, "When we choose to be uncaring, prideful, selfish, or even abusive, evil in the form of pain, suffering, and tragedy comes about. I am sure that you have heard the talks about gun control in the news. A gun is an inanimate object until somebody pulls the trigger. Can a gun be blamed for a person's death, or is it the fault of the person who pulled the trigger?"

"It's the person who pulled the trigger." Tara said.

"But, why?" Travis asked.

"Because he made the choice to pull the trigger," she responded.

"That's what it's like with sin. A person's choice affects others. When a man cheats on his wife and has an affair, that not only affects his wife, but his children as well. When a person drinks and gets behind the wheel, that choice can affect a stranger driving down the road. When Jack chose to be abusive to you, the result was pain and suffering in your life. Can God be blamed for free will actions?"

Hannah looked at Tara as she handed her an open Bible turned to Romans 3:23. "God didn't make us robots, Tara. He wanted us to choose Him and to choose love out of free will. Yet, He knows as it says here 'everyone has sinned; we all fall short of God's glorious standard.' Sin entered the world through Adam and Eve. It is impossible for us to live a perfect life."

Jonathan cleared his throat.

"That brings me to my next point," he said. "Even though pain and suffering is not good, God can use it to accomplish good. Since you have that Bible in your lap, Tara, read Romans 8:28 please."

Tara struggled to find where Romans was in the Bible that she had just closed and was embarrassed by Wendy's help as she gently turned to the correct page. Tara read, "And we know that God causes everything to work together for the good of those who love God and are called according to his purpose for them." Confused, she looked at Jonathan. "What does that mean?"

"I want you to notice two things here. One, this verse only promises to cause good to emerge from evil. It does not say that God caused the evil and suffering to occur. Two, it doesn't say that we will necessarily see in this life how God will cause good to emerge from a bad circumstance. We may never see the good that comes about in our lifetime. That is a promise we have to cling to in hard times, however, that God will somehow make something good come out of it.

"Do you remember the story of Joseph in the Old Testament? Joseph was the spoiled younger brother who was sold into slavery by his older brothers who were jealous of him. While a slave, he was falsely accused of a crime and imprisoned. His story kept going from bad to worse. Thrown in a pit, sold into slavery, imprisoned! Yet, after many years, Joseph was placed in a leadership position and given powerful authority which allowed him to save the lives of his family and many others during a great famine.

"He said something very important to his brothers in Genesis 50:20. Will you read that, Wendy?

Wendy quickly turned to the reference and read, "You intended to harm me, but God intended it all for good. He brought me to this position so I could save the lives of many people."

Jonathan smiled at Tara. "Bad things happened in Joseph's life. There must have been times when he wondered why he was so alone and why so much bad was happening to him. He didn't deserve to be treated the way he had. Joseph ended up a slave because of the actions of his brothers. He was a victim of circumstance. I'm sure that he felt forsaken and abandoned during those years of slavery. Yet, God did not abandon him. God used Joseph's circumstances. He used the choice of Joseph's brothers to sell him into slavery and placed him in a position to help others. God caused something good to come out of what was intended for bad!"

Tara frowned at Jonathan as she asked, "How can God use what happened to me for good? I am too messed up and permanently, emotionally, scarred. There is no way God can make anything good come out of my life!"

Wendy patted Tara on the shoulder. "Nothing is impossible with God, Tara. Absolutely nothing! God can use our suffering to draw us to Him, to mold our character, and to influence and encourage others who may be going through the same thing and need hope that it gets better.

"Tara, I have shared my story countless times, and I know that it helps others because they tell me or write me notes. It gives them encouragement to know that they are not alone in their suffering and that there is hope. I used to be a victim and have a victim's mentality, Tara. Now, I am a survivor. I am a survivor of childhood sexual abuse! I am no longer a victim! I used to be in bondage to the shame and guilt that came from that, but I am not anymore. I have been set free by the blood and love of Jesus Christ. He freed me from that bondage, and I am freed more and more each time I share my story. There is healing in speaking about it. You have made that first step toward healing today with your courage to share. I am proud of you!

"Tara, we have all been through hard times. I could sit and ask questions all day. Why did God allow my grandfather to molest me? Why did He allow my fiancé to be killed in an accident? Why didn't He stop that driver from having that drink? Why didn't He stop him from driving drunk?

"The answer is, 'I don't know.' Yes, God could have intervened in those circumstances, but for whatever reason, He chose not to. I have to have faith that God loves me and that He is in charge. I have to believe that He will make something good come out of the tragedies and hard times in my life. Will I ever truly understand it? Probably not! But, I can't blame God for what happened. I can't blame him for people's choices."

Jonathan smiled at Tara. "God loves you, Tara. He loves you! And, I believe he was sad when those things happened to you. I don't know why He didn't choose to intervene, but it's not because He didn't love you. It's not because He didn't think you had value in His eyes. God doesn't always choose to intervene in circumstances. I do believe that God is going to make something good come out of what you have experienced though just like He did with Wendy. I believe He will give you a beauty from ashes experience."

Travis stifled a yawn. It was getting late. "Tara, it's been great talking with you tonight, and I admire your vulnerability. I think I speak for all of us when I say that we would like to be your friends. We would like to talk with you some more and help you find your identity in Christ. We want to help you unplug from what you have been taught about God and help you plug into the true God through Scripture. Would you be open to that?"

Tara stared in shock at the group. She couldn't believe that they had heard her shameful secrets and still wanted to spend time with her much less be her friend. Stunned, she quietly answered, "I'd like that."

"How about Wednesday evening?" Jonathan asked. "Does that work for everyone? We could meet here at the church or at someone's house?"

Wendy smiled. She loved entertaining company. "How about at our place? I could cook a dinner for everyone too!"

"Your place it is," said Jonathan rubbing his stomach in anticipation of the meal. Wendy was a wonderful cook. "Let's pray before we go." The group all placed their hands on Tara as Jonathan prayed.

"Father, You are mighty, and You have done a mighty work in Tara this evening. You gave her the courage to break the silence of this secret that she has held for many years. Your Word says in Isaiah that You have come to set the prisoners free, and I believe with all my heart that You will set Tara free from her past. I thank You for the work You are doing in her. I ask that You will continue to draw her to You and help her find her identity in You alone. Help her to no longer feel worthless but valued and loved. I ask that You will help us to be the friends she needs in her life. Help us to encourage her and to be a light that shines in the darkness for You. In Jesus's name, Amen."

~CHAPTER 11~

Tara smiled as Wendy gave her a hug goodnight then closed her bedroom door. Wendy and her friends truly seemed to care about her, and that felt really good. She was amazed at how freeing sharing her story had felt. She had always been afraid of how people would react if they only knew, yet she didn't feel judged at all by the group at New Life.

As she lay in bed, however, negative thoughts suddenly filled her mind. *You are just a project for them. You are worthless. They are actually disgusted by you. Nobody can care about you.* As Tara tossed and turned while wrestling with the thoughts, she was confused. Wendy and her friends truly did seem to care, but why. The negative thoughts continued with intensity. *Nobody cares about you. You are garbage. Worthless!*

Tara reached under her bed for her secret stash of junk food and quickly gorged herself on an entire bag of potato chips. Food always soothed her. As she looked down at the empty bag, she felt instantly repulsed and ran to the bathroom. Sobbing, she stuck her finger down her throat and waited for the relief to come. Instead of relief, she was flooded with guilt over her binging. Suddenly, the thought came to her to drink the bathroom cleaner that was in the cabinet under the sink. *Might as well. There is no point in you being here. Nobody cares about you. Drink it now!* The thoughts egged her on as she sat on the bathroom floor staring at the toilet. Memories of Jack forcing her head in a similar toilet flashed in her mind as she shuddered.

Wendy, who was laying in her bed reading her Bible in the adjoining bedroom, heard the sounds of retching. She pondered for a moment if she should intervene. After all, Tara was embarrassed and angry at her the last time she did. She said a quick prayer for wisdom and felt God telling her to get involved. Taking a deep breath, she lightly tapped on the bathroom door. There was no response, so Wendy quietly entered. Tara sat on the floor staring at the toilet seemingly in a daze. Remembering how Tara had reacted the other night, Wendy was afraid to touch her in this state, so she softly called her name.

"Tara."

There was no reaction. Wendy tried once more. "Tara, look at me."

Tara fixed her glazed eyes on Wendy. "Leave me alone!"

"I can't," Wendy said. "What's wrong?"

"I shouldn't have told y'all!" Tara yelled. "Now it's worse."

"What's worse?" asked Wendy as she sat next to Tara on the bathroom floor.

Tara began to sob. "I thought it would get better if I told, but it was a mistake. I still feel worthless."

Wendy wrapped her arm around Tara as she said, "The enemy is going to attack you because he wants you to stay in bondage. You made the first step tonight to be set free, so he is going to do his best to wrap the chains of insecurity around you. It is a spiritual battle, and we have to use spiritual warfare to fight it."

At Tara's confused look, Wendy added, "We fight with prayer. Let's pray. Father, I ask that You will give Tara peace tonight. The enemy has had her in bondage over her past, and he does not want her to be set free. Father, You came to set the captives free, and I know that You want that for Tara. Help her to seek Your face. Help her to believe that You are trustworthy and that Your love is without any type of fault. Draw her to You and help her to cling to You and Your truths. Release her from this bondage. In Jesus's name, Amen."

Embarrassed, Tara stared at the floor as Wendy gave her a hug.

"Do you want to talk about it?" Wendy asked.

Tara hesitated for a moment. The random thoughts she was having about ending her life were scary and not normal. If it was depression, wouldn't she be having the thoughts all of the time instead of randomly? What was wrong with her? Would Wendy understand? Or, would she demand that she get professional help? Tara decided that she wasn't willing to risk it. She didn't want Wendy's pity.

"No, I'm okay now. Thanks for being there for me," she simply said. It was true. When Wendy was around, the dark thoughts Tara had seemed to go away. It was like she truly was a light for God. God's light shone in Wendy so much that the darkness that seemed to surround her fled when Wendy prayed. Tara made her way back to her bedroom and soon fell into an exhausted sleep.

~CHAPTER 12~

Tara slept in the next morning and didn't get out of bed until ten. Wendy had left her a note on the refrigerator.

"Good morning! I am volunteering at the nursing home today with Hannah. Enjoy the quiet and have a wonderful day!"

Tara felt a brief moment of jealousy arise. Why wasn't she invited too? She tried to reason to herself that Wendy volunteered at the nursing home twice a month and had asked her several times before to join them. However, her feelings were still hurt at not being asked this time.

The negative tape instantly began to play in her head. *Wendy doesn't really want to be friends with me*, she thought. *I am just a project to her.* She quickly pulled out her cell phone. The desire to hurt Wendy back was very strong as she angrily typed out a text message.

"Thanks for thinking of me this morning!"

Her phone vibrated with a sunny response from Wendy a few moments later.

"Sure! How r u doing?"

Tara glared at the phone. Was Wendy too stupid to realize that she was being sarcastic? She quickly responded.

"Like u care!"

A long pause passed then Tara's phone vibrated once more with a text message from Wendy.

"R u ok?"

Tara angrily typed, *"Watever!"* She waited for Wendy to respond, but she never did. *Some friend she is,* she thought. *She doesn't really want me around.*

Wendy stared at her phone in dismay as she showed the text messages to Hannah. "I don't know how to respond," she exclaimed.

Hannah smiled at her. "She's probably just feeling embarrassed about talking to us last night. Just let it go."

Wendy shrugged. "I guess. I just don't know how to be a friend to her or to reach her."

Hannah paused as she raised her hand to knock on the door of Mr. John's room. "Wendy, I remember a similar person who was angry at the world and took it out on everyone around her." She looked at Wendy pointedly. "She's one of my best friends now, and the nicest person I know!"

Wendy smiled. "I guess that's what it is. Tara reminds me of me. She just needs time and lots of love."

Hannah nodded her head in affirmation. "She needs Jesus, and she needs friends who can show her God's love.

Now, let's go be a blessing to Mr. John. I am sure he is waiting on us."

At Mr. John's weak "Come in," they entered the room bearing their gifts of cookies and doughnuts. He smiled at them as he extended a shaky hand in greeting. "I've been waiting for my favorite visitors," he said. "Sit down, and let's catch up."

~CHAPTER 13~

Tara glared at her phone for the twentieth time. Wendy had still not responded. Granted, she probably didn't even know why Tara was upset, but she still should have responded. *She doesn't really care about me,* she thought again. *Nobody does.*

Tara angrily sat down and opened her philosophy book. Her assignment was to read and write a paper on Plato's "Allegory of the Cave." Plato, a Greek philosopher, wrote it in an attempt to answer philosophical questions about the nature of reality. In it, the reader is asked to imagine a cave in which prisoners are kept chained together from birth and forced to look at a wall in front of them. A fire is constantly roaring behind the prisoners. Since they are unable to turn their heads, all they could see were the shadowy representations along the cave wall caused by the guards moving and carrying objects behind them. For the prisoners, the shadows are their reality.

Plato presents a dilemma. What would happen if one of the prisoners was freed and forced to look at the fire after spending his entire life staring at the cave wall full of flickering images? Of course, the light would hurt his eyes, and he would naturally turn around to look at the shadows once more. In doing so, he would question reality. There was more to life than what he had known on the cave wall.

The plot thickens. What if the prisoner was then released outside in the daylight? After an initial period of discomfort from being exposed to the sunlight for the first time in his life, he would visualize dimensions and reflections. He would see green trees growing tall and reflections upon the water of a nearby lake. He would hear birds singing as they flew by and the sounds of frogs croaking by the lake's shore. His senses would be delighted by the sight and smells of wildflowers growing tall in the grass.

The prisoner would be amazed at what he saw. If he were forced to return to the cave, he would no longer be satisfied by the shadowy images on the cave wall as he once was. He had been given a taste of true reality. As the man would try to convince his fellow prisoners that there is more to life than what they had experienced, they would scoff at him and think he was insane. After all, the shadows were their only reality. They couldn't possibly imagine a world such as the man described.

Tara's forehead creased, deep in thought. What was true reality? How could she know? Did God truly exist? If He did, which image of Him was true: the one Jack had taught her about or the one New Life portrayed?

Just then, Wendy bounced in the door. "Hi Tara!" she called. "I brought you back a peanut butter fudge milkshake! We made them at the nursing home today with some of the residents."

Tara turned around, surprised that Wendy had thought of her since she hadn't invited her along. "Thanks," she muttered as she accepted the slightly melted shake.

"Sure," Wendy said as she washed her hands. "What are you working on?"

"A paper for philosophy," Tara replied as she took a long sip of the shake. It was delicious! "Can I ask you a question?"

Wendy nodded. "Of course!"

"How can I know what true reality is?"

At Wendy's confused look, Tara added. "I have been reading the 'Allegory of the Cave', and I am confused as to how I can know what the true reality about God is? How can I know that He isn't just something that you perceive to be just because you don't know any better?"

Wendy sat down on the couch and motioned Tara to do the same. "I know that God exists because everything in nature testifies to that: the mountains, the ocean, the sunrises and the sunsets, the wind, the flowers, the beauty that surrounds us. That's all the work of God."

She hurried to her room to get her Bible and opened it to Romans 1:20. She began to read, "Through everything God made, they can clearly see His invisible qualities – His eternal power and divine nature. So they have no excuse for not knowing God."

Wendy then turned in her Bible to Psalm 19. "There is also a reference that is related here as well. Listen to this. 'The heavens proclaim the glory of God. The skies display His craftsmanship. Day after day they continue to speak; night after night they make Him known. They speak without a word; their voice is never heard. Yet their message has gone throughout the earth, and their words to all the world.'

"All of nature reveals the glory of God! It's always there pointing to the Creator! Tara, the enemy wants us to have doubts about God's existence. He wants to keep us in bondage. But, Jesus came to set us free! He can and will set you free from the grip the past has on you, Tara! I know the story of the 'Allegory of the Cave.' For those who don't know God, yes, we look foolish just like the prisoner who left the cave. We look like the ones who don't know the true reality or have been brainwashed. And, people don't want to believe us when we share the Good News because they are still looking at the images on their cave walls believing that's all life is. You're born. You live. You die. And, you make the best of it. The end.

"But, it's not the end, Tara. Death is not the end! There is more to come if you will accept Jesus's gift of eternal life. His gift isn't just for when you die though. It is for now. He can change your life in ways you never imagined. He will give you courage instead of fear and doubt! He will give you confidence and the ability to do all things through Jesus who gives you strength. And, He will show you what love, true love, really looks like."

Wendy closed her Bible. "Does that make sense Tara?"

Tara sighed as she stood up. "I wish I could believe you, but I don't think I can. Every time I think of God, I see Him as Jack portrayed Him: mean and angry. You talk about God as if He is totally different. How can I know which is the true reality?"

Wendy opened up her Bible to Jeremiah 29:13. "This is where you start, Tara. God never lies! Listen to what He promises here. 'If you look for Me wholeheartedly, You will find Me.' That's a promise, Tara! God always keeps His promises! He will never abandon you! In fact, the only thing He has ever abandoned was the grave. He left behind an empty tomb! Seek Him! Ask Him to show you who He truly is, and He will."

Wendy stood up. "I'd love to talk with you some more later. Right now, I've got to hit the books. Would you want to go for a hike next weekend? I could invite Jonathan and the gang to join us as we get out in nature and see God's creation. I already have plans with Hannah after church tomorrow, so it would have to be next weekend though."

Tara frowned as an instant wave of rejection hit her. So, Wendy was once again not inviting her along with Hannah for wherever they were going. She could feel the tears of rejection that threatened to fall burning her eyes as she faked a smile and said, "Sure that would be great."

She quickly walked to her room and closed the door as the sobs took over. She was so tired of being rejected by everyone in her life. Wendy didn't really want to be friends with her. She was just being nice and treating her as a project. Tara reached under her bed for a bag of chocolate candy and stuffed piece after piece in her mouth until the bag was empty.

~CHAPTER 14~

"How is Tara doing?" Jonathan asked Wendy the following morning at church. "I hoped that she would come this morning."

"Me too," said Wendy studying Jonathan intently. "Be careful not to get feelings for her. She's lost remember."

Jonathan blushed. "Am I that obvious?" he asked.

"I could tell she won your heart the minute she opened up with her story. You feel sorry for the girl who feels that nobody loves her, and you want to be the person to show her love."

Jonathan gaped at Wendy. "Is it wrong to want to be a knight to a damsel in distress?" he teased. At Wendy's stern look, he became serious. "Of course, I won't act upon my feelings. She doesn't know Christ. I can't even think of having an unequally yoked relationship. However, if I am to be perfectly honest with you, I should share that I do feel that she is the woman for me, the woman that God has in store for me. I'm willing to wait as long as I have to until the timing is right."

Wendy stared at Jonathan. "Are you serious?" she asked.

He smiled. "Yes, I knew it the moment she began to tell her story the other night. It was like I felt God saying 'This is the one!' I have never felt that way before, Wendy. I have been praying for a while now that God would not only put the woman He has in store for me to marry in my life but also that I would know it instantly."

Picturing Tara's unkempt appearance, he chuckled. "Believe me, I was more surprised than you. To be honest, she wouldn't have been a candidate I would have even been attracted to physically at first, but it's her heart that got my attention. I think she is beautiful on the inside even though she doesn't realize it. And, she is on the outside too. That unkempt look has grown on me."

Wendy stared at Jonathan in shock. She knew that he had been praying specifically for a wife, but she never would have imagined that Tara would have been the answer to his prayer. She tried to imagine Tara as a preacher's wife with her standoffish behavior and just couldn't picture it.

Changing the subject, she asked, "Do you want to join me and Hannah today after church? We are going to the cemetery to visit Gary's grave."

Jonathan instantly sobered. "Oh, Wendy, I'm so sorry. It slipped my mind that today is the one year anniversary of his death. Of course, I will come. Can I invite Travis too?"

Wendy's eyes filled with tears. "Sure," she replied. "I can't believe it's been a year already. It seems like just yesterday he was leading the worship team here. We had so many plans for our life together. I can't believe he is gone. I know I will see him again one day in heaven, but I miss him."

"Me too. I miss our talks together. I know he was your fiancé, but he was my best friend. He is the one that helped me out of legalism and taught me the truth of grace. I loved how he brought his guitar with him everywhere he went and made up songs. He was great at making people laugh."

Wendy smiled sadly. "Remember that road trip we all went on together on our way to the missions conference a few years ago? Gary made up lyrics to every song that played on the radio. I have never laughed so hard in my entire life. My stomach was literally hurting by the time we got there."

Jonathan chuckled. "I remember it vividly. I was laughing so hard that I could hardly focus on the road. That's what we have to remember – the good times. Gary wouldn't want it any other way."

Wendy smiled as Hannah approached and enveloped her in a hug. "I'll see you after church. Thanks for being there!" she called to Jonathan as they walked away to find a seat in the sanctuary.

Travis already had two seats saved for them by the time they arrived. Wendy didn't miss the surreptitious glances he and Hannah gave one another during the service. It seemed like romance was in the air everywhere. Hannah deserved a good man after that loser she had dated who had gotten another girl pregnant while dating her. Travis was honorable and trustworthy. There would never be a question as to his fidelity.

As Jonathan opened up with the sermon, Wendy briefly thought of Tara. She hadn't come out of her room this morning. She wondered if Tara was purposely avoiding her or if she had just overslept.

After the service, the group gathered in the foyer while waiting for Jonathan to shake hands with the congregation as they exited the building. As the young adult pastor, he only preached once a month on Sunday mornings in addition to his weekly Unplugged sermons. Yet, he still had responsibilities for making everyone feel welcome.

Wendy thought it was a good idea that Jonathan had been praying for a wife. Although Jonathan lived an exemplary life, quite a few members of the church had loudly voiced their opinion that a pastor shouldn't be single – especially a young adult pastor. The entire congregation knew about Jonathan's past as a player, and some had used his vulnerability in sharing about his past against him. He made sure to never be alone in a room with any member of the opposite sex to avoid any judgment or scandal.

The group piled into Travis's sport utility vehicle and headed to the cemetery. As Wendy opened the door of the vehicle, her phone vibrated with a text from Tara.

"Thanks for inviting me today."

Wendy sighed. Tara knew it was Sunday and that she went to church every Sunday morning. If she had wanted to go, why didn't she come out of her room that morning?

"I'm sorry," she typed as her brows creased in frustration. *"I thought u were sleeping."*

Her phone vibrated with another text almost instantly.

"Well, I'm not sleeping now. Do u want to go get lunch?"

Wendy glanced at her friends who were waiting for her to walk with them to Gary's grave as she typed a quick response.

"I'm sorry. I can't today. We are doing something right now."

She placed her phone in her purse and left it on the seat as she walked over to where her friends were standing and accepted a hug from Hannah.

Tara stared in anger at her phone. She had finally got the courage to reach out, to ask Wendy to hang out, and Wendy had flat out rejected her. Wendy didn't really want to be friends with her. Nobody did.

~CHAPTER 15~

The silence of the empty apartment was getting to Tara as she tried to concentrate on Plato's "Allegory of the Cave." She tried to imagine how overjoyed the prisoner who left the cave must have felt when he saw the real world for the first time instead of the shadows he had lived his entire life in. She wondered if she too had spent her entire life in a cave of darkness and illusions while missing out on the real world outside of it. Wendy would say that she should step into the light – the light of God's love. But, is God love? How could she know for sure?

As she pondered those questions, the old tapes of insecurity and negativity began playing in her head over and over. *Nobody cares about you. You are worthless. Garbage! Unlovable!* She tried to shrug the negativity off, but the tapes began intensifying. *Wendy is just pretending to be a friend to you. So are the rest of her friends. They just feel sorry for you. You are just a project to them. You are everything Jack said you are. Tease! Sinner!*

Tara just wanted the tapes in her head to stop, so she grabbed her phone and quickly sent Wendy an emotional text message.

"U don't really care about me. Nobody does."

She waited for a response, hoping that Wendy would respond back with "Of course I care." But, no response came.

The tapes continued playing their frequent and redundant messages. *You are ugly. Nobody likes you. Reject. Worthless. Trash. Loser.* Jack's sweaty face appeared in her mind screaming his obscenities at her. *It's all your fault! You have been a bad girl! You are going to burn in hell forever!*

Tara hurried to the kitchen and grabbed a bag of chips. She quickly scarfed down the entire contents of the bag. Looking around for something else to eat, she settled on a bag of chocolate candy. After eating all that remained in that bag too, she hurried to the bathroom and stuck her finger down her throat. She waited for the relief to come and the negative messages to stop. But, they didn't. The tape continued to play.

God hates you. You are a mistake. You are so worthless.

Tara began sobbing uncontrollably and typed out another emotional text message to Wendy hoping that Wendy would say something to ease the pain that she was feeling. She just wanted to feel loved and wanted.

"U hate me, don't u? I am a horrible roommate to u."

She stared at her phone willing Wendy to respond, but she didn't. She quickly sent several more messages in succession.

"U r going to write me off, aren't u?"

"I am just a project."

"You think I am so annoying."

The negative tapes continued playing in her head as flashbacks of Jack consumed her thoughts. She shivered at the messages that seemed to strike with vehemence. *You are a mistake. You don't belong here. You never have. You should just end your life now and make everyone else happy. Why don't you go get your gun and do it? Come on. Do something right for a change. Get the gun!*

Tara's body shook with emotion. It was true. She didn't belong here. She had nobody in her life that she was close to or who truly cared about her. Wendy and her friends had just been pretending to care. She walked to her closet and grabbed her handgun that she kept on the top shelf.

~CHAPTER 16~

Wendy wiped the tears from her eyes as her friends released her from their embrace.

"Thank you so much for being here today. I needed this time to focus on the good times we all had with Gary. I don't know why God let me fall in love with him only to have him taken from my life. I don't know what God's plan is for me or what the future holds, but I am choosing to trust God and His plan for me even if it is lonely right now."

Travis straightened his glasses on his nose as he grinned at Wendy. "Gary told me the very same thing the day before he was killed in that accident."

Wendy stared in shock. "He told you he was lonely?"

Travis laughed. "No, he told me that he didn't know what the future held or what God had in store for him. He said that He was just choosing to trust God with his life and not worry about finances or how he was going to support you."

Wendy gave Travis a quick hug. "Thank you! Thank you for sharing that memory, Travis. I know you miss him too." She opened the door to Travis's vehicle and heard the unmistakable sound of her phone vibrating. Looking at it, she frowned. There were twenty texts from Tara.

As she began to read text after text telling her how much she didn't care about Tara or how she was just pretending to be her friend, she began to get angry. She had been doing everything she could think of to reach out and make Tara feel love and accepted. What had she done to deserve all of this hatred from her?

Jonathan saw her staring in consternation at her phone.

"Problems?" he asked.

She began typing as she vented, "I don't what to do. I have tried so hard to be a friend to her. She doesn't trust me. She thinks the worst of me. I can't take it anymore." She finished typing four words and hit send.

~CHAPTER 17~

Tara jumped as her phone vibrated with a text. She had been staring at the shiny black barrel of the handgun while trying to muster the courage to pull the trigger. Finally, Wendy was responding. She would make her feel wanted and make the negative tapes stop playing. Tara frowned as she read Wendy's reply.

"You need professional help!"

Suddenly furious, she typed out a quick response.

"Professional help? Isn't that being judgmental? Some friend u are!"

She stared at the gun again. It seemed to beckon her as the thoughts in her head intensified. *Do it! Do it now! Do something right in your life for a change. It would serve Wendy right to come home and see what she made you do because she didn't care enough to be there. You might as well. You don't belong here. You are a mistake!*

She quickly picked up the phone again and sent another text to Wendy. *"Hypocrite!"*

~CHAPTER 18~

Wendy's eyes filled with tears as she stared at her phone. She didn't want to go home now and have to face Tara after all of the hateful messages she had received. Jonathan looked at her. "What is going on?" he asked.

"What's wrong?" Wendy asked angrily. "It's an emotional enough day having to remember the anniversary of Gary's death, and now Tara has decided to use my phone as her punching bag."

"Let me see," Jonathan asked as he reached for her phone. He began to scroll through the texts and frowned. "We need to get to your house now," he said. "Call her and tell her we are on our way."

"I don't want to go home after reading these," Wendy complained.

"We need to. Call her," he demanded.

Wendy dialed Tara's number and waited for her to pick up.

~CHAPTER 19~

Tara stared at her phone as it rang. She gently put the gun down on the dresser beside her as she answered.

"Professional counseling? You are such a hypocrite, Wendy! I thought you were my friend."

Wendy sighed. "I am your friend, Tara. I think you need some help to deal with your emotions. Nobody sends that many texts in a row, and you haven't been very nice to me in them."

Tara rolled her eyes as she picked up the gun once again. It would serve Wendy right for her to hear the gunshot over the phone. She deserved it for being such a fake and pretending to be such a caring person.

"I was having a bad day, and I reached out to you just like you said I should do. Like you really care about me. I'm just your latest project!"

Tara hung up the phone hoping that Wendy would call her back. She just wanted Wendy to tell her that she truly did care. Instead, Wendy was acting defensive. Tara sobbed as she stared at the phone. "Call me back, please" she whispered. "I need a lifeline, or I'm going to do this." She stuck the barrel in her mouth and reached for the trigger.

~CHAPTER 20~

Jonathan was fervently praying as Travis drove towards Wendy and Tara's apartment. He had a strong feeling that spiritual warfare was taking place and was behind Tara's hateful texts to Wendy. As Travis turned into the apartment complex's parking lot, Jonathan shouted, "Stop!"

Travis hit the brakes and stared in shock as Jonathan opened the door and began running up the steps to the building like it was on fire. Wendy hesitated for a moment and followed suit. Apparently, Jonathan knew something she didn't. She hurried to catch up to him. "Wait," she called. "Slow down!"

Jonathan paused on a step for a moment. "Hand me your keys," he yelled. "Quick!"

"What is the matter with you?" Wendy demanded as she sought to catch her breath.

"I don't know. I just have this sense of urgency from God," he called as he dashed up the remaining steps to the third floor. Finally reaching the girls' apartment, he turned the key in the lock and ran inside. "Tara," he called. "Tara, where are you?"

There was no answer as he dashed from room to room with Wendy on his heels. Reaching Tara's bedroom, he hesitated for a moment then flung the door wide open. Tara was seated on her bed with a handgun pointed at her face.

"Tara," he called softly. "Put the gun down."

Tears streamed down Tara's face. "I can't take it anymore. Nobody cares about me. I am a mistake!"

"I care," Jonathan insisted. "So does Wendy." He took a tentative step towards Tara and held out his hand. "Tara, hand me the gun. It's going to be okay."

Tara's hand shook as Wendy stared in horror at the scene playing out in front of her. "Tara," she sobbed. "Please put the gun down. I'm sorry. I didn't know what was going on. I didn't know your texts were a cry for help. Please, hand Jonathan the gun."

Travis and Hannah, who had run up the stairs after parking his vehicle, came to an abrupt halt behind Wendy as they surveyed the situation.

Jonathan cautiously sat on the bed beside Tara. "We are here for you, Tara. Let us be your friends. Let us help you."

Tara lowered the gun but kept a tight grip on it instead of giving it to Jonathan. He kept his hand outstretched and began to pray.

"Father, Your timing is always perfect. I thank You for giving me that sense of urgency to get here. I ask that You speak Your truth to Tara. Let her feel Your presence and sense Your love for her. Help her to realize that she is not a mistake, and that You knew her before she was even born. You created her, and nothing You create is a mistake for You are perfect.

"I praise You that You accept us as we are, and I thank You that You accept Tara. She may think she is messed up and too far gone, but she can never be too messed up for You in Your grace and mercy to cleanse from the inside out. Cleanse her Father! Cleanse her from her past and the emotions that she deals with from that. Help her to see herself as You see her.

"Father, You know everything about us. You know every hair on our head, and You know what we are going to say before we even say it. You know how lonely and isolated Tara feels. Open the eyes of her heart and let her feel Your love and realize that not only is nothing impossible with You but also that Your love is so deep, so wide, and so large that she can never understand the depths of it. The enemy is attacking her and trying to drag her down. The enemy doesn't want her to step out of the cave of darkness that she has been trapped in and feel the warmth and love of Your light. The enemy wants to keep her in bondage. Free her Lord! Free Tara from her past! Free her from her insecurities! Free her from her emotions! Set her free Lord! In Jesus's name, Amen."

Jonathan was openly weeping as he finished praying and gently reached for the gun once more. This time, Tara released it to him as she crumpled herself on his shoulders. Wendy hurried over and sat beside her rubbing her back. "We love you, Tara. We love you," she said over and over as Travis and Hannah joined in.

~CHAPTER 21~

Wendy began leading the group in praise songs as her heart continued to rapidly pound. She inwardly blamed herself for the situation. She knew Tara had been struggling, but she had no idea just how bad until now. The "if-onlys" began to play in her head. *If I had only been a better friend. If I had only invited her to more events. If I had only.*

She suddenly paused in her thinking. *Here I am mouthing the words to the praise songs while my heart and mind are elsewhere focused on the situation instead of focused on You.* As she struggled to turn her attention from the gun on the windowsill where Jonathan had placed it, she recalled Gary's words to her a few years ago.

"When you are overcome by anxiety about something, instead of letting those anxious thoughts consume you, start praying and praising and thanking God for His goodness. It is hard to focus on the negative when you turn your thoughts to God."

Wendy smiled as she stopped automatically singing. Jonathan looked at her quizzically.

"I'm sorry. I can't get my mind off what just happened or almost happened. I'm just mouthing the words. I'm just so in shock. I would like to do something y'all. Something that Gary taught me long ago when I was struggling with my past and with believing God is who He says He is and that I am who God says I am. I would like us to pray the attributes of God together right now."

Travis stared at her in confusion. "You want us to do what?"

Wendy stood up and began to nervously pace around the room.

"I want us to think of the attributes or qualities of God and praise Him for that. He deserves our praise! He just did a miracle here! He saved Tara's life. He saved your life, Tara, whether you realize it or not. I was annoyed and upset by your text messages, but God spoke to Jonathan and gave him a sense of urgency to come here. He didn't speak in an audible voice, yet the Holy Spirit spoke to his heart and convinced him of the seriousness of this situation. That is a God thing!"

Jonathan nodded in agreement. "It definitely was!"

Wendy continued. "Let's praise God using the alphabet. I'll go first."

All of the group closed their eyes except for Tara who was still openly weeping. Wendy began.

"Father, I praise You for You are acceptance. You accepted me just as I am! I didn't have to get cleaned up for You. I praise You because You accepted me and then changed the desires of my heart to reflect You more."

Jonathan took the cue. "God, I praise You for You are beautiful. Your love is beautiful! Your Creation is beautiful!"

Hannah joined in. "Father, I praise You for You are compassionate."

Travis removed his glasses and wiped his eyes as he said, "Lord, I praise You for You are my Deliverer. You have rescued me! And, You just rescued Tara in Your own perfect timing."

Tara listened in astonishment as the group continued to praise God for who He is.

"God, I praise You for You are eternal."

"Lord, I praise You for You are forgiveness."

"Father, I praise You for You are grace."

"I praise You for You are holy. You are indescribable. You are just. You are kind. You are love."

Tears openly ran down Tara's face as she pondered. *Who is God? Is He the cruel dictator that I have always imagined Him to be? Or, is He truly the characteristics the group is listing?* She focused her attention back to the praise.

Wendy was on the letter "m" and was praising God for being merciful. Tara listened in astonishment as Wendy prayed.

"Father, I praise You that You are merciful and not mean as I once thought You were. I praise You for Your mercy that You have shown me. I praise You for Your grace and forgiveness."

Tara hadn't realized that Wendy had once had the same conflicting thoughts about God as she did. On second thought, Wendy had tried to explain her faith several times, but she hadn't wanted to listen. She stared openly at Travis whom she had dubbed in her mind, "Richie Rich". He wasn't like the other wealthy guys she knew. He didn't flaunt his family's wealth. Instead, he sat there with his head bowed, praying and openly weeping as he said,

"Lord, I praise You for You are never failing. People may fail me. People have failed me, but You never will. You have never abandoned me. You will never let me down! You are the only One in my life who has never failed me."

Travis broke down in sobs as Hannah comforted him. Tara stared in amazement.

Jonathan continued the praise. "Father, I praise You for You are omnipresent. You are everywhere. I don't have to compete for your attention."

Voices chimed in.

"I praise You for You are perfect."

"I praise You for You are quiet. You don't scream and badger us. You quietly speak to our hearts."

"I praise You for You are rest. You give us rest because of Your righteousness."

" You are my salvation."

" You are trust."

"I praise You for You are understanding."

" You are victorious."

Tara chuckled as Jonathan prayed. "I praise You for Your perfect wisdom. You know what is best for our lives, our hearts, and our relationships. You are the God of wisdom, and You also are so wise that You know a word and a characteristic about Yourself that begins with the letters "x" and "z" even though we can't think of any."

Jonathan looked around the room as he asked, "Seriously, what characteristics about God begin with the letters "x" and "z"?

Wendy shrugged. "We will have to pray that God will reveal that to us. I personally can't think of any." She glanced at the handgun sitting on the windowsill. The sight of it no longer made her flinch. She felt more at peace after praising God for His attributes. She led the group once more in a praise song, and this time her heart was actually into it.

~CHAPTER 22~

As Jonathan began to stand up, Tara reached for his arm. "Wait!" He paused and looked at her.

"What if I have been wrong all this time?" she asked as the tears ran down her face uninhibited. "Y'all seem so sure of who God is, and you don't describe Him as the monster I have always seen him as. All of the words that were used to describe Him – love, grace, mercy, acceptance. He really is all of those things, isn't He? It's like the 'Allegory of the Cave.' What if I'm actually the prisoner, and what if what I have always pictured or perceived God to be is based upon my circumstances and not based on the reality of who He truly is?"

Wendy sat down beside Tara on the bed and put an arm around her. "Tara, how serious were you about killing yourself? If we hadn't got here when we did, do you think you would have gone through with it? Be absolutely honest."

Tara hung her head. "Yes, I have no doubt in my mind. I was just about to pull the trigger when Jonathan burst in and interrupted me." She looked pleadingly at Wendy. "I'm not mental, ok. I just am tired of life. I'm tired of being unwanted. I just want people in my life to truly care about me."

Wendy's eyes filled with tears. "Tara, we do care about you. I care about you! I wasn't trying to ignore you today. Maybe I should have invited you along, but I didn't think you would want to come. After all, you didn't know Gary."

"Gary?" Tara questioned.

"My fiancé. We were visiting his grave today." Wendy took a deep breath. "Today marked a year since he died." She nodded her head towards her friends.

"They came along to support me today and help me remember the good moments that we all shared with Gary. I left my phone in the vehicle – not because I was trying to avoid you. It had nothing to do with you at all. Then, when I realized I had twenty texts from you, I didn't know what to say. I was already emotional, and you were basically telling me how I wasn't a good friend. I should have reacted differently. I should have been more understanding. But, Tara, you are not the only person who has struggles. I am human too! As much as I care about you, I can't be everything to you! Nor can Hannah or Travis or even Jonathan. Only God can!"

Jonathan sat down on the floor by Tara's feet and looked up at her. "You know how frustrating it can be when you call a company and get a recorded message stating something like this." He put on a slightly nasal tone as he imitated a recording.

"Your call is very important to us. Due to being busier than normal, there is an average forty-five minute wait time for the next available representative. Please stay on the line, and your call will be answered in the order it was received."

At Tara's chuckle, Jonathan continued his point. "Then, the boring elevator music plays over and over while you wait and wait and wait to finally reach a live person instead of a recording. Do you know what I mean?"

Tara smiled and nodded.

"God is not like that! He is everywhere at all times. When we want to talk to Him, we never have to wait. He doesn't give us a wait time to be acknowledged. We are important to Him! We are His children! We have a direct line to God through prayer! Even people who have the best intentions are not always going to be able to be there for you when you need it. Life gets in the way. But, God is just a prayer away! He is always there for each and every one of us, and He promises in His Word to never leave us or forsake us. He won't ever abandon you. He loves you! He loves you so much that He gave you another chance at life today! You admitted that you were going to go through with it – that you had no doubt in your mind. Yet, you are still alive! You are sitting right here in front of us and breathing! That is a God thing!"

Jonathan excused himself and hurried down to Travis's SUV to get his Bible. Busy praying, he was startled to hear Travis's voice behind him. Turning, he saw Travis standing there holding the gun and the bullets he had removed from it.

"I want to lock this in the glove compartment for now." Travis nervously said as he straightened his glasses. "Do you want to put the bullets in your pocket or something? I don't want them anywhere near the gun."

Jonathan nodded in affirmation as he reached for the bullets and stuffed them deep in the pockets of his jeans.

Travis cleared his throat. "Man, I don't know how you were able to stay so calm in there. I was a nervous wreck. I didn't know what to do or say. I was scared out of my wits! I thought she was going to do it."

"Me too," Jonathan admitted. "If we had been even a few minutes later getting there, I don't want to even think about what we would have found. The enemy has convinced her that she is unworthy for so long that she has that constant negative tape running in her head. It's a spiritual battle, Travis, and we need to gear up." He pointed at his Bible.

Travis nodded and reached for his as well as he hurried to catch up to Jonathan who was already heading back to the girls' apartment.

~CHAPTER 23~

The girls were in the kitchen when Jonathan and Travis came back in. Wendy had a pot of coffee brewing and was arranging a snack tray of cheese and cookies that she had found in the cupboards. Meanwhile, Hannah was in quiet conversation with Tara. Hannah looked up and smiled at Travis as he entered the kitchen. He could see the relief in her eyes. He longed to embrace her but stopped himself. He couldn't let their friendship go any further than that – just friendship. *"What if I turn out like my father?"* he thought. *"It's better to keep Hannah at arm's length to protect her from getting hurt."*

Travis realized he was staring at Hannah and quickly turned his attention to Wendy. "Do you need any help?" he asked. "What can I do?"

Wendy nodded towards the coffee pot. "You could pour it," she said. Travis frowned as he noticed her hand trembling as she handed him some mugs. He hoped she was okay. This day had been hard on everyone, but especially Wendy. He turned his attention back to Hannah who was gently patting Tara's hand. Hannah was the most compassionate person he had ever met. Between Wendy and Hannah, Tara was in good hands. Travis took a seat as Jonathan began to speak.

"Tara, you said something about Plato's 'Allegory of the Cave' earlier and wondered if you were like the prisoner in it who had been given a false reality most of his life. I want to read you this verse here from Isaiah 61, verse one."

Jonathan waited while Travis located the Scripture in his Bible too and then began to read.

"The Spirit of the Sovereign Lord is upon Me, for the Lord has anointed Me to bring good news to the poor. He has sent Me to comfort the brokenhearted and to proclaim that captives will be released and prisoners will be freed."

Jonathan looked directly at Tara who was fiddling with her coffee mug. "Do you know who this verse is talking about?" he asked her.

Tara shook her head. "No." She then stared defiantly at Jonathan as she added. "Look, I appreciate the concern, but I am not interested in a Bible study. I was feeling down earlier, but I am fine now. I don't need all of this attention. Just leave me alone."

She began to rise up out of her seat as Wendy looked helplessly as Jonathan. Before he could say anything, Hannah stood as well and gently pushed Tara back into her chair.

"Tara, like it or not, we are not going anywhere right now. We are kidnapping you until you at least listen to what we have to say. Every one of us here, except you maybe, recognizes the fact that you are in a spiritual battle right now, and we are prepared to go to war with our spiritual armor for you. We are going to fight with you! You don't have to fight this battle by yourself."

Wendy joined in. "She's right, Tara. For too long, you have gone through life as a lone ranger fighting your battles alone because that is all you knew. You have erected walls around your heart the size of Mount Everest, but guess what, we are rock climbing in the name of the Lord Jesus today! We are scaling those walls because we care about you. We want you to experience the love of God.

"Those text messages you sent me today were a cry for help – a cry for attention, a cry to be noticed, a cry to be included. Well, we are going to do just that! You do not have to fight your battles alone anymore. We are going to fight with you! That means that you don't have to fight the battle of an eating disorder alone anymore! That means that you don't have to fight the battle of shame alone anymore! That means that you don't have to fight the battle of depression alone anymore! And, it means that you don't have to fight the battle of loneliness anymore because we are going to be around you so much that you are going to start begging us to leave you alone!

"That is what friends do for each other! That is what the Bible tells us to do for each other. God tells us to fight for each other in prayer. He tells us to share our struggles with one another so that we can encourage one another. Well, we cannot truly encourage one another unless we are vulnerable with one another! You took that first step, Tara, when you talked to us at church the other night and shared your past. You tried today through those text messages, but I didn't realize what they were. You have reached out to us, and we are going to be here for you from now on."

Tara stared at her coffee cup. She was totally humiliated and wanted to leave but Wendy and Hannah each physically had a hold on her. The only way she could leave was to punch them off of her, and she didn't really want to do that. She slid deeper down into her chair and waited for Jonathan to continue his sermon.

~CHAPTER 24~

Jonathan cleared his throat.

"Tara, I can't imagine what you are thinking or feeling right now. There is nothing to be embarrassed about though. We all struggle! We may struggle with different things and in different ways, but every one of us struggles with something. You are not alone in that! I am going to be very transparent here and share that I struggle with my past.

"I used to be a player. I wasn't happy until I felt that I had conquered a woman. Then, when I got what I wanted, I moved on to my next conquest. I was never satisfied. As a result, I hurt a lot of women and caused a lot of heartbreak. For all I know, I may have fathered some children at some point that I don't know anything about.

"I was a prisoner to that lifestyle. It was fun and involved no commitment on my part. I lied and told women what they wanted to hear all the while knowing, yet not caring, that I was scum. I have never been held in an actual jail cell, but I know what it is like to be a prisoner to sin because I was. That is not easy to say, and my past is definitely not something I am proud of. That verse I read to you in Isaiah has meaning to me. Jesus brought me the good news of His message. He showed His love, grace, and mercy for me despite my behavior, and he freed me from that lifestyle. Not only did he free me, but He changed me. He completely changed me from the inside out. The person I was is gone. The old me no longer exists! I am a new person in Christ!

"Yet, I still struggle. I struggle with shame over who I was and what I did. Even though I know that God has forgiven me and has removed my sins as far as the east is from the west and even forgotten my sins, I have not been able to forgive myself. The enemy, Satan, likes to remind me of my past. He invites himself over for popcorn and reruns of what I like to call "The Facts of Life" where he reminds me of scenes of my life over and over in an attempt to bring me down.

"That is where Travis comes in. He is my accountability partner. When I feel an attack coming on from the enemy, I call him, and we pray together because the Bible says in Matthew 19:20, 'Where two or three are gathered in My name, I am there among them.'

"That's not saying that God isn't there when we pray individually. It simply means that there is power in praying together. God uses our willingness to be humble and to be vulnerable. He doesn't expect us to be Christian lone rangers and fight our battles alone – just us and God. He wants us to put on our spiritual armor and fight together!

"I tell Travis when I feel those spiritual attacks coming on. I tell him when the enemy tries to convince me that I am worthless as a pastor because of my past. We pray together in the name of the Lord Jesus for the Bible also says in James 4, verse 7, 'Humble yourself before God. Resist the devil, and he will flee from you.' And, he does!"

Wendy shouted "Amen" at that.

Jonathan smiled as he continued.

"This verse in Isaiah 61 is a prophecy that refers to Jesus. He actually referenced it in Luke 4:18-19 and said that it was about Him. The good news that He is talking about is the Gospel. It is the fact that Jesus fulfilled all of the prophecies in the Old Testament in His birth, life, and death. He was God in a human form sent to die for our sins on the cross. But, the story didn't end there. He conquered the grave and rose again. That is the good news! Jesus allowed Himself to be a living sacrifice to pay our sin penalty so that in Him we can have eternal life. He came to set the prisoners free! He is the light that shines in the darkness!

"Tara, you are right. We are all like prisoners in a cave chained to sin. I was! In fact, everyone in this room was before we came to know Christ. Jesus set us all free by His blood on the cross. The enemy wants us to have a distorted view of God just like the prisoners in the 'Allegory of the Cave' only saw distorted shadows on the wall and thought they were reality. The enemy wants to keep us trapped in the darkness believing all of the false things we were taught or perceived about God. All the while, all we have to do is turn around, and we would see God's light for ourselves."

Tara's body shook with sobs. "What if it's too late? I have made a mess of my life, and I have hated God with a passion. Why would He want anything to do with me now?"

Hannah patted Tara's shoulder. "Have you heard of the story of the Prodigal Son?"

Tara shook her head.

Travis excitedly stood up as he turned his Bible to Luke 15.

"This is my favorite story in the Bible! You gotta hear this, Tara! It's so awesome!"

Tara smiled at Travis's boyish enthusiasm as he began to read.

"A man had two sons. The younger son told his father, 'I want my share of your estate now before you die.' So his father agreed to divide his wealth between his sons."

Tara rolled her eyes at Travis as he read. Of course, his favorite story would be about money! He didn't notice, but Wendy did and frowned at her.

"A few days later, this younger son packed all his belongings and moved to a distant land, and there he wasted all his money in wild living. About the time his money ran out, a great famine swept over the land, and he began to starve. He persuaded a local farmer to hire him, and the man sent him into his fields to feed the pigs. The young man became so hungry that even the pods he was feeding the pigs looked good to him. But, no one gave him anything.

"When he finally came to his senses, he said to himself, 'At home even the hired servants have food enough to spare, and here I am dying of hunger! I will go home to my father and say, "Father, I have sinned against both heaven and you, and I am no longer worthy of being called your son. Please take me on as a hired servant."'

Travis was nearly jumping up and down with excitement. "Don't miss this, Tara! Here this guy has gone as low as you can get. So low that pig food was looking good to him! This prideful man had physically hit rock bottom. He was starving! He was in such a low place that he was willing to beg his father to take him on as a servant. He knew he no longer deserved to be treated as the spoiled son he once was after how he had treated his family. Yet, he hoped that his father would find it in his heart to at least let him work in exchange for food. He had a repentance speech planned to beg his father for mercy."

Travis adjusted his glasses as he continued. They always seemed to slip down his nose.

"So he returned home to his father. And while he was still a long way off, his father saw him coming. Filled with love and compassion, he ran to his son, embraced him, and kissed him. His son said to him, 'Father, I have sinned against both heaven and you, and I am no longer worthy of being called your son.'"

Travis was practically doing jumping jacks at this point. "Do you see it, Tara?"

Tara wasn't sure what he was talking about or why he was so excited.

Travis reread verse 20.

"So he returned home to his father. And while he was still a long way off, his father saw him coming. Filled with love and compassion, he ran to his son, embraced him, and kissed him."

Wendy and Hannah were smiling at Tara. She still didn't get it.

"Wait!" she finally said. "The guy's father ran to him? Is that what you are so excited about? Why would he do that? The son didn't deserve his kindness after how he had treated him! And, what does this story have to do with God?"

Travis looked like Tigger from Winnie the Pooh the way he was bouncing up and down.

"This story is a picture of God! The father in the story is God. And, the wayward son is us. You are right. The prodigal son did not deserve his father's kindness. He sure didn't deserve his grace or forgiveness. Neither do we!

That's what makes it so awesome! We don't have to run to God because He is running to us with His arms open wide full of forgiveness!

"His son had been living among pigs. He was dirty and smelled disgusting. He didn't have to get cleaned up to go to his father. His father accepted him just as he was – unkempt and stinky. You are never too dirty for God to cleanse! You have never messed up too much for God's grace to handle! God is patiently waiting for you to turn around and step out of that cave of darkness, and when you do, He will run to you with arms outstretched and embrace you in the biggest and best hug ever!"

~CHAPTER 25~

Tara listened quietly as thoughts filled her mind. This sounded too good to be true. Was this just a feel good story of a father who showed grace and mercy to a wayward son? Or, was this a picture of God who was also known as the Father?

"What happened next?" she asked. "After the father runs to the son and hugs him. Does he hire him on as a servant like the son wanted?"

Travis's eyes danced with excitement.

"No, listen to this!" he exclaimed.

"His father said to the servants, 'Quick! Bring the finest robe in the house and put it on him. Get a ring for his finger and sandals for his feet. And kill the calf we have been fattening. We must celebrate with a feast, for this son of mine was dead and has now returned to life. He was lost, but now he is found.' So the party began."

Tara shook her head in confusion.

"That makes no sense at all!" she declared. "I can understand the father hugging the son and maybe even running out to meet him. He missed his child. But, to throw him a party after everything he did? Was he insane?"

"No, that is what true love is all about," Jonathan said as he opened his Bible to the book of John. "The father threw a party to celebrate the return of his son. I believe that God throws a party every time we repent and turn to Him. He celebrates the victory of life over death. Listen to this verse from John 3:16.

'For God loved the world so much that He gave His one and only Son, so that everyone who believes in Him will not perish but have eternal life.'

"God wants us to spend eternity with Him. He enjoys spending time with us because He loves us. Just as the father in the story celebrated when the wayward son repented and turned back to him, God the Father does as well."

Tara's eyes filled with tears once more. "Do you really think that after all these years of my hating God that He would just accept me? That He would run to me and embrace me and even throw a party in celebration for me of all people?"

Wendy nodded as she took a sip of coffee. "Yes! I believe that with all my heart!"

Hannah patted Tara's hand.

"Tara, something you probably don't know about me is that I explore caves. It's a hobby of mine. I also have a dog – a border collie/lab mix that I rescued – that I take hiking with me. I don't take her caving because that doesn't work well, but sometimes when I am out hiking, I feel some air flow coming from the ground and decide to check it out.

"So, I tell Sassy - my dog - to stay while I go check out the cave. Sometimes, it is just a grotto and doesn't have any significant passageway, but other times, it leads to a huge cavern with all kinds of tunnels to explore."

Hannah looked a little shamefaced as she added, "I know that you are not supposed to cave alone, but my sense of adventure wins in those situations. Sometimes, I am exploring underground for several hours before I realize that I haven't told anyone where I'm at. So, I drag myself out of the cave that I have just discovered only to find Sassy waiting anxiously by the cave entrance. She never moves from it while I am underground. She just waits patiently for me to turn around and come back to her.

"If I were her, I would be angry at being left behind for that long. But, she never is. She is just always so happy to see me. Her tail wags as she bounces up and down in excitement. It doesn't matter to her how long she has had to wait. All she cares about is that I'm back.

"To me, that is a picture of God. When we go on our own way, He hasn't left us. He just patiently waits for us to turn around and step out of that spiritual cave we were living in and step into His light and His love. Just like Sassy, He is so excited when we do that He spiritually embraces us and throws a party. He doesn't nag us for how long it took us to come to Him. Rather, He just shows us love.

"And, Tara, one thing you should know. When I cave, I get disgusting just like the prodigal son. I crawl around in mud and guano and pack rat feces in the caves. I smell, and I'm covered head to toe in dirt. I'm so dirty that when I blow my nose, dirt comes out that I've been inhaling in the cave while breathing. I am literally disgusting.

"That is what we look like on the inside without Jesus to cleanse us. We look on the inside how I look on the outside when I cave."

Hannah paused, and Travis took over.

"You see we can try to clean ourselves up, but..." Travis stopped himself. "I want to show you something," he said. "I'll be right back."

Travis sprinted down the stairs to his SUV and opened the back. He dug around in a duffel bag for a shirt and hurried back inside after locking his vehicle.

Tara stared at him. What was so important about the shirt he was carrying?

"I wanted to show you this," he said as he held the shirt out. It was a dirty, white t-shirt covered in black stains. "This shirt is actually clean," he said as he held it out for Tara to take.

Tara wrinkled her nose. The shirt sure didn't look clean.

Travis laughed. "It's clean. I promise! Take a good look at it."

Tara carefully held the shirt with the tips of her fingers. She didn't notice a smell emanating from it, but it sure did look dirty.

Hannah laughed. "Travis, why did you bring your caving shirt in here?"

Tara dropped the shirt on the table as Travis explained.

"Hannah talked me into going caving with her a few months ago. The first cave we went into had manganese deposits in it which left all of these black stains on my shirt. I wore a white t-shirt that day because I didn't really know what I was getting myself into. I had no idea just how dirty I would get. Hannah conveniently left that part out when she invited me along!"

Tears rolled down Hannah's cheeks as she giggled. "You should have seen Travis's facial expression that day when I asked him to crawl through some wet mud while he squeezed through a tiny tunnel!"

"I can only imagine," Jonathan said as he chuckled. "I heard about that adventure!"

"Anyway," Travis continued. "That happens to be one of my favorite t-shirts, so I did everything I could to get the stains out. I washed it, bleached it, and used several types of stain remover. But, the stains never came out. The shirt is clean, but it is stained forever. That is what we look like on the inside when we try to clean ourselves up without God. We can put on a front and make ourselves look presentable and respectable. However, inwardly, we are covered in sin stains. We can fool people, but we can never fool God. The only way to get rid of those stains is to allow Jesus to cleanse us from the inside out. He can make us truly clean on the inside. He turns us into a whole new person!"

Hannah added. "It's simple. When we try to do things independently of God, we end up with a result like Travis's shirt here. We are clean – but only partially." She wrinkled her nose at the shirt. "However, Jesus can make you truly clean. Just like Travis said, He will remove those stains and make you pure white on the inside. He gives you a fresh start!"

Travis cleared his throat as he awkwardly added. "This may be too much information. But, I can't wait to take a shower after I go caving. Like Hannah said, you get absolutely disgusting when you cave. The best feeling for me is to get cleaned up when I am that dirty. Yet, Tara, it is even better when we allow Jesus to cleanse us from the inside out. A physical shower when you are dirty feels wonderful, but a Jesus cleansing – man, there is nothing like it in the world!"

~CHAPTER 26~

Tara thought of the gun she had pointed at her head just hours before.

"That sounds great and all, but I just can't see why God would want anything to do with me. Even if He could forgive me for hating Him all of these years, it doesn't change the fact that I am worthless. I am a mistake!"

"God doesn't make mistakes," Jonathan quietly said. "The Bible says that you are the apple of His eye. He adores you. He created you to have meaning and purpose."

Wendy began rubbing Tara's back as she said, "What happened to you in the past was horrible. That pastor was terrible to manipulate you and abuse you in that way. I know that you feel unlovable, but God loves you in ways that you could never even imagine. He loves you higher than the tallest mountain and deeper and wider than the ocean! In fact, God's love for us is so great that it is hard to comprehend just how deep, how wide, how long, and how high His love for us goes. I want you to read something with me."

Wendy motioned to Travis to pass his Bible to her. She opened it up to Romans 5:8. "I want you to read this aloud, Tara. Whenever you see a pronoun like 'us' or 'we', I want you to replace it with your name instead."

Tara began to read. "But God showed His great love for Tara by sending Christ to die for Tara." She began to giggle. "This sounds funny," she said.

"I know," Wendy said as she suppressed a grin. "But, go ahead and finish the verse."

"While Tara was still a sinner." Tara's brow creased. "Are we really supposed to personalize the Bible in this way?"

"Yes," Travis said with a grin. "The Bible is the way God communicates personally with each of us. Now read Romans 8:38-39, and do the same thing. Insert your name or a pronoun about yourself."

Tara slowly turned the pages to the correct verse. "And I am convinced that nothing can ever separate me from God's love. Neither death nor life, neither angels nor demons, neither my fears for today nor my worries about tomorrow – not even the powers of hell can separate me from God's love. No power in the sky above or in the earth below – indeed nothing in all creation will ever be able to separate me from the love of God which is revealed in Christ Jesus my Lord."

Tara stared at Travis in astonishment. "Wow!" she declared. "Making it personalized sure does give it more meaning. I like those verses because they give a clear picture of the love of God. Nothing can separate us from God's love!" She corrected herself. "Nothing can separate me from God's love! That's true, isn't it? All of those characteristics of God that y'all were praying earlier gave me a whole new picture of God. It's like for the first time in my life I'm seeing something besides the image I had of Him on the cave wall of my heart. Do you have any others that I can personalize?"

Jonathan chuckled. "Sure! How about you look up John 3:16 again – only this time make it personal?"

Tara slowly turned to John 3:16. She hadn't picked up a Bible in years, and her memory of what order the books were in had faded somewhat. She smiled as she began. "For God so loved me so much that He gave His one and only Son, so that if I believe in Him, I will not perish but have eternal life."

Her hands began to tremble. "Jesus died for me? For me personally? I've always pictured him hanging on the cross, but I thought of his sacrifice in general terms - never personally. Wow! That brings the cross new meaning! He gave His life for me! He really did, didn't He? Jesus actually thought I was worth dying for! That is so amazing!"

Tears began to run down Wendy's face. "That's why we call it amazing grace," she exclaimed. "The cross is meaningless until you really get it. Then, the cross becomes everything to you! Your sins, my sins – they were nailed to the cross. Jesus was perfect. He was innocent. He was the only one who had never sinned. Yet, He took it upon himself to pay the price for our sins. It was huge. Listen to these verses from Isaiah 53."

"My Servant grew up in the Lord's presence like a tender green shoot, like a root in dry ground. There was nothing beautiful or majestic about His appearance, nothing to attract us to Him. He was despised and rejected – a man of sorrows, acquainted with deepest grief. We turned our backs on Him and looked the other way. He was despised, and we did not care. Yet, it was our weaknesses He carried; it was our sorrows that weighed Him down. And we thought His troubles were a punishment from God, a punishment for His own sins!

"But He was pierced for our rebellion, crushed for our sins. He was beaten so we could be whole. He was whipped so we could be healed. All of us, like sheep, have strayed away. We have left God's paths to follow our own. Yet the Lord laid on Him the sins of us all.

"He was oppressed and treated harshly, yet He never said a word. He was led like a lamb to the slaughter. And as a sheep is silent before the shearers, He did not open His mouth. Unjustly condemned, He was led away."

Wendy paused and wiped the tears from her eyes. "Those verses are about Jesus. That's what true grace is." That's how big God's love for you is!"

For the first time in her life, Tara got it. God wasn't a monster! He wasn't a copy of Jack waiting to manipulate and torment her. God was simply love! He was grace, mercy, and forgiveness. Her heart pounded as she realized that this was the moment of choice. Humbly, she asked, "How can I invite Jesus into my heart?"

Jonathan's eyes danced with gladness. "Let's read Romans 10:9 and personalize it," he said.

"If I will confess with my mouth that Jesus is Lord and believe in my heart that God raised Him from the dead, I will be saved."

Tara stared at Jonathan. "Is it really as simple as that?" she asked.

"Yep, let's read verse 13," he said with a grin.

"For everyone who calls on the name of the Lord will be saved."

"That's all I have to do?" Tara questioned. "Just confess with my mouth that Jesus is Lord and believe in my heart that He rose from the grave?"

Hannah reached for Tara's hand. Wendy grabbed the other one. Soon, the entire group was holding hands.

"Pray along with me," Jonathan instructed. "Don't just repeat in your head what I am saying, rather personalize it and make it your own words."

"Dear Jesus, I confess that I am a sinner, and I am sorry for what I have done wrong. I realize that no matter how hard I try, I can't wipe away my sin stains, but You can. I believe You are King of Kings and Lord of Lords and that You gave Your Son, Jesus, as a living sacrifice on my behalf out of Your love for me. I believe He died on the cross for my sins and rose victorious from the grave. I ask You to forgive my sins and come into my heart. I want to know You and have a relationship with You. By faith, I thank You for saving me and for giving me the gift of eternal life. In Jesus's name, Amen!"

Tears streamed down Tara's face as she felt a weight lifting from her. A peacefulness that she had never experienced came over her.

"I did it! I did it!" she exclaimed. "I asked Jesus into my heart! I suddenly feel this love that I have never felt before!"

Travis let out a loud yell and clapped his hands! "Whoo-hoo! Now we have something to celebrate for you were lost and now you are found! You are now my sister in Christ!"

Tara smiled. "Thank you! Thank you all for showing me the way! Wow! This is an amazing feeling!"

~PART 2~

ONE YEAR LATER

~CHAPTER 27~

Tara nervously typed out her profile on the Christian dating site.

"New Christian seeks godly Christian man to be a spiritual leader. Must love the outdoors. Non-smoker. Non-drinker."

She attached a picture of herself that she had taken with her cell phone. Done! Now, the big question was, would it draw anyone's interest?

A few minutes later, her computer beeped. She had a wink already! Excitedly, she clicked on the man's profile. Sixty years old in California. Eww! Definitely not! Several other winks followed, all by men in their sixties. Disappointed, Tara walked away from her computer.

Later that evening, Tara checked her computer once again. This time she had a message on the dating site in addition to a wink. The man lived right there in Savannah, and his profile name was "Walkingtall". Tara stared at his picture as she read his profile.

"My idea of a perfect date is a hike in the woods. I would bring a picnic lunch along, and we would find a quiet spot and just sit and listen to the sounds of nature as we view the beauty of God's creation."

"Walkingtall" was bald, but in a good sort of way. Some guys could pull off the bald look, and apparently "Walkingtall" was one of them. His brown eyes seemed to look straight into her, and his goatee completed his look. "Walkingtall" was hot! Why was he on a dating website? Tara clicked on the message he had sent her.

Hi "NewChild", I liked your profile and would like to get to know you better. To tell you a little about myself, I am twenty-five years old and a paramedic. I was raised in a church and am a believer, but I drifted away from God after my fiancé committed suicide. I am seeking to know Him again and to be around other believers. I love taking road trips and exploring outdoors. I hope to hear back from you.

Tara smiled as she hit the reply button. "Walkingtall" sounded great! A paramedic! She frowned as she thought of what to write.

Hi "WalkingTall"! Thank you for your message. You sound like someone I would like to get to know. I am twenty-two and a student at Bridger with an undeclared major so far. As I mentioned in my profile, I am a new Christian, a new creation in Christ, and I am seeking a friendship leading to a relationship with a godly, Christian man. I don't want to waste either of our time, so I would like to meet in a public place to get to know each other in person instead of chatting back and forth on here. You can text me at 503-1647 if that works for you.

Tara took a deep breath as she sent the message to "WalkingTall". Would he think her too forward? A few minutes later her phone vibrated with a text from a number she didn't recognize. Tara quickly picked it up and read it.

"Hi, I'm Stewart - 'Walking Tall' - would u like 2 meet 2morrow @ the Peachtree coffee shop? 5 pm?"

The Peachtree was a popular, college hangout only a ten minute walk from her apartment. "Sure!" she responded excitedly. Just then, Wendy walked in the door. Tara jumped up and wrapped Wendy in a hug.

"Guess what! I have a date tomorrow!"

"A date? With who?" Wendy asked.

"His name is Stewart, and I met him on a Christian dating site. He is going to meet me at the Peachtree tomorrow. He lives right here in Savannah! He looks so hot, and he is a paramedic!" Tara gushed.

Wendy looked worried. "Tara, you didn't give him any personal information, did you?"

"Just what I wrote on my profile," Tara explained. "Besides, he is a Christian and a paramedic. He is safe."

"You don't know if anything he wrote on his profile is true. Just be careful. Do you want me to go with you? I could hang out at a nearby table – just in case."

Tara frowned. Wendy acted like she was a naïve child. "No Mom!" she said snidely. "I'm meeting him at a public place. I will be fine. Besides, I am a good judge of character. I don't need you looking after me all the time."

"I just worry about you is all. Besides, I think Jonathan likes you."

"Well don't! I can take care of myself. I appreciate all that you have done for me, but back off some and give me some space. And, all Jonathan sees when he looks at me is a project – nothing else. He doesn't see me as a woman. He just sees me as someone to mentor. Geez, I'm finally ready to date, and you are trying to talk me out of it! I thought you would be more supportive."

Wendy's eyes filled with tears. "Tara, I am supportive of you, and I think it is a great idea for you to date. I'm just not so sure meeting guys off the internet is a good idea is all. You are a baby Christian. I don't want you to be misled."

"I might be a baby Christian, but I am an adult, Wendy. I can take care of myself! Why can't you just be happy for me?" Tara threw herself onto her bed as she crossed her arms and stared at Wendy.

"I am happy for you. Just remember I am here for you - no matter what." Wendy said as she walked to the bathroom.

Tara stared after Wendy in disgust. She was so sensitive. *Why couldn't she just be happy for me?* Wendy was ruining Tara's excitement over meeting Stewart with all of her reservations about internet dating.

~CHAPTER 28~

Tara avoided Wendy the next morning as she got ready for class. She was still angry at Wendy for not being more supportive of her meeting Stewart that evening. But, she was not about to let Wendy's attitude ruin her day. She carefully picked out one of her favorite new outfits: khaki pants with a white button-up shirt. She left the buttons unbuttoned and layered a gray t-shirt underneath. She was dressed like one of the mannequins at the popular clothing stores now. No more baggy clothes for her! It felt good to wear nice clothes. She felt stylish as she straightened her blonde hair. The brown lowlights she had added were a nice touch.

Tara frowned as she remembered the day Wendy took her to the salon to get her lowlights put in. It had been Wendy's treat. It was nice to have a best friend to hang out with. Wendy had taught her how to apply makeup as well. Tara felt a twinge of guilt for how she had treated Wendy last night. Oh well, Wendy would get over it. She always did. Tara shrugged as she finished getting ready for the day.

The hours seemed to pass by slowly as Tara kept an eye on her watch all day. She was jittery by the time her last class ended at 4:30 and couldn't recall anything any of what the teachers had said. As she made her way across campus and headed to the Peachtree, Tara wondered if she should have taken Wendy up on her offer to wait at another table there just in case the meeting with Stewart didn't go well. Oh well, it was too late now.

Tara nervously walked in the door and glanced around. The Peachtree was packed as normal, and most of the tables were already taken. She looked around for someone who resembled Stewart's profile picture, but didn't see a bald head anywhere.

Just then, she noticed a hand waving at her. A handsome man sporting a baseball cap and a goatee was looking her way. He stood up as she approached.

"Are you, umm, New Child?" he asked.

At her nod, he smiled. "Oh, thank goodness! I realized I didn't ask you your name. Asking if you are 'New Child' would have sounded really weird to the wrong person! Would you like some coffee or chai?"

"Chai sounds good," Tara said. Stewart pulled a chair out for her at the table where he had been sitting. "My treat! I will be right back." As he headed to the counter to order her drink, Tara subtlety checked him out. He was cute!

Stewart returned to the table with her Chai and sat down opposite Tara. "I have to admit that I have never done anything like this before," he said.

"Nor have I," Tara explained as she took a sip. "But, it's just so hard to meet new people these days since I don't go to a bar. There are guys in the church I attend, but the majority of them are already in a relationship."

"Where do you go?" Stewart asked as he stirred his coffee.

"I go to New Life. It's a non-denominational church on the outskirts of Savannah. How about you?"

Stewart looked embarrassed as he replied. "Well, I'm officially Methodist, but I haven't been to church in a long time. I kind of got down on church after Rosemary died."

"Was she the fiancé you mentioned on your profile? The one who committed suicide?" Tara asked.

"Yes, it was horrible to watch. My job is to save lives, but I couldn't save hers. She shot herself right in front of me."

"Wow! That must have been horrible!" Tara said softly. "I'm so sorry!"

"Nobody ever saw it coming. She had isolated herself from her friendships, but I never thought she was so unhappy that she would end her life."

"How long ago did that happen?" Tara asked.

"Two years". Stewart smiled sadly. "Enough about her though. Tell me about you."

Tara wondered what to share. She had learned to be vulnerable and share with Wendy, but what would Stewart think if he knew her past. She decided to gloss over the details.

"Well, I have junk in my past. Who doesn't? To make a long story short, I ran from God most of my life because I had a false image of Him. I didn't see Him as love. I saw Him as torturous and as cruel. I was angry at the world and had walls as high as a mountain around me. Impenetrable! I had a self-fulfilling prophecy that nobody cared about me and didn't allow anyone to get close enough to me to care about me. Until my roommate bribed me to go to Unplugged that is. That's where I saw God for who He truly was for the first time."

Stewart looked confused as he asked, "Unplugged?"

"Yes, Unplugged is this great young adult ministry at New Life. It's all about unplugging from previous notions you have about God and searching the Scriptures to get to know the one true God – the God of love. You should come sometime with me!"

Stewart smiled. "I'd like to! It sounds fun. So you went to Unplugged, and it changed your life?"

"It sure did! I didn't want to go at first. I hated church, and I hated any mention of God. But, Wendy offered me three hundred dollars if I would go, and well I needed a new computer, so I took her up on it."

Stewart chuckled. "Who is Wendy? The more important question is why did she pay you three hundred dollars to go to church? Is she loaded or something?"

"She comes from an old family. They are actually struggling financially. She did it because she is one of the most spiritual people I know. She wants to be, as she puts it, 'God's girl'. She felt that God wanted her to get me to Unplugged, and she was willing to do what it took to accomplish that." Tara explained as she took a long drink of her chai.

"But, three hundred dollars to go to a church event! That's a little extreme!"

Tara noticed that Stewart had cute dimples when he smiled. "Well, actually she paid me five hundred dollars. Three hundred the first time and two hundred the second time."

"Wow! She really wanted you to go to this Unplugged thing!"

"Yeah, I'm glad she pushed me into going. I feel a little guilty now about taking all of that money from her though." Tara sighed as she thought of Wendy and all of the ways she had taken advantage of her in the past. She quickly turned her attention back to Stewart.

"Wendy has been a great roommate and a friend. If you go to Unplugged with me this Friday, you will get to meet her. But, enough about her, tell me about yourself. Did you grow up here in Savannah?"

"I grew up in a lot of places. My father was in the military, and we moved around a lot. I think the longest we were in one place was a year in Colorado. That's where I found my love for hiking. The mountains are so huge there that they seem to touch the sky, and the snow in winter blankets everything in a sheet of white. It's peaceful and refreshing!"

"Wow! That sounds awesome! I would love to see it. I've never been out of Georgia," Tara explained.

"I will have to take you sometime." Stewart looked pointedly at Tara.

The two sat at the Peachtree and talked for several hours. Finally, they took the hint that the restaurant was trying to close. Stewart agreed to go to Unplugged Friday night and offered to pick Tara up at the apartment and give her a ride.

~CHAPTER 29~

Stewart arrived promptly at 6:30 to pick Tara up for Unplugged. After a brief introduction to Wendy, they were on their way in his bright red Mustang. Tara felt momentarily guilty for not inviting Wendy to ride with them since she and Wendy always rode together, but, after all, this was a date. Surely, Wendy would understand.

As they pulled up to New Life, Stewart reached over and grabbed Tara's hand. "You look beautiful tonight," he said. Tara smiled. She wasn't used to being complimented in that manner after years of dressing in baggy, frumpy clothes to avoid attention. Stewart looked handsome in a white polo shirt and jeans. She had never been attracted to the bald look before, but Stewart really pulled it off.

They walked inside holding hands, and Tara introduced him to her friends while beaming at their curious looks. After introducing Stewart to Travis and Hannah, Tara led him over to a corner where Wendy and Jonathan were talking quietly.

"Hi, this is Stewart," Tara gushed. "He is a paramedic."

Jonathan smiled as he extended his hand. "Nice to meet you Stewart. How long have you been a paramedic?"

"Only a few years, sir. Before that, I was an EMT for a while until a spot opened up. There are more people who want to be paramedics than there are spots available."

Jonathan chuckled, "Well, that's a good thing. I'm glad you are able to serve our community in this way. It's good to know we have help here tonight if anyone needs it. How did you and Tara meet?"

Stewart's face reddened. "Online, sir. On a Christian dating sight. It's hard to meet people these days if you don't go to bars or clubs. I liked her profile, and we met over at the Peachtree the other night. We really seem to be hitting it off. She invited me to come tonight."

"Well, I'm glad you did. Unplugged is a great way to get to know people and to learn the truth about God." Jonathan glanced around. "It looks like we are ready to start. I'd better get up there. It was nice to meet you. And, good to see you, Tara." He blushed as he shook her hand.

Tara began leading Stewart toward a seat in the middle of the room. She and Wendy sat with Travis and Hannah each week. As Wendy began to scoot over to make room for Stewart, he balked.

"Let's sit closer to the back of the room," he suggested in her ear.

"Why? I always sit here with my friends," Tara said.

"Well, that's just it. I don't care about meeting your friends to be honest. I just want to spend time with you. Let's sit in the back."

Tara agreed. If a guy like Stewart wanted to sit with her alone, she wasn't going to say no. Wendy gave her a concerned look as she walked away, but Tara ignored it.

As usual the crowd cheered when Jonathan came on stage and boomed, "Welcome to Unplugged!" Tara smiled at Stewart. God had used Unplugged to change her life in a huge way. She hoped it would impact him as well.

As the band began to play, Tara stood and sang along to the words on the screen. She really enjoyed the music here. Tara noticed that Stewart wasn't singing, but then, he had mentioned that he hadn't been to church in a long time.

While the band was putting away their instruments, Jonathan came on stage and led the audience in a prayer.

"Father, we thank You for Your truth. We thank You that our identities are found in You alone and not in others. We ask that You help us to see ourselves as You see us and not as others see us or as we see ourselves. Help us to fully see and recognize who we truly are in You. The enemy tries to devalue us and make us constantly feel less than. We pray that we will see the truth about our real identity in Christ tonight as we prepare ourselves for battle – spiritual battle – with the enemy. Gird us with Your belt of truth for we are not fighting against flesh and blood enemies but against evil rulers and authorities of the unseen world, against mighty powers in this dark world, and against evil spirits in the heavenly places as Your Word states in Ephesians 6:12.

"I pray specifically for our new believers here tonight that they will put on spiritual armor, so that they may be able to stand firm against the enemy's attacks to draw them away from God. Help us to live in righteousness, applying Your truth to our daily lives, behaving in a way that is honoring and pleasing to You. Help us to walk in peace with one another as we courageously hold up the shield of faith while we walk in our belief and knowledge of You. Protect our minds with the security and hope of salvation in You and the reward to come as You give us strength for battle. Your Word is our sword to fight with! Help us to ingrain it in our hearts and minds and remember Your Word in times of trouble. In Jesus's name, Amen!"

Jonathan cleared his voice as he looked around the room. "War! We are in a war right now. The enemy does not like what we are doing here at Unplugged. He wants us to come for the music, the food, and the fellowship. None of that bothers him. He wants us distracted by the fun that we can have here. There's nothing wrong with coming here for fun. But, the enemy does not want us to unplug. He does not want us to rid our minds of preconceived notions of God and learn the truth of God.

"He wants us to keep God in a box where we can limit Him in our minds. He doesn't want us growing closer to God. The enemy does not want us to have a passion for God – a passion to draw closer to God. He wants us busy, even busy doing good things, because it will take our focus off of God. It's easy to lose perspective. Turn in your Bibles to 1 Kings 18. The title of the sermon tonight is 'A Crisis of Faith'.

"Elijah was a confident prophet of God. He believed that God was going to work through him because He had in the past. Ahab was a wicked king who ruled Israel and had taken up following the Canaanite's practice of worshipping Baal who was known as the storm god. Baal, the most significant deity in Canaanite religion, was attributed to bringing rain and life to the land, in particular through weather, wind, lightning, rain, and fertility. Canaan, which depended upon rainfall for its agriculture, focused attention on Baal's role as the storm god. The worship of Baal began to spread throughout Israel through Ahab's time.

"The followers of Baal believed that he was the weather god, and God became angry at the Israelites for worshipping him. Elijah appeared with prophetic authority in 1 Kings 17:1 when he made the following startling command to King Ahab.

'As surely as the Lord, the God of Israel, lives – the God I serve – there will be no dew or rain during the next few years until I give the word!'

"One can only imagine King Ahab's reaction to this prophecy. Disbelief! He believed in the power of Baal. Who was Elijah to make this dire prediction?

"God wanted to demonstrate through Elijah that He alone was the sole Creator of the world and that He alone had the power to control the weather. Even though Ahab disbelieved the prophecy, time would prove it. Three long years passed as the land was in drought.

"In the third year of the drought, God sent Elijah to King Ahab to tell him that He would soon send rain upon the dry and parched land. The land was so dry that King Ahab had sent men to check every spring and valley to try to find enough grass to save some of the horses and mules.

"When Ahab saw Elijah, he exclaimed, 'Is it really you, you troublemaker of Israel?' in 1 Kings 18:16. He blamed Elijah for the drought and famine. Times were hard. His anger was focused in the wrong place – on the man Elijah instead of God the Creator.

"Elijah didn't mince words in his response and accused Ahab and his family of being the true troublemakers for worshipping Baal and refusing to obey God's commands. I imagine Ahab's face turned bright red as Elijah issued him a challenge to summon all of Israel to Mt. Carmel along with the 450 prophets of Baal and the 400 prophets of Asherah. Why did Ahab obey? Perhaps he was curious as to what Elijah planned to do. Not many people would have had the audacity to approach the king in this manner. Perhaps Ahab hoped that Elijah would revoke his no rain prophecy and send rain.

"In the next scene, all of the people of Israel and all of the prophets are at Mt. Carmel as per Elijah's demand. Elijah issued a challenge to the people to choose who they will follow. 'How much longer will you waver, hobbling between two opinions? If the Lord is God, follow Him! But if Baal is God, then follow him!' But, the people were silent. They were torn between the two. They wanted to see what happened first before they chose who they would serve.

"Then in verse 22: Elijah said to them, 'I am the only prophet of the Lord who is left, but Baal has 450 prophets. Now bring two bulls. The prophets of Baal may choose whichever one they wish and cut it into pieces and lay it on the wood of their altar, but without setting fire to it. I will prepare the other bull and lay it on the wood of the altar, but not set fire to it. Then call on the name of your god, and I will call on the name of the Lord. The god who answers by setting fire to the wood is the true God!' And the people agreed.

"Then Elijah said to the prophets of Baal, 'You go first, for there are many of you. Choose one of the bulls, and prepare it and call on the name of your god. But do not set fire to the wood.'

"So they prepared one of the bulls and placed it on the altar. Then they called on the name of Baal from morning until noontime shouting, 'O Baal, answer us!' But, there was no reply of any kind. Then they danced, hobbling around the altar they had made.

"About noontime, Elijah began mocking them. 'You'll have to shout louder,' he scoffed, 'for surely he is a god! Perhaps he is daydreaming or relieving himself. Or maybe he is away on a trip, or is asleep and needs to be wakened!'"

The audience broke out in laughter at the picture of a god of storms relieving himself.

"Watch out! That's what it means when 'yer in storm!" a witty guy called out. The audience roared with laughter. Tara lightly elbowed Stewart who seemed confused.

"Yer in storm! Get it!" she asked. At his quizzical expression, she said the phrase more slowly. "Yer is southern slang for your. Yer in storm!" He smiled.

"I've seen that a time or two on the job when we encountered some serious drunk dudes. I'll have to tell the team that."

Jonathan waited for the room to quiet down before he continued reading from 1 Kings 18:28.

"So they shouted louder, and following their normal custom, they cut themselves with knives and swords until the blood gushed out. They raved all afternoon until the time of the evening sacrifice, but still there was no sound, no reply, no response.

"Then Elijah called to the people, 'Come over here!' They all crowded around him as he repaired the altar of the Lord that had been torn down. He took twelve stones, one to represent each of the tribes of Israel, and he used the stones to rebuild the altar in the name of the Lord. Then he dug a trench around the altar large enough to hold about three gallons. He piled wood on the altar, cut the bull into pieces, and laid the pieces on the wood.

"Then he said, 'Fill four large jugs with water, and pour the water over the offering and the wood.' After they had done this, he said, 'Do the same thing again!' And, when they were finished he said, 'Now do it a third time!' So they did as he said, and the water ran around the altar and even filled the trench."

Jonathan paused. "What was Elijah thinking? Water was precious! They were in the middle of a three year drought. And, Elijah was pouring it on the altar! Can you imagine the thunderous expressions on the people as they watched this? I picture some very angry looks being tossed

Elijah's way. He was wasting water that they needed for their crops, livestock, and even themselves in what they thought was a foolish contest. Whether or not Baal chose to respond, it was a no-lose situation: 450 prophets versus one. Elijah was clearly outnumbered. When he failed to call down fire from heaven, the 450 prophets would kill him. But, there was no need to waste precious water in the process. Twelve barrels of water were used. The sacrifice was soaked, and the trench around it was running over."

Tara was intrigued by the story. Jonathan had a way of preaching that captured the audience's attention. In her mind, she pictured a cocky Elijah pouring bucket after bucket of precious water on the altar, using so much water that it filled the trench. The people must have been beyond angry. She turned her attention back to Jonathan as he continued with verse 36.

"At the usual time for offering the evening sacrifice, Elijah the prophet walked up to the altar and prayed, 'O Lord, God of Abraham, Isaac, and Jacob, prove today that You are God in Israel and that I am Your servant. Prove that I have done all this at Your command. O Lord, answer me! Answer me so these people will know that You, O Lord, are God and that You have brought them back to Yourself."

Jonathan took a sip of water as he paused. "We can learn a lot from Elijah here. He did not want to be the center of attention. He wanted God to get the credit for what was about to happen. He prayed, 'Prove that You are God and that I am Your servant.' Elijah was bold and confident in his actions and in God, yet He was humble. He wanted the credit to go where credit was due. In essence, he was saying, 'Steal the show! Prove that it's You doing this, and not me!' That is something I have to pray every time I get up here to speak. 'Let me not take the praise God. Let the praise go only to You! Use me as Your vessel but help me not to get a swelled head.' Elijah prayed that the people would know without a doubt that what is about to happen is all God. Look in verse 38."

"Immediately the fire of the Lord flashed down from heaven and burned up the young bull, the wood, the stones, and the dust. It even licked up all the water in the trench!"

Jonathan explained, "The fact that the fire was so hot that it burned everything up even when everything was soaked proves that this was a miracle! Continue in verse 39." He paused for a moment to let the miracle of the fire soak into everyone's head.

"And when all the people saw it, they fell face down on the ground and cried out, 'The Lord – He is God! Yes, the Lord is God!' Then Elijah commanded, 'Seize all the prophets of Baal. Don't let a single one escape! So the people seized them all, and Elijah took them down to the Kishon Valley and killed them there."

Jonathan cleared his throat. "Elijah had just had a mountaintop experience. He proved to Ahab and the people that God is the one, true living God. He was more powerful than the silent Baal and his prophets. God made the impossible happen! He sent a fire from heaven so hot that it literally burned up water and everything in its path. The result was that the people who were sitting on the fence, the ones who were undecided about who to follow, believed. The story doesn't end there; it gets even better. The land still needed rain. It had been three long years without rain! So, Elijah climbed to the top of the mountain and prayed for rain.

"God answered his prayer right away for the fire, yet Elijah had to pray seven times before the rain came. Each time he prayed, he sent his servant to go look out toward the sea for clouds. It makes me think of the cell phone ads on television, only instead of asking 'Do you hear me now?', Elijah was asking, 'Do you see it yet? Do you see a cloud? How about now? Do you see it now? No, okay, I will pray some more.'

"Elijah must have felt frustrated and wondered what God was doing. Why was God being silent after He had shown off in such a huge, mighty way with the fire? Seven times Elijah prayed for rain. He didn't give up praying even though it seemed that God was not answering because he still believed that God was in control. On the seventh time, the servant returned and said, 'I see a little cloud about the size of a man's hand rising from the sea.' Relief! God had finally answered his prayer!

"You see we are going to have mountaintop experiences where God answers specifically and right away. We are also going to have times when God seems silent. Those are the times we have to keep praying and trusting that God is in control and allow those times to increase our faith.

"Elijah had just had that mountaintop experience where God answered his prayer for fire specifically right away, and he had a time of waiting for God to answer his prayer for rain. Through it all, he never lost his faith. He believed without a doubt that God would answer his prayers. Even when he stood as one man against 450 prophets, Elijah remained confident in God. Yet, in chapter 19, when Jezebel, Ahab's wife, threatened him, he lost his focus. He was tired, afraid, discouraged, and even depressed enough to ask God to take his life. Elijah experienced a crisis of faith. Instead of focusing on God, he focused on his circumstances which looked bleak.

"The enemy wants to steal our focus. Elijah took his eyes off of what he knew God could do and instead turned his focus to the current situation. He knew of Jezebel's reputation and character. He knew that she would be persistent in her threat to seek revenge on his life. She had armies at her disposal and would stop at nothing.

"Standing up to the prophets of Baal and praying for rain had taken a physical and emotional toll on Elijah. He was tired. What happens when we are physically tired? We don't have the strength to fight. Elijah looked at his circumstances and said, 'God, I've had enough. Take my life!'

"God didn't take his life. Instead, He provided a meal for him. God gave him nutrition and led him on a forty day journey to a cave. There, Elijah whined and complained to God in chapter 19, verse 10."

'I have zealously served the Lord God Almighty. But the people of Israel have broken their covenant with You, torn down Your altars, and killed every one of Your prophets. I am the only one left, and now they are trying to kill me, too.'

"Elijah was tired and wanted to quit. He had allowed the enemy to steal his focus. You see, when Elijah fled for his life, it wasn't because God told him to run. He acted on his own. He responded to Jezebel's threats with his own solution rather than waiting for God's. When we lose our focus, we become disappointed, angry, full of self-pity, and depressed. What happened to the confident, bold prophet that we first saw in chapter 17? He turned into the depressed, whiny man that we see begging God to take his life in chapter 19 because he had a crisis of faith.

"Every single one of us is going to experience a crisis of faith at some point in our lives. The enemy is going to do his best to cause us to lose our focus on God and His truths and to instead focus more on our situations and circumstances. He knows just where to attack which is why it is so important that we prepare for spiritual battle now. It's important that we memorize God's Word, the sword of the Spirit, so that we can recall it and cling to God's promises when we need them. We are in a battle, and it's time to go to war.

"I'd like everyone to break off into small groups and talk about focus and how we can lift our eyes from our circumstances and keep our focus on God."

The room filled with noise as the audience got up and began to shift their chairs around. Tara was about to join her friends, when Stewart grabbed her arm.

"Let's go!" he said with a grin.

"Go?" Tara questioned. "But, it's not over yet. It's group discussion time."

"I know," Stewart said. "But, I want to spend some time alone with you. I'm busy at work the next few days. This is my only chance to hang out with you for a while. Can't we just skip the discussion and head over to the Peachtree instead?"

Tara glanced over at the table where Wendy, Travis, and Hannah were already waiting. She loved Unplugged and got as much out of the group discussions as she did from Jonathan's sermons. But, Stewart acted like he really wanted to spend time getting to know her and that couldn't really happen at a group function. Hanging out at the Peachtree again did sound fun. She nodded at Stewart. "Ok, let's go!"

~CHAPTER 30~

The Peachtree was crowded when they arrived, so Stewart suggested that they go to a club on Main Street called Nightlife. Tara felt uncomfortable as they walked inside. There were some obviously intoxicated people milling around. Stewart led her to a table in the corner and ordered a beer for himself. The waitress looked questioningly at her.

"Water please," she said as she glanced at her phone. She had just got a text message from Wendy. *"Where are u?"* Tara ignored it.

"Don't you want a drink?" Stewart asked.

"I don't drink," Tara responded.

"Wow! You really are uptight," Stewart declared. "There's nothing wrong with having a beer."

"Maybe not," Tara said. "But, as a new Christian, I want to make choices that glorify God." She glanced at her phone again as it vibrated with another text message from

Wendy. *"R u ok?"* She ignored it once more and turned her attention back to Stewart.

An uncomfortable silence followed that seemed to have been caused by Tara's choice not to drink. Tara broke the ice and asked, "What did you think of Unplugged? I thought Jonathan had a great message on keeping our focus on God tonight."

"Yeah, it was a good message. I liked the story." Stewart took a long drink and signaled to the waitress to bring another bottle. "It is interesting how one can feel so close to God and then so far away."

"Have you ever felt that way?" Tara asked glancing at her phone once more. Wendy was getting on her nerves texting like this.

"When I was in high school I did. I carried my Bible to school with me every day. Since we moved around a lot, I never got to stay involved in one church very long. But, there was this one youth group that really made an impact on me. They lived their faith like it was real. It wasn't an act for them. They really made an impression on me."

"In what way?"

The waitress handed Stewart another beer, and he took a long drink before responding.

"Well, God always seemed like mere words on a page until then. Somehow, they made Him real. I believed it. But, after Rosemary," Stewart began to choke a little on the words. "After Rosemary err died, I'm just not so sure what I believe anymore. But, somehow I think that you are going to lead me back to Christ."

Tara smiled. God was already giving her a job to do. She couldn't believe how much God had changed her life in such a short period of time. New friends and now a potential boyfriend! Life was looking up! She felt good about herself in her new clothes and hairdo, and that confidence showed in her actions. It was awesome.

Stewart and Tara talked for a few hours before he drove her home. As he walked her to the door of the apartment, Tara thought he might kiss her, but just then the door opened.

"Oh thank God! I was getting worried about you," Wendy gushed. "Where did you go? Why didn't you answer my texts?" She seemed to ignore Stewart who was leaning against the door.

"We decided to go hang out for a while," Tara explained. Stewart leaned in to give her a hug goodnight, and Wendy stepped back with a frown on her face. As soon as he left, Wendy lit into her.

"Was he drinking and driving?" Wendy angrily asked. "He smelled like alcohol. How much did he have?"

"He only had a few beers," Tara explained. "I wasn't really keeping track of how many, but I don't think it was that much."

"Tara," Wendy said in a loud voice, "you don't even know this guy. You ditched part of Unplugged to go to – where did you go?"

"We went to Nightlife."

"To Nightlife!" Wendy exclaimed. "You ditched Unplugged to go to a club with a man you just met, and you didn't bother to tell anyone where you were going! What were you thinking? Then, you allowed him to drive you home – drunk! I thought you had better sense than that!"

"You're the one who told me that I need to be more outgoing and make friends," Tara said defiantly as she plopped on the couch. "Now you are mad at me for doing just that."

"I'm not mad at you," Wendy said gently as she eased into a chair. "I'm disappointed. I thought you would make better choices than this. Weren't you listening tonight when Jonathan was talking about focus? The enemy is going to try to take our focus off of God. We have to be cautious with our choices. You love Unplugged, yet you allowed Stewart to influence you tonight into skipping out on the discussion and going to a club instead."

Tara crossed her arms and stared at Wendy. "So, are you saying that you think Stewart is bad for me? You don't even know what we talked about there. We talked about God there, Wendy. Stewart wants me to lead him back to Christ."

Wendy paused for a moment to collect her thoughts. "Tara," she said softly, "Stewart was drunk tonight. He probably won't even recall your conversation. And, it's never a good idea for a woman to try to lead a man back to Christ. That creates conflict. He needs to find another male to be a spiritual mentor, not you."

Tara angrily got off the couch and stomped to her room. Before slamming the door, she said, "You're just jealous, Wendy. You want me to be your little pet project, so you can show me off." Her voice assumed a high pitch as she exclaimed, "Oh, look how much I have done for Tara. Look at how she dresses now and how much better her appearance is." Tara paused. "I appreciate all you did; I really do. But, I don't need you anymore. I have Stewart now!"

Wendy stared at the closed door and began to pray. "Father, please protect Tara. She is a baby Christian and easily influenced. Help her to keep her focus on You." As a side thought she added, "And, be with Stewart too. Only You know his heart. Draw him to You. In Jesus's name, Amen."

~CHAPTER 31~

Tara awoke in the morning to streams of sunlight on her face feeling slightly ashamed at how she had talked to Wendy the night before. It was nice of Wendy to be concerned about her, but Wendy just didn't know Stewart the way she did. Even though she had only met him a few days before, Tara felt like she had known him her whole life. Stewart was everything she had dreamed of in a man, and, best of all, he was interested in her. Tara deserved to be happy and to be in a relationship. Not that she and Stewart were officially a couple yet, but he definitely seemed interested. She longed to heal the pain Rosemary had caused with her sudden death.

Just then, Tara's cell phone vibrated interrupting her daydreaming. It was a text message from Stewart!

"Had a great time last night. Can I take you to dinner this evening at the Red Rose?"

The Red Rose was an upscale steakhouse in the heart of Savannah. It was known for its dark, romantic interior lit only with soft candlelight. Red roses framed each table setting the mood. It was also known to be quite pricey.

Tara quickly responded, *"I would love that!"*

"Great!" came Stewart's response. *"Make sure to wear a red dress."*

Tara thought Stewart was joking, so she laughingly responded, *"Ok!"* and then ran to the kitchen where she could hear Wendy making breakfast.

"Guess what! Stewart is taking me to the Red Rose tonight!"

"That place is really fancy. You will love it!" Wendy replied as she scrambled some eggs in the cast iron skillet. "Want some?" she asked.

"Just a little bit. I want to save my appetite for tonight." Tara said while getting some plates down from the cupboard. "And don't go getting on me about my eating habits. I will eat tonight. I promise!"

Wendy turned, spatula in hand. "Tara, I don't want to fight with you. I just worry about you is all."

"Well, don't! I'm a big girl, and I can take care of myself!" Tara exclaimed as she scooped some eggs onto her plate. "Anyway, I am excited about going to the Red Rose with Stewart. That sounds like a really romantic gesture, doesn't it?"

Wendy bit her lip to keep from replying and quickly changed the subject. "What are you going to wear tonight?"

Tara laughed. "Well, Stewart asked me to wear a red dress, but, of course, I don't own any dresses. I thought I might wear a white cashmere sweater with some khaki pants. Can I borrow some of your jewelry to accentuate it?"

"Of course," Wendy responded as she scarfed down her breakfast. "Well, I've got to run. I have to get to work a little early today for a meeting."

The day passed by slowly for Tara. She tried to concentrate on her studies, but all she could picture was Stewart's face. He was so cute! She couldn't believe he was interested in her. After spending two hours straightening her hair and completing her ensemble, she heard a knock at the door. Stewart had arrived a few minutes early!

Tara rushed to the door, pausing before the mirror in the hallway to check her hair one final time before opening the door. Stewart was dressed in a black suit and tie with a white shirt underneath. Tara suddenly felt underdressed.

Stewart frowned at Tara. "Where's the red dress I asked you to wear?" he asked.

Tara suddenly felt uncomfortable. "I don't own any dresses, much less a red one," she explained.

Stewart frowned. "I specifically asked you to wear a red dress tonight, and you responded that you would. You should have been honest with me and said that you didn't have one."

"I'm sorry," Tara said nervously. "I thought you were joking. I didn't know you were serious. Does the Red Rose require formal attire or something?"

"No," Stewart said as he reached for her hand. "I just wanted to show you off tonight."

Tara melted. Stewart thought she was beautiful. He didn't say it in so many words, but he wanted to show her off.

"Well, let's go," Stewart said as he gave her a once-over. "That outfit will have to do."

Tara suddenly felt a little awkward like she had somehow disappointed Stewart by not wearing the red dress he had requested. She shrugged that feeling off as she followed him out to his Mustang.

As Stewart pulled up to the Red Rose, Tara felt like a princess. She couldn't believe that someone as handsome as Stewart was interested in her. Tara felt in a dream as they entered the restaurant. Her eyes took a moment to adjust to the darkness as a hostess led them to the table that Stewart had reserved. The warm glow of the candlelight combined with the wonderful aromas drifting from the kitchen created a cozy, romantic atmosphere. Stewart pulled out a chair for her as she sat down. The sweet smell of the signature red roses on the table in front of her delighted her senses. Stewart smiled as he sat across from her.

"It's lovely, isn't it?"

Tara beamed. "Yes, it's wonderful!"

A server appeared to take their drink order. Stewart ordered a bottle of sweet, white wine with two glasses. He noticed Tara's hesitation as the server walked away.

"I know you don't want to drink beer, but this is what sophisticated people do," he said with a smile. " A little wine never hurt anyone. Besides, if Jesus thought it was so bad, He wouldn't have turned the water into wine, would he?"

Tara chuckled. Stewart had a point. It was just a little wine. She took a hesitant sip and smiled as the wine entered her taste buds. It was delicious. At the sound of a man clearing his throat, Tara looked up. The server was back to take their order. Frantically, she looked for the menu, but Stewart took it out of her hands.

"We will both have the New York strip and lobster. Medium rare on the steak with a baked potato and ranch dressing on the salad."

The server looked at Tara for confirmation. Astounded, she just nodded. She didn't like her steaks medium rare, but she didn't want to embarrass Stewart. Tara took a few more sips of wine. Soon, she began to feel as if she were speaking from a cloud. She felt very light-headed. Was she drunk already?

Stewart reached across the table for her hand. "Wow! You really are a lightweight! Once our food gets here, you will feel better."

Tara remembered that all she had eaten all day was that little bit of scrambled eggs she had for breakfast. That was probably why the wine affected her so quickly. He was probably right. Once she got some food in her system, she would be fine.

Soon, their steaks arrived. Tara stared at her steak. The bloody juice oozing from it made her stomach lurch. She always ate her steaks medium well. Stewart was waiting for her to take a bite first. She took her knife, cut off a small piece, and forced it into her mouth.

Stewart didn't say much during dinner. He just kept staring at her which was fine with Tara. She didn't feel up to making small talk. She felt dizzy from the wine, and her stomach rolled in disgust every time she took a bite of the steak. Stewart finally broke the silence.

"Tell me more about yourself," he said.

Tara tried to focus her eyes on him. "What do you want to know?" she asked.

"You told me the other night that you had junk in your life. What kind of junk?"

Tara hesitated. Was it too soon to tell him? Wendy had been preaching vulnerability to her for a long time now, and she had learned to be transparent with her. Could she trust Stewart with her secrets? The wine seemed to loosen her tongue as she began to share her story.

"I shouldn't be here, well not here, but I shouldn't be alive." Tara paused at Stewart's confused expression. "About a year ago, I tried to kill myself. I was feeling so lonely and confused. I just felt like garbage all the time. I starved myself to ease the pain. I felt like I was a mistake. Wendy convinced me to go to Unplugged with her, well she paid me to go, but the more I went and learned about God the more confused I got."

"Confused?" Stewart questioned.

"Yeah, I, umm, well I was raised in foster homes since I was four years old. At this one particular home, my foster dad was a preacher, and he physically beat me and sexually molested me all in the name of God. He misquoted Scripture from the Bible for his own misguided purposes. As a result, I had a very warped view of God as a cruel tormentor."

"That's understandable."

"The more I went to Unplugged with Wendy, the more messed up and unloved I felt. God was trying to draw me to Him, but the enemy was doing his best to pull me away. And, he almost succeeded. I had the gun ready to kill myself. If Jonathan hadn't convinced Wendy to get home in time," Tara shuddered, "I wouldn't be here. I know it without a doubt. God used them to save my life." Tara nervously waited for Stewart's response.

"So that's why she is so controlling with you," Stewart said.

"She's not controlling; she just worries about me is all. I know that God cured me from the suicidal thoughts and that He has helped and is helping me deal with the insecurity and low self-worth. But, she still worries that I'm going to slip up. I'm not though. I tell my story to whoever will listen because I've finally learned that I'm only as sick as my secrets. God can use my story to help others who have gone through abuse to show them that there is hope for a better life. A year ago, I wouldn't have been able to hold your hand because I couldn't stand to be touched. God is in the process of healing me, and I will shout my story from the mountaintops for all to hear what He has done for me."

Stewart gave Tara a long look. "Wow! That is an incredible story. I'm glad that Wendy found you in time. I wish, I wish that I had found Rosemary in time to stop her. But, are you sure you are better? You don't have thoughts of ending your life anymore?"

"No, not in the past year! I believe with all my heart that what I called dark days, the days where I felt so down, so alone, and so ugly, were attacks from the enemy. My friends prayed for me at Unplugged. Wendy, Jonathan, Hannah, Travis, and others. They all put their hands on me and prayed that I would be healed from those thoughts and that I would have protection from the enemy. I didn't expect results at first. I had experienced what I call 'dark days' for years. Yet, they ended just like that, and so did the nightmares of Jack, my foster dad. God healed me, Stewart!" Tara pleaded with her eyes for him to believe her. She didn't want him to look at her with pity the way Wendy so often did.

Stewart smiled as he took her hand. "I believe you, Tara. God did a miracle in your life!"

~CHAPTER 32~

Tara stumbled into the apartment after ten p.m. Wendy, who was sitting in the easy chair reading a book, looked up in concern.

"Tara, you're drunk!" she exclaimed.

"I'm not drunk. I'm just a little tipsy." Tara defended herself as she slurred her words. "I wasn't drinking beer; I had wine – wine, Wendy! It's what sophisticated people do. There's nothing wrong with having a little wine with dinner. If Jesus thought it was so bad, He wouldn't have turned the water into wine, would He?"

Wendy looked at her in concern but said nothing.

"Wendy, I don't feel so good. My stomach really hurts, and my head is spinning out of control. All I had was a little wine. Why do I feel so bad?"

Wendy refrained from reminding Tara that she was drunk as she helped her to the bathroom. She held Tara's hair back as she began to spew.

"Wendy, I love you." Tara slurred. "You're always here for me, you know. I love you. I do. You're the greatest friend I could ever have. In fact, you're the sister I never had."

Wendy smiled as the odor of vomit hit her nostrils. Tara was never sappy in her words. The last time Tara had told her what she meant to her was a year ago when Wendy and her friends had walked in Tara's room and saw her pointing a gun at her head and somehow convinced her to not take her life. Wendy helped Tara to her feet and to her bedroom where she promptly passed out.

As Wendy returned to the living room to her easy chair, she bowed her head and began to pray fervently for Tara.

"Lord, Tara is caught in a battle right now. She has fallen head over heels for Stewart, and he is not good for her. Open her eyes, Lord. Let her see her true friends and those who care about her. Give her strength to reject Stewart's efforts to corrupt her. In Jesus's name, Amen."

Tara awoke Sunday morning to the sounds of birds happily chirping outside her window and groaned. Her head hurt, and the sound of the birds' happy cries was not helping. She stumbled to the kitchen holding her head and inhaled the aroma of bacon and eggs cooking in the cast iron skillet.

Wendy turned at the sound of her footsteps. "Good morning!"

"Aaagh," Tara said.

"Headache?" Wendy asked.

Tara sat at the table. "Yeah."

Wendy handed her a plate of steaming food. "Eat up. We need to leave for New Life soon for services."

Tara groaned again. "I think I'm going to pass today. I don't feel so good."

Wendy smiled. "That's all the more reason why you need to go, Tara. You need to get your focus back on the Lord. You have been letting Stewart steal your focus in ways that aren't healthy for you."

Tara immediately became defensive. "What is it you have against Stewart, Wendy? He likes me, okay. And, I like him. It's not his fault I got drunk last night. He didn't force me to drink the wine. I drank it of my own free will. I didn't realize I was such a lightweight that I couldn't keep up with him."

"That's just it," Wendy said. "You shouldn't have to keep up with him. He is influencing you in unhealthy ways."

"You're not my mom, Wendy. Stop telling me what to do!" Tara argued. "Geez, I appreciate all you have done for me in the past, but stop treating me like I am your project. Just be my friend and be happy for me."

Wendy took a deep breath. "Tara, as your friend, I am trying to warn you that Stewart is not healthy for you. He talked you out of staying for group discussion at Unplugged Friday night and got you drunk last night. He is not the man for you!"

Tara angrily stood up, her chair scraping the floor in the process. "You don't know anything about him, Wendy. We talked about God again last night at the Red Rose. I told him what God has done in my life and how much He has changed me. Stewart wants that for his life too. I believe God is going to use me in Stewart's life to help him just like you did for me." Tara shook her head and shouted over her shoulder as she walked away. "Don't judge him before you know him, Wendy. You know nothing about Stewart!" Her bedroom door banged closed as she slammed it.

Wendy looked at the door and quietly asked, "Do you?", as she finished her breakfast.

~CHAPTER 33~

Tara went back to bed while Wendy was at New Life. Why was she always up in her business? As usual, Tara felt a hint of guilt over how she had treated her but quickly let the moment pass. Wendy should be happy for her. A real friend would be supportive. Stewart was right. Wendy was controlling of her. She closed her eyes and blissfully drifted off to dreamland.

The vibrating noise of her cell phone signaling that she had a new text message awoke her. Tara rolled over and glanced at the phone then quickly sat up. It was Stewart.

"Hi babe! Had a great time last night. Want to get together again tonight at Nightlife?"

Tara thought briefly of Wendy's warnings about Stewart then quickly put them out of her mind.

"I'd love to!" she responded.

"Pick u up at 7," he wrote back.

Tara smiled then went back to sleep. Hopefully, her head would stop pounding by this evening. She awoke again to the sounds of laughter. It sounded like Wendy had invited some friends over for lunch. Tara quickly got dressed and went out to see who was there. Travis and Hannah were sitting in the living room with Wendy playing a board game and eating pizza.

"Hey Tara, we sure missed you at church this morning," Travis called as he rolled the dice.

"Are you feeling better?" Hannah asked. "Wendy said you weren't feeling good this morning."

Tara stared suspiciously at Wendy. Had she told them that she was nursing a hangover?

Wendy smiled at Tara and got up to get a plate out of the kitchen.

"Here," she said extending the plate towards Tara. "Help yourself to some pizza before Travis eats it all."

"Hey, I take offense at that!" Travis joked.

Hannah and Wendy looked pointedly at his beanpole body. "Where does all that food you eat go?" Hannah asked.

"I wish I could eat as much as you do and never gain weight," Wendy said.

Tara smiled at their good natured teasing and began to relax. It looked like Wendy hadn't said anything about the real reason that Tara wasn't at church.

Travis changed the subject. "Where have you been lately, Tara? We missed you at group discussion at Unplugged. Who was that guy that was with you?"

"His name is Stewart, and he is a paramedic. We wanted to have some time alone to get to know each other so we left after the message that night and went to Nightlife."

Hannah's brows knit together in a concerned expression. "You left Unplugged to go to Nightlife?" she asked.

"Well, we were going to go to the Peachtree, but they were packed. So, we went to Nightlife. No big deal."

"No big deal," Travis echoed. "Tara, you ditched church to go to a club. How long have you known this guy anyway?"

Tara crossed her arms in a defensive manner. "A few days. I met him on the internet. Don't worry. He is a Christian."

Travis exchanged glances with Hannah and Wendy. "Umm, Tara, if this guy really is a Christian, he should be encouraging you to go to church, not skip it to go to a nightclub."

Tara stood up and cast an angry look at Wendy. "You told them, didn't you? You couldn't wait to tell them what a bad influence Stewart is. Did you tell them that I got drunk last night too? What is this – an intervention for poor Tara who can't make choices for herself?"

Travis cleared his throat. "Wait a minute, Tara. Wendy didn't say a word to us. In fact, she was remarkably quiet when we asked her where you were this morning. And, you know Wendy is never quiet!" he added as an icebreaker.

Tara raised her voice as she exclaimed, "Why don't any of you wait to get to know Stewart before you judge him? Y'all think he is such a bad influence on me, but you don't even know him."

Hannah looked pointedly at Tara. "Do you? How well do you know him?"

Tara angrily stomped out the door and went for a walk. What was with her friends, and why wouldn't they give Stewart a chance?

~CHAPTER 34~

Tara was quiet on the drive over to Nightlife. Stewart tried to make small talk with her but gave up once he realized she wasn't listening anyway. As they sat down, he ordered two beers and slid one across to her.

"What's up? Something is bothering you."

Tara's eyes filled with tears. "It's my friends. They – well they don't like me hanging out with you. They think you are a bad influence on me and that I can't make that judgment call for myself."

"Do you think I am a bad influence?" Stewart asked as he took a swig.

"No, I like being around you. It just bothers me that they think so negatively of you when they don't even know you." Tara took a hesitant sip of the beer and tried not to grimace at the taste.

"I'm used to it." Stewart said sadly. "People have been judging me all my life for failing to live up to their expectations."

Tara waited for Stewart to expound, but he didn't. Instead, he changed the subject.

"You know what I think?" he asked. "I think it's time for you to get out of Wendy's apron strings and get your own place. Have some independence. She's too controlling over you, and you know what, I think that she may be emotionally abusive toward you. Making you feel bad for the choices you make – that's abusive!"

"Wendy's not abusive," Tara defended. "She just cares about me."

"If she truly cares about you, then she would want you to be happy. But, she doesn't. She wants you in her control like a puppet on strings. She probably gets her kicks out of you being a project for her. It sounds like she is co-dependent to me. She needs to take care of you in order to feel good about herself." Stewart signaled the server to bring him another beer.

Tara frowned. It was obvious that Wendy didn't like Stewart, and he didn't seem to think very positively of Wendy either. She needed to find a way that the two of them could get to know each other so that they would see one another's good qualities. Sure, Stewart drank more than he had let on at first. But, he always seemed in control. His job as a paramedic had to be stressful; it was probably just his way of relieving the stress somewhat. Plus, he really seemed to like her. She didn't want to have to make a choice between spending time with her best friend or with Stewart. She just had to get them to like each other somehow.

"I don't think Wendy is co-dependent, Stewart. She cares about me and looks at me as a sister. She doesn't want me to get hurt. Besides, alcohol is kind of a sore point with Wendy. Her fiancé was killed in an accident that was caused by a drunk driver. That is why she freaked out when she smelled the alcohol on you the other night when you drove me home."

"I only had a couple of drinks, Tara." Stewart said sarcastically. "I was still in control."

"I know that you know what you can handle. But, Wendy doesn't. She was just scared for me. We left Unplugged Friday without telling her where we were going. She tried texting and calling a few times, and I ignored her because I was talking to you. She knew I had met you off the internet. For all she knew that night when she didn't hear from me, you might have abducted me. She was worried. Then, when we did get back to the house, she could smell the alcohol and knew you had been drinking and driving. Wendy is a good friend – my best friend. She is just concerned that maybe we are moving too fast."

Stewart threw back his head and laughed heartily. "Abducted you? She thought I abducted you? Did she actually say that? Wait until I tell the guys at the station that this Christian goody two shoes roommate of yours thinks that I meet women off the internet and abduct them. Boy, will they get a laugh out of that! I put in long hours and see things no person ever should see on the job all for the sake of saving lives. Yet, she thinks that I'm some crazy, twisted internet guy who drinks too much and is a bad influence. Ha Ha!"

Tara frowned again. Christian goody two shoes? Wasn't Stewart a Christian too? Why would he mock Wendy in that way? He seemed to think her concerns were hilarious. She tried again.

"Well, Wendy just hasn't spent any time with you yet. I can see why she would be concerned. You see stuff like that on the news all the time. Listen, come over later this week and hang out with the two of us. I want you to like each other."

~ 171 ~

Stewart took a long drink and frowned. "Tara, she has already judged me as bad news, and nothing I do is going to change her mind. From the sounds of it, she has already poisoned your friends against me too. What's the use? I like you, but maybe this isn't going to work out for us. You are going to start listening to your friends at some point and think lowly of me too. I don't need that in my life again. Rosemary already did that to me once, and it was hurtful. I poured myself into her, yet she let her friends brainwash her into thinking negative things about me. Just because I called her frequently during the day to check up on her, they convinced her that I was controlling. I see the worst kind of scenarios all the time on the job. I called her because I wanted to know she was okay, but they refused to see it that way. I'm not going to go through being judged like that again."

Tara's heart pounded. What was Stewart saying? Was he giving up on her already? She pleaded. "Stewart, I am sorry for how Rosemary and her friends treated you. My friends aren't like that; just give them a chance. Come over on Thursday night for dinner and spend some time getting to know my friends. I will invite Travis, Hannah, and Jonathan over to the house. Let them get to know you, and their opinion of you will change. I know it."

Stewart reached his hand out across the table and grasped hers. "I like you. I really do. I think this can be good between us and that God will use you to bring healing in my life from Rosemary's death. We will figure out a way to work out this friend problem."

Tara smiled and started planning out her conversation with Wendy about having a get-to-know Stewart gathering.

~CHAPTER 35~

Tara hesitantly walked into the door of the apartment she and Wendy shared that evening. She had been careful to only drink half of the beer that Stewart had bought her. She didn't want to cause an argument with Wendy over drinking again. Besides, she remembered all too well her hangover and didn't want to experience that ever again. Wendy was sitting at the computer typing out something. She must have been deep in thought because she didn't even turn around at the sound of the door opening.

Tara cleared her throat. "Hi," she said softly.

Startled, Wendy looked up. Tara noticed her eyes were red and swollen like she had been crying for a long time.

"Hey, how was your date?" Wendy asked.

"It was good," Tara said as she took a seat near the computer desk. "How was your evening?"

Wendy smiled sadly. "Today was the second anniversary of Gary's death. I've just been sitting here feeling sad thinking of what might have been. I thought I had my life planned out. All I have ever wanted to be is a wife and a mother. If Gary hadn't died in that crash, I could be both by now. I loved him so much, Tara. He is the only man I have ever loved. Do you think that maybe you only get that one chance at true love? Maybe I missed mine. Maybe Gary was the only man that God had in store for me, and I'm going to be single the rest of my life." She sniffed.

"I look around, and I just feel so lonely. I miss him, Tara. I miss the way we danced in the rain and strolled through fields of wildflowers. I miss his gentle hugs and kisses. I miss his spirit of service. He always inspired me. He was always willing to help anyone in need. I thought we would sit on our rocking chairs on the front porch of a cabin and grow old together after a lifetime of missionary work. Instead, he is gone, and I'm here at Bridger studying for a degree that I have no interest in pursuing. I just wanted to be a wife and a mother."

Tears were rolling down Wendy's cheeks as Tara gently put her arms around her and hugged her. Wendy's body shook as she continued.

"I've been sitting here trying to write a letter to Gary's mom. I know this day is always hard for her. I would call her, but she won't answer her phone for several weeks this time of year. His death just hit her so hard. He was her only child. It must have been so rough to lose both her husband and her son at once like that."

Tara was confused. "Wasn't Gary alone in his car when he was hit by the drunk driver?" she asked.

"Yes," Wendy said.

"Then, what happened to his father?" Tara asked.

Wendy's voice choked up as she explained. "His father is the one who crashed into him. Ted had a drinking problem. He thought he could manage it. He thought he was in control. He thought he could tell when he had too much to drink, but he couldn't. He was going seventy miles an hour when he ran the stop sign just ten minutes from their home. Ted hadn't been answering his phone, and Gary was on his way to the bar to check on him. Ted must have decided to head home for some reason. They both died at the scene."

Tara's eyes filled with tears. She couldn't imagine the pain that Gary's mom must feel knowing her own husband had caused the accident that killed her son. Ted's choice to drink had huge consequences. She was angry with herself for forgetting what this day meant to Wendy. No wonder Travis and Hannah had come over after church. She should have been there to support Wendy in her grief too instead of fighting with her over Stewart.

"Wendy, I'm sorry I wasn't here for you today. I have been so excited about dating that I forgot this day was coming for you. Please forgive me."

Wendy smiled. "Of course! And, I'm sorry for overreacting about Stewart. I do think he is not being a good influence on you, but part of that feeling is because I could smell the alcohol on him when he brought you home Friday night. You weren't answering your phone, and I was so worried that something had happened. I even called the hospitals to see if they had any news."

Tara picked up a bottle of lotion and began rubbing it on her hands. "Wendy, I understand why you have reservations about Stewart. I met him on the internet, and I ignored your worried texts when I left Unplugged early with him. Plus, he drove me home after a few drinks. I should have insisted that he not drive for the safety of both of us. I can see why you don't have a good impression of him. But, he is such a nice guy, and he has been through so much. I think you will like him if you give him a chance. In fact, we talked about that tonight. I'd like to invite Travis, Hannah, and Jonathan over here on Thursday evening to spend time with Stewart and get to know him. And, you too of course. I want you to like him," she pleaded.

Wendy rubbed her neck that ached after sitting for several hours at the computer. "That's a great idea! I would love for us all to get to know him. Do you want me to cook dinner for us? Or, would you like to prepare something special?" She smiled knowing Tara's cooking tended to be somewhat inedible most of the time.

Tara nodded. "Yes please! I'd like to impress Stewart – not scare him off. How about you make your famous chicken alfredo, and I'll prepare the salads?

Wendy agreed and turned her focus back to the letter to Gary's mom. She never quite knew what to write at the end. Finally, she typed, "I just wanted you to know I was thinking of you. I miss him too. Love, Wendy." As she hit the "send" button, she allowed the memories to flood her once more. She smiled as she remembered Gary excitedly talking about getting involved in mission work and helping children overseas. He had really wanted to make a difference in such a big way. Why did God allow her to fall in love with such a wonderful man and then take him away so soon? It didn't seem fair.

She cringed as she could feel the dark feeling of despair and grief wash over her and quickly prayed, "Lord Jesus, I'm feeling down and alone. I miss Gary. I miss the life that we could have had. There is so much that I don't understand, yet I know that You are good. I know that bad things happen because we live in a fallen world but that the truth about Your love is that You are right here beside me walking with me through it all. You are with me through my doubts, fears, questions, and even my loneliness. Is Tara right, God? Am I jealous that she is developing a relationship with Stewart while I'm still single? But, I don't think that's it. There's something wrong here in the picture about him. Guide us to the truth Father. Open our eyes. In Jesus's name, Amen."

~CHAPTER 36~

Tara smiled as she walked into the kitchen and smelled the wonderful aroma of garlic and basil Thursday evening. Wendy stood at the stove stirring a large pot filled with her famous homemade alfredo sauce. She already had the table set and glasses chilled in the freezer ready for sweet tea to be poured into them. Wendy was always the perfect hostess. She never seemed to get frazzled when guests showed up early as it seemed would happen tonight.

Tara recalled a strange text she had received from Stewart earlier in the day. *"I sent u a present. Wear it 2nite."* She wondered what he had sent her and asked Wendy if she had received a package.

"Yes, I put it in your room," Wendy said as she sautéed the chicken.

Tara hurried to her room. She had imagined that Stewart had sent her a piece of jewelry and was surprised to see a large box sitting on the floor. It was much too large for jewelry. She frowned as she opened it. It was a red dress – or at least she thought that was what it was. There wasn't much to the material, and it seemed very short.

Frowning, she walked into the kitchen holding it. "What do you think of this?" she asked Wendy.

Wendy frowned too. "It looks like it would be very revealing," she warned. "Is that what Stewart sent you?"

"I'm sure the store made a mistake or maybe Stewart guessed the wrong size," Tara defended. In her mind, the material looked slutty. Why would Stewart have picked this out for her? Surely, it was a mistake. "He sent me a text saying that he was going to send me a present and asked me to wear it tonight. I'm sure it was a mix-up."

Wendy opened her mouth in response but was interrupted by a knock at the door. Tara rushed to the door to open it. Stewart stood there looking spiffy in a suit and tie. His grin faded as he looked her over.

"Didn't you get my package?" he asked. "I checked the delivery time on it, and it said that it was delivered this afternoon."

"Yes," Tara said, "but, I think there was some mistake."

"Mistake?" Stewart repeated as his face reddened. "What kind of mistake?"

"I think the store sent the wrong dress. The one I got was – well, umm, very revealing to say the least."

Stewart's eyes hardened as he stared at her. "Well, did you try it on to see what it looks like on you?"

"Of course not. The dress was so tiny that I wasn't even sure I could fit into it. Besides, I don't wear dresses, remember. I appreciate the thought though."

Stewart angrily put both of his hands on Tara's shoulders as he pushed her back into the corner of the wall. "I got you a gift. The least you could do was try it on," he whispered angrily. "You don't even know if it fits you or not."

Tara's heart pounded, but she decided to stand her ground. "I appreciate the gesture, Stewart. I really do. But, I don't like to wear dresses in the first place much less a dress like that. I honestly thought it was a mistake."

Stewart's eyes hardened as he angrily whispered. "You should have tried it on at least. You rejected my gift without even trying it on!"

Tara's eyes began to well with tears. Why was Stewart so angry over the dress? "I'm sorry," she apologized. "I didn't know it was such a big deal to you. I wasn't rejecting your gift. I just..."

The sound of Wendy clearing her throat in the entryway between the living room and kitchen cut her off. "Hey there, Stewart. I thought I heard you knock. How are you?" She looked pointedly at Tara. "I guess Tara told you the store goofed up your order, huh?"

Stewart smiled as he straightened himself. "Yeah, she said it looked a little short. No worries. I'll take it back tomorrow and get them to return my money."

"That happens sometimes. Well, make yourself at home. I'm just finishing get everything ready. Tara, can you come help me get something out of my closet please?"

Stewart started forward. "I can help."

"Oh, that's okay. I'd rather Tara. I don't want you to see my messy room," Wendy laughed. "You can help get the salad ready. Tara was going to, but she was running late. Everything is on the counter."

Tara followed Wendy into her bedroom and silently stood as Wendy quickly closed the door.

"I saw Stewart with his hands on you in the corner. Are you okay?" she asked. "He looked pretty angry. What's going on?"

"Nothing," Tara lied. "He was just mad when I told him what the store had sent. He definitely didn't pick that dress out for me. He was ready to call the manager and let him really have it."

Wendy stared at Tara in concern. "Is that really what was going on?" she asked.

"Of course, Wendy! You are already judging Stewart, and he just got here. He is very embarrassed that I was sent that revealing dress is all."

"I'm just concerned. Why would he buy you a dress to wear to hang out with friends at your own home anyway? And, what is he dressed up for? Who goes to dinner at someone's house in a suit and tie?"

"Do you have a problem with him looking nice?"

"Of course not. It just seems weird to me."

Tara sighed. "What seems weird to me is that you automatically think the worst of Stewart. Now you are judging him for dressing up! He is right. Nothing he does is going to be good enough for you. He was probably just trying to make a good impression. He is out there making salad for us while you are in here talking behind his back. Did you even need anything out of the closet anyway? Or was it just a ruse to tell me once more how Stewart is no good? Tell me the truth, Wendy. You seem so concerned about the truth when it comes to Stewart. How about yourself? Did you lie about needing help?"

Wendy nodded her head in affirmation as Tara stormed from the room. "God, open my eyes to see and give me the words to say to get through to Tara. The right words. Something is really wrong here," she prayed.

~CHAPTER 37~

Stewart looked up as Tara entered the kitchen. "Everything ok?" he asked pointedly.

Tara shrugged. "Yeah, Wendy was just being Wendy. She didn't really need my help. She just wanted to tell me what to do and control my life."

Stewart raised his eyebrows in an "I told you so" manner. "I could tell she was faking about needing help."

Tara frowned and was about to say something when she was interrupted by her friends letting themselves in the door.

"What's up?" Travis cheerfully called as he plopped himself down on the couch.

As Wendy came out of her room to greet them, Hannah could tell that she had been crying. She looked quizzically at her and nodded her head toward the kitchen where Stewart and Tara remained. They hadn't come out to greet anyone.

Jonathan frowned as he walked into the kitchen and noticed Stewart holding tightly to one of Tara's wrists. "Hey, how ya doing?" he asked as he lightly patted Stewart on the back. "Good to see you again!"

Stewart turned around, clearly annoyed.

"I was just telling Tara. I'm so sorry, but we can't stay for dinner. I forgot that there is a gala tonight for emergency service personnel."

Jonathan frowned. "You're both leaving?"

"Yes," Stewart admitted. "I got my nights confused. I already told the guys I was bringing the most beautiful woman in the world with me."

Wendy entered the kitchen and overheard. She angrily put her hands on her hips as she looked pointedly at Tara.

"This dinner is for you and Stewart! You asked me to put this together. You can't leave!"

Tara was torn. She didn't want to hurt Wendy's feelings and those of her friends, but Stewart had been pretty adamant about skipping out on dinner after she admitted that Wendy hadn't really needed help earlier. She wavered.

"She's right, Stewart. Wendy has gone to a lot of work to prepare this for us. Maybe we should stay."

Stewart grabbed Tara's arm. "No, we are leaving. Go put that dress on that I got you."

"But, I think it is too small." Tara protested.

"At least try it on," Stewart demanded. "And, come out here and model it for us." Stewart made his way to the couch and sat down as Jonathan and Wendy exchanged worried glances with one another.

Tara hung her head and headed for her room. She frowned at the dress. There was no doubt about it in her mind. It looked slutty. But, she didn't want to disappoint Stewart any further. He was already angry about Wendy.

Travis attempted to make small talk with Stewart while Wendy and Hannah excused themselves. They went into Wendy's bedroom and through the shared bathroom exiting into Tara's bedroom. As they entered her room, they paused in shock. The dress was so short and skin tight that Tara looked like a prostitute in it!

"Tara," Hannah exclaimed. "You can't wear that!"

"It would hurt Stewart's feelings if I don't," she explained.

Wendy was angry. "Let his feelings be hurt! You can't go out looking like that! You look like a tramp in it!"

Hannah was confused. "Why would Stewart buy you this?" she asked with a frown.

"I'm sure the store just goofed up on the size." Tara protested. "This can't be what he had in mind for me."

Wendy and Hannah exchanged knowing glances, which Tara caught.

"Don't judge him. He's not like that! I'm sure this dress was a mistake!" she protested.

"Then, test it," Hannah said. "Walk out there and see what he says when he sees you in it. If he is a gentleman, he won't ask you to leave the house in that thing."

Tara suddenly felt apprehensive. "But, Jonathan and Travis are out there too. I don't want them to see me like this."

Wendy sighed. "Then, take it off, and tell Stewart that you tried it on and that it doesn't fit."

Tara debated what to do. She didn't want to make Stewart upset at her again.

Suddenly, there was a knock on her door.

"Are you dressed yet?" Stewart called. "Come on out and model it for us."

"I umm don't think it is the right fit," Tara called back. "I'm going to take it off and put another outfit on."

Stewart looked at the guys sitting on the couch and laughed.

"At least let us see you in it and decide for ourselves."

Travis stared at Jonathan. What game was Stewart playing? If Tara didn't want them to see her in it, he should respect her wishes.

Jonathan interjected. "Stewart, she said it was too small. Just drop it."

Stewart laughed once again as he demanded, "Come on out and let us see!"

Hannah grabbed Tara's arm and pulled her away from the door. "You don't have to do this. He should respect that you don't want to wear it."

Tara brushed Hannah aside. "Mind your own business," she said as she opened the door and walked out.

Jonathan and Travis stared at Tara in shock. The red dress, if it could even be called a dress, clung tightly to her body accentuating her curves. Jonathan quickly looked away. Travis's jaw dropped as Stewart woofed at Tara.

"I thought you said it didn't fit. It fits you perfectly," he declared as he put his arm around her. "Let's go!"

Tara stared at the guys who were both carefully avoiding looking at her. Their faces were bright red in embarrassment.

"I don't think I want to go out in this," she nervously said as she felt Stewart's fingers digging into her back.

"You look wonderful! Now everyone will know that you are my red rose!" Stewart steered her towards the door. He looked mockingly at the group staring in disbelief at him and Tara. "Don't wait up!"

~CHAPTER 38 ~

There was a brief period of stunned silence after the door closed. Wendy broke the ice.

"What was that?" she angrily sputtered. "I can't believe that man! Why doesn't Tara see what he is up to?"

"What is he up to?" Hannah softly asked with a worried expression on her face.

"He is trying to establish his control over her," Travis sadly explained. "He can tell that she is desperate for a relationship, and he wants to see what is more important to her – him or her values and friends. It's a manipulative game that guys like him play. He will do his best to isolate her and convince her that he is the only person who truly cares about her. Then, he will break her heart after changing her into a person who is completely dependent upon him for her every need. As soon as he gets what he wants, he will move on to his next conquest."

Hannah stared at Travis. He seemed so certain. "What makes you say that? How can you tell?"

Travis frowned and glanced at Jonathan. "Because my dad was like that. I watched him at his game for years – the controlling, the manipulating, the isolating. It's sick."

Wendy made eye contact with Hannah. They had had many discussions about Travis in the past. Hannah felt sure that he liked her, but he never seemed to want to move forward past the friend stage. She took a deep breath and asked the question she had wanted to ask for a long time.

"Travis, is that why you don't date?"

Travis's face reddened. "I just worry that I might end up like my dad somehow. I don't want to hurt Han – anyone."

Hannah reached for Travis's hand and looked him in the eye. "Travis, you are not your dad. You love God and do your best to live for Him. That is the difference between you and your father. You are sweet, and you truly care about people. You aren't manipulative in any way."

Travis pulled his hand free and stood up. His face was bright red as he walked into the kitchen and opened the fridge. Hannah was everything he could want in a woman – in a wife. But, he couldn't take the risk of hurting her. *Like father, like son*, he thought.

He grabbed a soda and hurried back into the living room as he pasted a smile on his face.

"What are we going to do about Stewart?" he asked as he sat on the floor instead of on the couch next to Hannah.

"The big question is – what are we going to do about Tara?" asked Jonathan. "It was obvious that she was uncomfortable in that thing. I don't understand why she is so willing to fall head over heels in love with this guy that she just met and knows nothing about. I'm concerned for her. We need to somehow show her that we support her while making it clear that we don't support her choice of Stewart. That's going to be tricky because he has already convinced her that we don't like him."

Wendy huffed. "That part is true at least! I can't stand him! He has somehow convinced her to toss her values and morals out the window. I have never known Tara to touch a drop of alcohol before, yet he has been getting her to drink and get drunk with him. He tried to convince her that it was okay because Jesus turned the water into wine in the Bible. She already experienced that psychotic preacher in her childhood twisting Scripture in his favor to condone his sinful actions. Now Stewart is doing the same."

Jonathan snapped his fingers. "That's what it is! That's why she is being so gullible! You're right, Wendy! Because she is a new Christian, she doesn't yet have a firm foundation in the faith. So, she is extremely gullible to anyone twisting Scripture right now. Maybe more so than others because of her background with that Jack character."

Wendy sighed as she leaned back in her chair. "Yes, she keeps telling me that she thinks she is supposed to bring Stewart back to the faith. Her intentions are good, but she doesn't realize that his are not. We need to pray that God will reveal the truth about Stewart to her before this goes too far."

"Let's pray now," Jonathan suggested as he bowed his head.

"Father, we are all in shock right now. Tara was doing so good and growing in the faith. She has been allowing You to work in her life, and I do believe that Wendy is right. Tara thinks that You have given her a job with Stewart to lead Him back to You. And, that may be true, but at the same time, she is confused and desperate for a relationship. She is desperate to feel loved and wanted. We are worried that desperation is going to allow Tara to get in over her head with Stewart.

"We pray that You would guide her and show her the way. Let her know with certainty as You promise in Your Word that she will hear Your voice guiding her clearly saying, 'This is the way. Walk in it.' We pray for Tara because we love her and are worried about her and the choices she has been making.

"However, we also pray for Stewart. It is quite clear that none of us like him. But, he is Your child too. I pray that You will change his heart and his desires from whatever purposes they may be and lead Him to You. I pray that you will give us a love for Stewart. Help us to see him with Your eyes and with Your heart. Draw him to You. In Jesus's name, Amen."

~CHAPTER 39~

Tara felt ashamed as she allowed Stewart to guide her into the passenger seat of his Mustang. She hated the dress she was wearing. It was way too revealing. She also hated how Stewart had convinced her to brush off her friends. Wendy had put a lot of effort into making the dinner, and they didn't even bother to stay for it. She turned to Stewart to give him a piece of her mind. Just as she did, he leaned in for a rough kiss.

"I love you. You are so beautiful!" he exclaimed in her ear. "You are drop dead gorgeous!"

All thoughts of telling Stewart off went out the window as he began to drive.

"So, where is this gala?" Tara innocently asked as Stewart stopped at a red light.

He laughed. "There is no gala. I just wanted you all to myself. I thought I would take you back to the Red Rose and then we could go from there."

Tara was confused. "But, don't you have to have reservations for the Red Rose? We can't just drop in at the last minute and expect to get a table."

Stewart chuckled. "I already made reservations. You didn't wear a red dress like I asked you to wear there Sunday night, so I made another reservation. I wanted to show you off, and I always get what I want."

Stewart's words somehow felt chilling to Tara, but she was confused by his smiling face and his warm hand that gripped hers. "But, I thought we were leaving because you were upset with Wendy. Do you mean that you never planned on staying for dinner? Wendy went to a lot of trouble for us."

Stewart's hand gripped hers with more pressure. "I don't want to talk about Wendy. She is a controlling busybody, and you are better off without her. The truth is that I never planned on staying for dinner. I don't like your friends. I'm sorry if that hurts you, but the truth is I can't stand them, especially Wendy. I agreed to go to her dinner tonight. I never agreed to stay and eat there though. I want us to go have some fun together – just you and me. I want to show you off and for everyone to look at you and know you are with me."

Tara felt uncomfortable. Stewart was gripping her hand tightly now. "Stewart, I don't want to go into the Red Rose looking like this. The dress is too tight and way too short. Please, let's just go back to my place and have dinner with Wendy and the gang."

Stewart loosened his grip on her hand and a visible tension came over him. Seconds later his fist pounded into her ribcage with a force. She cried out in pain and gripped her side as he turned into the Red Rose parking lot.

"That dress was a gift from me," he yelled. "I was thinking of you when I bought it. And, I haven't heard a single word of appreciation for the gesture. Instead, all you have given me are complaints. It's too short. It's too tight." His voice rose. "You didn't even want to try it on to see if it fit. You rejected it from the start!"

Tears streamed down Tara's face as she fumbled with her seatbelt. Stewart was scaring her.

She shrank back as Stewart reached for her.

"I'm sorry," he said. "I'm so sorry. I don't know what came over me. I've been feeling a lot of tension with the job lately, and I guess it all just built up. Please forgive me. I won't ever do that again. Are you okay?"

Tara glanced warily at Stewart. Her side hurt where his fist had punched her. She wondered if she should call Wendy and ask her to pick her up. As she reached in her purse for her phone, Stewart grabbed it.

"Please don't. I'm so sorry. I will never do that again. Please stay. Let's go have a wonderful dinner. I need you, Tara. I need you in my life. You are the most beautiful woman I have ever met. Please don't go."

Stewart looked sincerely sorry. Tara relented and walked inside the restaurant with him while thinking to herself: *he is a paramedic and a Christian. He's safe. He is just under a lot of stress like he said.*

~CHAPTER 40~

Stewart portrayed himself as the perfect gentleman as he escorted Tara inside. He put his arm around her and beamed at the looks patrons gave Tara as they made their way to a reserved table. Tara felt uncomfortable with the attention and made futile attempts at stretching the thin fabric down. She hated feeling exposed in this manner. Stewart, however, seemed to thrive on the attention they were getting.

He immediately ordered a bottle of white wine for the two of them and urged Tara to take a sip. Feeling uncomfortable and wanting to please Stewart, she did so and soon became lightheaded after two glasses. Stewart noticed but didn't say a word. He began his tirade.

"You need to move out!" he demanded.

Tara raised bleary eyes at him. "I like where I live."

"Move in with me. We can get a place that's big enough for the two of us on the south side of town for fairly cheap."

Tara's head began to spin as the wine's effect became noticeable. "I really don't want to move," she weakly insisted.

Stewart smiled as he took her hand. "Who is more important to you? Your friends...or me? If you want to be with me, I need your full attention. I don't want to share that with anyone. I want you to love me. I don't want your attention or love divided. Do you think I don't see the way that pastor looks at you?"

Tara was confused. "Do you mean Jonathan?"

Stewart sneered. "Of course I mean him. How many pastor friends do you have? It's obvious that he has a crush on you."

Tara's face reddened. "We are just friends. He doesn't see me in that way."

Stewart sneered once again. "He had better not. I will not share you with anyone."

"Share me? What are you talking about?" Tara asked as the waiter delivered two platters steaming with fresh lobster.

Stewart's smile brightened. "Never mind. We will talk about it later. Doesn't this look delicious?"

Tara's stomach lurched. "Excuse me," she said as she hurried to the restroom. As she bent over the toilet, she heard her cell phone in her purse vibrate. Wendy had sent a text.

"Tara, are you ok? I am worried about you. Please come home. We are all worried about you."

Tara's side still hurt from where Stewart had hit her, and the wine was making her sick. Stewart would be upset, but all she wanted to do was go home and lie down. She pushed the voice recognition button on her phone and let it type out her text as she spoke the words.

"I don't feel so good. Can you come and get me?"

Wendy sent an immediate response back. *"Where is the gala at?"*

Tara hesitated. If she told her that she was at the Red Rose, Wendy would know that Stewart had lied about the gala. She decided to ask Stewart to take her home instead. She lingered in front of the bathroom mirror as she washed her hands and felt a dry heave coming on.

When Tara finally returned to the table, Stewart was fuming. "Took you long enough."

"I'm sorry. I don't feel so good. I want to go home."

Stewart frowned. "I thought we would go dancing after this."

Tara tried to focus on Stewart but her eyes kept seeing double. "I really don't feel good. I'm sorry."

The soft glow of the candlelight did nothing to ease Stewart's mood. "You're sorry!" he exclaimed. "I planned a wonderful evening for us, bought you this expensive lobster, and you haven't even tried a bite of it! Drink some water, and you'll be fine!"

"I don't think so," Tara whined. The double vision was making her dizzy. "I want to go home."

Just then, her phone rang. She had forgotten to send Wendy a response. She automatically reached for it and answered it to Stewart's disappointment. He glared at her as she hiccupped and fumbled over her words.

"I'm coming to get you. I mean you're getting me."

Wendy frowned in concern on the other end. "Where are you?"

"I don't feel so good."

Stewart's brows creased in anger.

"I understand," said Wendy as she repeated, "Where are you? I'll come and get you."

"You're coming for me? I don't feel good."

"Tara, where are you?" Wendy practically shouted in frustration.

"You'll be mad at me if I tell you," Tara whined.

"No, I won't. Just tell me where you are." Wendy frantically looked at Hannah for guidance.

Stewart reached across the table for the phone, but Tara held tightly to it. "I'm at the Red Rose," she whispered.

"Okay," Wendy breathed deeply. "I will be there as soon as I can." She shoved aside her chicken alfredo and stood up.

"Want us to go with you?" asked Jonathan.

Wendy paused. "Yes, but let's take separate cars. Just be there as back up in case there is any trouble. I don't want to scare her off from getting in the car with me. She's already worried that I will be upset with her."

Hannah frowned. "I thought they were going to a gala."

Wendy's voice rose in anger. "I've come to realize that you can't believe a word that Stewart says. He was deliberately trying to see how far he could manipulate her tonight."

Travis stood up so quickly that his chair tipped over. "Let's go before he talks her out of this."

The group hurried out the door.

~CHAPTER 41~

Stewart was fuming as Tara got off the phone. "How dare you?" he angrily asked. "How dare you answer your phone in front of me when you know I want your full attention? How dare you ask Wendy to pick you up? I would have brought you home if you felt that bad. It's your own fault for drinking the wine too fast."

Tara didn't feel like arguing. "I'm sorry," she blubbered. "I'm sorry for ruining the night I had planned. You, I mean. The night you had planned."

Stewart's face softened. "I'll let it go this time, but you are going to have to make a decision soon. Them or me! I won't be a second priority in your life!" He reached for her hand as he softly said, "I like you, Tara. I like you a lot. Maybe the wine was a bad idea since you are such a lightweight. I just wanted this evening to be perfect because you are perfect. You are my perfect woman."

Tears began streaming down Tara's face. She was so confused. Stewart's persona seemed to change so quickly. "I like you too," she said hesitantly. "I'm sorry I ruined tonight."

Stewart held Tara's hand tightly. "I'll make you fall in love with me. I'll be number one in your life, and you will be my number one."

Heart pounding, Wendy hurried into the Red Rose and brushed past the maître d'. She spotted Stewart and Tara at a table in the corner of the room. Stewart had his back to her, but she could see that Tara was crying. She prayed: *Help me, God. Show me how to be a friend.*

Stewart turned around and smiled at her as she approached the table.

"I'm glad you came. Tara is feeling a little sick."

Wendy looked at the empty bottle of wine on the table and bit back a response.

Stewart continued. "I would have brought her home, but I know that you are such good friend to her. I appreciate that."

Wendy was biting her lip so hard to refrain from making a scene that she could taste blood. She patted Tara's arm.

"Are you ready?"

Tara nodded and shakily stood up. She leaned over and whispered in Wendy's ear.

"I don't want people to see you in this." She corrected herself as she grimaced in agony. "To see me."

Wendy took off her jacket and draped it around Tara. Stewart stood up and enveloped Tara in a long hug.

"I'll see you soon," he softly said. "I love you."

Wendy reached for Tara to steady her as Stewart released her. The two of them slowly made their way to the front of the building where Wendy had illegally left her vehicle. Travis's SUV was parked behind it still running. Tara began to heave as Wendy opened the passenger side door for her. Hannah jumped out of the SUV and began to rub her back. Together, the two of them helped Tara into Wendy's car.

Tears began filling Jonathan's eyes as he watched from Travis's passenger seat. Tara looked ridiculous in that dress. How had a guy she had just met convinced her to sacrifice her values in such a short amount of time? He never in a million years would have imagined her wearing something like that and getting drunk to boot. He began to quietly pray.

"Father, I am so confused by what is happening. I know that Tara loves you and that more importantly You love her. I don't understand the control this guy has over her or why she has allowed him to have that control. I am worried for her. I am worried that she is not strong enough in her faith to resist the work of the enemy which is what I feel is taking place here. I pray that You will strengthen her faith and remind her of who she is in You. Help her to put on her spiritual armor to stand her ground. Give her strength to hold up that shield of faith. This is a battle. Show us how to stand with her and fight for her. In Jesus's name, Amen."

~CHAPTER 42~

Tara woke up and grimaced. Her head was pounding. Last night was a blur. She frowned as she tried to remember. Scenes filled her mind of Stewart punching her and then begging for forgiveness. The last thing she remembered was sitting at the restaurant sipping on wine. She groaned as she made her way to the kitchen.

Wendy was sitting at the table sipping on coffee and studying. She looked up as Tara slumped down into the chair opposite her.

"How are you feeling?"

Tara groaned once more and rubbed her throbbing forehead.

"What happened last night?" she asked.

Wendy frowned. "You don't remember?"

"The last thing I remember was being at the restaurant. I don't remember anything after that."

Wendy bit back a snide remark. "You asked me to come pick you up," she explained.

Tara was confused. "Why didn't Stewart bring me home?"

Wendy frowned once more. "I guess you would have to ask him that question. Or, better yet, ask him why he got you so drunk last night. Ask him why he insisted that you humiliate yourself wearing that horrible dress. For a man who is supposedly a Christian, he sure doesn't act like one!"

Angry, Tara stood up and placed her hands on her hips. "I have had enough of you bad mouthing Stewart. That is all you have done since I met him. Why can't you be supportive? I really like him, and he likes me. Besides, he is proud of the way I look and just wanted to show me off. There is nothing wrong with that!"

Wendy couldn't help herself. "Nothing wrong with that?" she questioned. "Did you see the way Jonathan and Travis were purposely avoiding looking at you last night? They were embarrassed to see you dressed like that. And, what about us? What about your friends? Don't you care that you blew us off last night to go to the Red Rose with Stewart? Don't you care that I had to rush home after being at school all morning and at work all afternoon to prepare a special dinner for you – that you didn't even bother to stay for?"

Wendy stood up. "You are allowing Stewart to control your life! What about God? When is the last time that you prayed? Did you ask God what He thinks about Stewart? Have you asked Him what He thinks about the choices you are making lately – getting drunk and wearing slutty outfits? How do you think God feels about it? You obviously don't care how we, your friends who care about you, feel about it. At least ask yourself, how God feels about it. You need to pray, Tara!"

Tara began walking towards her room not even bothering to pour herself the cup of coffee she had come into the kitchen for. Before slamming her door, she shouted, "Mind your own business! Go on to class this morning and be the perfect little Christian. Make sure to tell all of *your* friends to pray for me since I am obviously so lost and confused! I'm going back to bed. I don't feel like going to class."

Wendy tensed as the door slammed. She stood up to go bang on Tara's door and talk some sense into her. Instead, she felt God gently talking to her.

"I love her too. Her choices are paining ME just as much as they are hurting you, if not more. Trust Me. I am still in control."

Wendy began to quietly sob. "Father, draw her back to You. I just don't understand how Stewart has so much control over her in such a short period of time. I'm so worried for my friend. Please forgive me for my outburst in anger at her. I should have guarded my speech better and spoke the truth in love instead of anger. Touch my heart too. My feelings are hurt. I was hurt when she ditched us last night for Stewart. I think of her as a sister, and her attitude towards me lately hurts. Help me to give that hurt to You and not cling to it. Amen."

Wendy sat quietly at the table for a few more minutes, then scribbled a note on a piece of paper before heading out the door for class.

Tara, I am sorry for my outburst. Please know that I care for you and love you as a sister. Have a wonderful day!

~CHAPTER 43~

Tara angrily sat on her bed and glared at her Bible on the nightstand next to it. She grabbed a pencil and began journaling her thoughts – something Wendy had taught her to do to release emotion.

How dare Wendy ask me if I have been praying about Stewart? Stewart is an answer to my prayer! She just can't see it because she is jealous. She is jealous because her fiancé died, and she has no one to love. Unlike me. I love Stewart, and he loves me. Sure, he has his faults. Hitting me last night was not acceptable, but he apologized and explained that he has been under a lot of pressure at work. He's a great guy, and he thinks I am beautiful. Well, I didn't like that dress he made me wear last night. He didn't actually make me wear it, but I could tell that he really wanted me to. I didn't want to disappoint him. He has been through enough heartbreak with Rosemary and her friends. I want to be there for him. I will be there for him. It doesn't matter what Wendy or anyone else thinks. All that matters is what I think, and I think Stewart is wonderful.

Just as Tara put the pencil down, her cell phone vibrated with a text message from Stewart.

"How do you feel this morning? I was worried about you last night. You've got to learn not to drink wine that fast. LOL!"

Tara frowned as she typed out a response with her fingers.

"My head really hurts, but otherwise I am fine. I stayed home this morning to rest."

A response came swiftly back.

"Good call! Want to go to lunch? I can pick you up."

Tara was confused. When did Stewart actually work? It seemed like he had a lot of free time.

"Don't you have to work today?"

After a short pause, another message from Stewart came.

"I took the day off. I wanted to check on you and maybe spend some time with you. I'm really sorry about last night."

Tara hesitated. What was he sorry for? Getting her drunk again, humiliating her in that dress, or hitting her? She mentally kicked herself for sounding like Wendy.

"Sure! Give me about an hour to get ready before you come."

Tara hurriedly grabbed some clean clothes and headed for the shower. She hoped the spray of the water would ease her pounding head. Stewart knocked on the apartment door as she was applying her makeup. He smiled in appreciation at her and whistled.

"You sure do look beautiful!"

Tara blushed. "I'll just be a few more minutes. There's coffee in the kitchen. Help yourself while you are waiting."

As Stewart opened the cupboard to reach for a coffee mug, he noticed a large vase decorated in flowers in the back that was filled with cash. He smiled to himself as he reached for a couple of twenties and stuffed them in his pocket.

Tara entered the kitchen to find Stewart sitting at the table reading a note. He held it out to her and sneered.

"Looks like Wendy left you a note."

Tara glanced at it. "Yeah, we kind of had a fight this morning. I guess she must have felt bad."

Stewart shrugged. "Hey, I found a vase full of money in your cupboard when I was getting a coffee mug. As many people as come in and out of this apartment, that's really not the safest place to keep it."

Tara nodded. "I agree, but it's not mine. It's Wendy's. She's too trusting, I guess."

Stewart sighed. "Well, the reason I brought it up is that I'm kind of low on cash. I'd like to take you somewhere nice for lunch, but I don't really have enough. Maybe we could just take some from the vase? It looked like a lot in there. I doubt she would notice."

Tara hesitated. She was angry at Wendy, but stealing from her was a different story.

Stewart noticed her hesitation. "Hey, we can put it back after I get paid. She'll never know."

Tara's heart pounded as she felt that once again she was torn between being a friend to Wendy and pleasing Stewart. "Ok," she yielded. "As long as we put it back next week.

~CHAPTER 44~

Stewart took Tara to a bar named Homer's for lunch. Tara looked at the building in disgust as they pulled up. Stewart noticed and reassured her.

"You have to get past the experience. The food is great here!"

Tara blinked her eyes in an effort to adjust them to the dim atmosphere as they walked inside. There were a few patrons sitting in the bar staring mindlessly at the large television hanging from the ceiling. The rest of the tables were empty.

Stewart led her to a table in the farthest corner from the bar. The bartender, a balding man in his mid-40's, hurried over.

"What will it be?" he drawled.

Stewart began to order two beers, but Tara quickly stopped him.

"Just one," she insisted. "I'll take a glass of water."

Stewart frowned at Tara. "I take it you have been listening to Wendy."

"No," she defended. "My head hurts still from last night, and I don't want any more alcohol right now."

Changing the subject, she asked him. "Where is your favorite place to hike around here?"

Stewart looked at Tara in confusion. "Hike?" he questioned.

"You said on your profile that your idea of a perfect date would be a hike in the woods. I was wondering where you like to hike and thinking we could do that after lunch maybe."

Stewart relaxed. "Oh, well, I haven't really spent much time hiking in this area, but I have hiked all over Colorado and Utah and some other states. We could find a trail to hike if you would like."

Tara smiled. "I would like that very much. I appreciate all the meals, but I really am just a simple girl. A hike in the woods and a picnic are all I need to be happy. Hannah actually has given me some tips on places to go in this area and directions for how to get there."

She reached in her purse for her notes from Hannah. She excitedly pointed to one that Hannah had placed a star by.

"How about this one? It's very remote. We have to take a ferry to the island, and on it are miles and miles of unspoiled beaches along with historic ruins! Doesn't that sound great?"

Hannah, Wendy, and Tara along with the guys had begun hiking together a few times a month, but they hadn't visited this particular island yet. Hannah had mentioned that it had great reviews though.

Stewart smiled at Tara's excitement. "Only if you will bring your swimsuit."

Tara nodded and quickly began to scarf down the chicken fried steak and sweet potatoes that she had ordered.

"Wow! You are right! The food here is really good!" she declared as she shoved another biscuit dripping with honey butter into her mouth. "This is delicious!"

"Would I steer you wrong?" Stewart asked playfully as he paid the bill. "Now, let's go for this island hike adventure!"

After a quick stop by Tara's apartment to get her swimming suit, the two began to follow Hannah's directions to the ferry that would take them to the remote island. Since it was the middle of a weekday and not quite the weekend for a few more hours, the place looked almost deserted as they drove Stewart's Mustang off of the ferry.

Once they parked, Stewart quickly linked hands with Tara as they approached the trailhead.

"Let's take the trail to the old manor ruins first," Tara suggested.

"Whatever you want," replied Stewart with a gleam in his eye. "I am just happy to be spending the day with the woman I love."

Tara blushed. Stewart loved her? She smiled and said, "Me too! I mean I'm happy to be spending the day with you. I feel like we got off on the wrong foot with all the bars and drinking and everything."

Stewart dropped her hand and looked hostilely at her. "I have been spending a lot of money on the bars and alcohol for you."

"That's just it, Stewart. You don't have to do that to make me happy. This is what makes me happy – spending time together outdoors in God's creation. Seeing the beautiful scenery and hearing the happy sounds of the birds singing – that's what it's about. Besides, I am a little confused about the drinking part. On my profile, I specifically wrote 'non-drinker'. And, you made it sound like you didn't frequent bars which is why you were on the dating website. Yet, most of our dates have centered around alcohol."

Stewart hung his head. "You're right. I was just feeling nervous and trying to impress you. Had I realized that all I needed to do was take you for a walk, that would have made things so much easier on both of us."

Tara sighed as she began walking. "Yes, it would have. The drinking has really messed up my friendship with Wendy and my other friends. Wendy especially."

Stewart sneered. "Can't we have a conversation without Wendy's name coming up?"

"I'm sorry, but she is my best friend, and I have really been hurting her lately. I should call her and apologize for this morning. She was just looking out for me." Tara reached for her phone, but Stewart quickly grabbed it.

"You can apologize to Wendy later if you want. But, for now, let's focus on each other. I told you before, I won't come second in your life. If you want to be with me, you have to make me your priority." He placed the phone in the pocket of his shorts as he put his arm around Tara. "Now, let's enjoy our day together."

The two of them walked in companionable silence to the stone ruins of an old plantation on the island. As they gazed at the foundation of the mansion, Tara had a brief thought. *God is my foundation. He saved me because of His love for me. He only has two commandments for me: to love Him and to love my neighbor as myself. I haven't been very loving to Wendy lately.*

She hesitantly asked Stewart as they leaned against a stone pillar, "Will you hand me my phone please? I need to call Wendy. God is really convicting me of that."

Stewart sneered. "God?" he questioned. "I don't think he is concerned about your and Wendy's little fight."

"God wants me to show love to others, and I haven't been very loving towards her, my best friend, lately. I need to apologize. Hand me my phone please."

Sullenly, Stewart relinquished the phone and watched in anger as Tara made the call.

Wendy must have been busy at work, or still angry, because she didn't answer the phone. Tara left a voicemail. *"Wendy, it's Tara. I just called to apologize for this morning. I know that you care about me and that you were trying to watch out for me. I'm so thankful for everything that you have done for me. I just wanted to call and say I'm sorry. Stewart and I are out hiking right now, and I've just been feeling so guilty over how childishly I reacted this morning. You were there for me. You are always there for me. I'm sorry."*

The hot Georgia sun beat down on them as Tara hung up the phone. She could tell that the sun was no match for the heat of Stewart's anger as he stormed away from her.

"Stewart," she called. "Come back."

He paused mid-step. The sun glistened off his shiny head making him appear ominous. "Why?" he asked. "You don't care about me. All you are concerned about is your friends. Do you care how much you hurt my feelings when you make phone calls like that in front of me? All I have asked is to be the center of your focus when we are together. Is that too hard to do?"

Tara was confused at Stewart's reaction. "I just wanted to do the right thing in God's eyes. He would want me to apologize and make amends."

Stewart frowned, "So, now I have to compete for your attention between Wendy and God?" His hand balled into a fist. Tara noticed and took a step back.

"Calm down, Stewart. You have my attention the rest of the day. I just needed to get that out of the way."

Stewart leaned against a tree that was growing in the middle of the foundation. "How much do you love me?" he asked.

"What do you mean?" Tara asked warily.

"How much do you love me?" he repeated. "Do you love me enough to take my advice and move out? Do you trust my judgment that Wendy and your friends are going to drive us apart instead of together? Do you love me enough to put me first and move in with me?"

Tara stared at Stewart in astonishment. "Move in with you?"

Stewart smiled grimly. "It's the perfect solution. Wendy is always going to be intruding into our relationship as long as you two are roommates. Besides it will be so much fun living together. We can get separate rooms if you want. I will respect your privacy, and we can see each other as often as we want with no interruptions. Can't you see how perfect it will be? We can pool our money together and get a cute apartment with a swimming pool and a hot tub. How awesome will that be!"

Tara hesitated. She wanted to make Stewart happy but moving in together was a huge step. She watched Stewart's pleading eyes fill with moisture before he looked away. She didn't want to hurt him. Life hadn't been kind to him. It must have been so hard losing Rosemary the way he did. She took a deep breath as she said, "Okay, let's do it!"

Stewart's eyes danced with delight.

~CHAPTER 45~

Heart pounding, Tara clutched Stewart's hand tightly as they walked into New Life. She had wanted to confront Wendy alone with the news, but Stewart felt that it would be better if she just told the whole gang all at once. The timing was perfect since everyone would be at Unplugged. They entered quietly and sat in the back as Jonathan wound his sermon down.

"In other words, don't put your faith more in people than in God. Despite their best intentions, people are going to let you down. But, God will never let you down. You might say, 'But Jonathan, I prayed specifically to get a job with more money, and that hasn't happened. God let me down! He must not care about me. Or, you might say, 'I prayed for that person I don't like to move, and she is still here getting on my nerves constantly. God let me down! He didn't answer my prayer.'

"Be careful not to misinterpret 1 John 5:15 and think that just because He always hears us when we pray our requests that He is going to give us what we specifically ask for. You will feel let down when the specific thing that you prayed for is not answered in the way that you wanted if you don't truly understand this verse.

"We have to read 1 John 5:14 in order to understand the context of verse 15. Listen to this: 'And we are confident that He hears us whenever we ask for anything that pleases Him.' Now listen to verse 15 again. 'And since we know He hears us when we make our requests, we also know that He will give us what we ask for.'

"Did you notice the key words in verse 14 that He hears us when we ask for what pleases Him? The clue is praying for what pleases Him. How do we know what pleases God?"

Jonathan pointed at his Bible. "This is how we know what pleases God. He tells us what pleases Him throughout this book. When we pray His will, His words, we are no longer praying our own thoughts and opinions. Instead, we are praying and agreeing with God's thoughts. These verses are telling us that when we pray God's Word, we can know that He is listening.

"For example, suppose you have a friend who struggles with insecurity." Jonathan began to dramatically pray. "God, I pray for Beth. She is so insecure, and she is driving me and everyone around her crazy. Fix her." The audience laughed.

He waited for the room to quiet. "Instead of praying somewhat selfish prayers like that, try praying Scripture over Beth like this. 'God, I lift Beth up to You. I pray that she will find security from her identity in You. I pray Romans 15:13 that You, the source of hope, will fill Beth completely with joy and peace. I pray that she will place her trust in You and that as she does she will overflow with confident hope through the power of the Holy Spirit.'

"Now which prayer about Beth do you think is more pleasing to God?"

The audience shouted, "The second one."

Jonathan smiled. "So, in conclusion, God is not Santa Claus. Remember to take 1 John 5:15 in context. He doesn't give us everything that we ask for because He knows that sometimes what we ask for is not what we need. Other times, He has a different plan than we have in mind – a better plan. Don't get discouraged when it seems that God has not answered your prayer. Instead, ask yourself, "Am I praying God's will? Am I praying what pleases God or what pleases me? God always answers our prayers! Sometimes it's 'yes', sometimes it's 'no', and sometimes it's 'wait'. When we pray for healing for someone, and that person dies anyway, you can trust that God will answer that prayer. When we see that person in heaven, he or she will be healed and whole! God will never let us down! Don't put a period where God has only put a comma!

"It's time for group discussion. Tonight, I want you to practice praying Scripture. Your group leaders have a list of verses. I would like you to each pick two verses and write a personalized prayer using those verses. Share those prayers with your table if you are comfortable and discuss why praying the Scriptures is so important."

As the audience made their way into small groups, Jonathan caught Wendy's eye and nodded toward the back of the room where Tara and Stewart were sitting. They had made no move to join the groups. Travis, who was sitting to the left of Wendy, turned to see what she was looking at. In shock, he said, "I can't believe Stewart is here!"

Hannah quickly chided Travis for staring as Wendy explained that she had received an apology on her voicemail from Tara that afternoon. "Maybe they both had a change of heart," she said hopefully as they walked to the back of the room to greet the couple.

Tara and Stewart remained seated as Wendy enveloped Tara in a huge hug. "I am so glad you came tonight. And, thank you for the message. I'm sorry too."

Tara sat stiffly and glanced at Stewart. "I, umm, we have something to tell you – all of you. We thought it best to tell you here since all of you are present. I didn't want to have to explain it over and over to each of you. I, umm, we just thought this way would be best."

Jonathan could tell that Tara was visibly nervous and tried to put her at ease while mentally thinking about what serious news she had decided. "We're glad you two are here. Would you like to come in the office to talk privately?"

Tara glanced at Stewart once more and wrung her hands nervously. He reached for her hand as he said, "We might as well just come out and say it. Tara is going to move in with me as of tonight. We have already moved most of her stuff out in the past hour while you have been here. We think that it's better for our relationship to grow if she doesn't have a roommate as a distraction." He glared at Wendy as he continued.

"We feel that God has brought us together and that you, as in all of you, have been doing your best to tear us apart. I know that none of you like me, and I feel that you have judged me unfairly. Tara is the only one who sees me as I really am. She is the sweetest, kindest person I know, yet all of you have been judgmental towards her. You've made her feel bad for spending time with me and treated her horribly just because you don't agree with the choices she has been making."

Wendy couldn't contain herself. "You are the reason that she is making those choices! You have done nothing but manipulate her!"

Jonathan put a hand on Wendy's shoulder as a warning to calm down. He looked pointedly at Tara. "Let's talk about this, Tara. Do you really feel this way? Do you really want to move in with Stewart?"

Tara's eyes filled with tears. She knew that her friends would be hurt even more with Stewart's next words.

He squeezed her hand forcibly while he demanded, "Tell them the rest."

Her mouth opened but no words came out. She looked at Stewart pleading for him to not make her say it, but he just squeezed her hand even tighter. "Tell them!" he demanded. "Let's get this over with!"

Lips quivering, Tara forced the words out. "Stewart feels, I mean we feel." Tears began to flow down Tara's face. "We feel that it would be best if we have no more contact with you, with any of you."

At Wendy's shocked expression, Tara explained, "I don't want to hurt you, especially you Wendy, but Stewart feels...I mean I feel...umm we feel that this is what is best for our relationship."

Stewart gleefully smiled as the group stood there dumbfounded. "I have already blocked all of your numbers from Tara's phone. We are serious about this. We will finish moving her stuff out of the apartment before you come home, Wendy."

Travis looked angrily at Stewart. "What are you doing man? Why are you trying to put a wedge between us and her? Wendy is right. You've done nothing but manipulate Tara since you met her."

"Watch your mouth," Stewart sneered. "You wouldn't want anyone else here to see me beat you up."

Travis balled his hand into a fist and stepped forward as Jonathan put his arm out to restrain him. "Don't stoop to his level, Travis."

"My level?" Stewart questioned as he stood up. "Look, Tara, there he goes insulting me again. Apparently he thinks he is better than me just because he is a preacher." He tugged on Tara's arm to pull her up as Hannah and Wendy grabbed Tara.

"Tara, let's talk about this. Let's just go have some girl talk," they pleaded.

Wavering, she made a move to go with them as Stewart glared at her. "It's me or them. You can't have both. I will ask you one more time, 'Do you love me enough to put me first?' I love you and will put you first always. I will do everything for you and treat you as a princess. What have your friends done for you besides make you feel bad for your choices? That's not love. I will show you what love is. You've got to make a decision. Me or them? What's it going to be?"

Tara hesitated then shook off the girls as she reached for Stewart's extended hand. He smirked at the group as he led her out the door.

"Tara, wait!" Wendy called frantically as she ran to catch up with the couple. "Please don't go like this. Don't cut us out of your life."

Stewart angrily turned around. "She's made her decision. She has asked all of you to leave her alone. If any of you make an attempt to contact her, I will be forced to call the police and ask for a restraining order for harassment."

"Tara," Wendy sobbed as Hannah wrapped her in a hug. "Tara, this is not love," she called as the door slammed leaving the four friends dumbfounded.

~CHAPTER 46~

Wendy angrily pushed Hannah away as she attempted to comfort her. She ran out the door and watched the red taillights of Stewart's Mustang fade into the night. "I'm going to the apartment to stop them," she cried.

Jonathan placed a restraining arm on her shoulder. "Tara is not going to listen to a word you or any of us say right now. I'm afraid that Stewart will manipulate the situation somehow and get the police involved if we go to the apartment right now."

"Well, let him get the police involved," Wendy huffed. "Maybe they will arrest him."

"On what grounds," asked Travis. "Legally, he has done nothing wrong. And, since he made Tara state that she wants no contact, he actually could file charges of harassment against us if we try to stop them from leaving the apartment." He shook his head in disgust. "Stewart has manipulated this situation beyond reason. Tara met him, what a week ago? How in the world has he twisted her around his fingers so quickly?"

Wendy nodded sadly. "I just don't understand. How can she just blow us off in this way?" She allowed Hannah to envelop her into a hug as she cried, "I just don't understand. We can all see she is making a huge mistake, yet there is nothing we can do about it."

Jonathan solemnly shook his head. "There is something we can do. Pray! I know sometimes, a lot of times, we tend to try to fix things on our own and then use prayer as a last resort, but prayer is an action. Stewart has manipulated it where we will get into trouble with the law if we try to do anything, but he cannot manipulate things with God. We can pray, and prayer is more powerful than anything Stewart can cook up!"

The four friends made their way back inside. Group time at Unplugged was winding down, and Jonathan needed to close. When he was finished, he quickly excused himself, and the four friends walked quietly to his office. Jonathan took the lead.

"I know right now it is easy to place blame on Stewart and Tara for their actions. However, I would like us to pray God's word over them just as I talked about in the message tonight. That is hard when we are feeling hurt and upset. Yet, this is the time to do it the most. I will go first."

Jonathan ran his fingers through his hair as he sat down. "Father, we are in shock and hurt at tonight's events. We simply do not understand. I pray the prayer of Paul in Ephesians 3:14-21. We know that You are the Creator of everything in heaven and on earth. You created Tara, and Stewart too. Tara needs Your strength right now to recognize the truth. I pray that You will fill her with inner strength through Your Spirit. I pray that she will place her trust in You to lead, guide, and direct her. I pray that she will understand, truly understand, just how deep, how wide, how long, and how high Your perfect love is for her. I pray that she experiences that love tonight and that she will be made complete in You. This situation may seem hopeless, impossible, and out of our hands, but we know that nothing is impossible with You. We praise You in advance that You can accomplish more than we could ever imagine in this situation. I don't know what is going to happen, but You do. We place Tara in Your hands. And, we pray for Stewart too. It is hard to pray for him, but he is Your child as well. Soften his heart, Lord. Turn his heart to You. In Jesus's name, Amen."

Travis took a turn. "God, I am confused. Well, we all are. I pray Colossians 1:9-10 over Tara. I pray that You will give her complete knowledge of Your will. I ask that You would give her spiritual wisdom and understanding so that the way she lives, the choices she makes, will always honor and please You. Actually, I pray that verse for all of us. Let our lives shine for You. We want our pictures hanging on Your giant refrigerator so that You can brag on us. Fill us with Your strength and guide us into what to do, if anything, right now. It's hard to be patient and just wait instead of acting, but maybe that is what You need us to do the most right now. Just wait. I pray for Your direction upon our lives and on Tara's. I don't really have anything good to say about Stewart, but I echo what Jonathan prayed. He is your child too. I ask that You turn His heart toward You. Amen."

Hannah sniffed softly as Travis handed her a tissue. "Father, this is hard because I too want to do something, anything to stop Tara from doing this, but I don't know what to do. I don't know the right thing to do. We have seen Tara grow so much in the past year as she has shaken off the bondage of her past and learned to trust in You. This just comes as such a shock. I pray Psalm 139 over her. You know all about her. You know when she stands up and sit downs. You know what she is going to say before she even says it. You know her so well that you even know how many hairs she has on her head. You know her anxieties. You know her struggles. I praise You for Your promise in Jeremiah 29:11 that not only do You know the plans You have for her, but that they are also good plans to give her a hope and a future. Even though things seem out of control in her life right now, we can trust that You are in control. I pray that she will respond as the Prodigal Son did and return to You and to us. Let her know that we care about her and will always be here for her."

Wendy cut in. "Yes, Lord. Open her eyes. Let her see Your love for her. Let her not be too ashamed to turn to You and to us as well. Please put forgiveness in our hearts and give us a loving acceptance for her. I pray Romans 8:11. Please let doubts, fears, and anxieties not occupy our hearts and mind more than our faith. I praise You that we can trust that the same power that resurrected You from the dead can resurrect our hearts and lives. You alone can give us courage instead of fear and doubt. I pray that You will resurrect Tara's heart. Open her eyes to see the truth about Stewart. I pray for Your protection over her. Amen."

The four friends were wiping their eyes as they closed by praising God for His goodness.

"What now?" asked Wendy.

"I want to escort you home, just to make sure Stewart is gone." Travis said.

"Maybe Tara will be there waiting for me," she said hopefully. "Maybe she changed her mind."

~CHAPTER 47~

Wendy tentatively unlocked her apartment door and stepped back. Travis and Jonathan had made it clear that they wanted to enter first. She stepped forward quickly at the sound of Travis exclaiming in dismay.

"Oh no," said Hannah who was right beside her. The living room was a mess. Lamps and picture frames had been shattered. The stuffing had been pulled out of her sofa and littered the floor. Bits of broken glass covered the kitchen. Wendy stared in horror. *How could Tara do this to me?* she thought. *How can she hate me this much? What have I done to her?*

"Is anything missing?" Travis asked as he carefully picked up a broken frame that contained a picture of Wendy and her former fiancé Gary. "This is all Stewart! I know it. How could Tara just stand by and allow to him to do this?"

"She probably helped him," Hannah bitterly replied. She looked carefully at Wendy who hadn't said a word. "Do you think they took anything of yours?"

Wendy shrugged her shoulders as she headed for her bedroom. She stood in shock in the doorway at the sight before her. Her camera, the one she had saved so carefully for and had just bought a few weeks ago, lay shattered on her dresser amidst broken glass from the telephoto lens. She had found a great deal for the camera online. The camera came with a kit lens and an extra telephoto lens to the tune of five hundred dollars. The cost had seemed like a lot, but Wendy was sure that she would more than make up for it with her new side business of portrait photography. Her last day at her part-time job was just yesterday. She wanted to focus solely on growing clients in between finishing up her last year of college. By averaging about two portrait shoots a week, she would make more than she had at her part-time job and have extra time to focus on studying and volunteering. She sat on the bed and covered her face with her hands. *What am I going to do now?* She asked herself as the tears began to flow. *How could Tara do this to me?*

Jonathan stared at the mess in dismay. It looked like a tornado had swept through the room. He couldn't imagine Tara doing something like this, but he also couldn't understand how she could just stand by and watch Stewart destroy Wendy's belongings and photography career. He pulled his phone out. "I guess we should call the police," he sadly said as he looked to Wendy for confirmation. "If you have renter's insurance, maybe that will help some with the costs of the damage."

Wendy nodded as he made the call. They sat quietly on the floor of Wendy's bedroom as they waited for the police to arrive. Jonathan took the lead and explained the situation to the police. "I don't know his last name," he said as he glanced at the others. "Do any of you?"

"I never heard Tara mention it," Wendy replied as she wiped her eyes once more with her hand. "All I know is that he is a paramedic."

"On the north side or the south side of town?" asked the kind officer.

Wendy shook her head once more. "I just don't know."

"Well, we can quickly find out," the officer said as he placed a call. He frowned at the voice on the other line. "No," he explained, "This guy's name is Stewart, and he is bald with a goatee. Around twenty-five. It can't be this hard to locate his address." He listened for a few moments and frowned again at his phone as he hung up.

"There is no record of a paramedic named Stewart on either the north side or the south side of town. Are you sure that he works in this area?"

"Yes," Wendy said as she looked worriedly at her friends.

The officer gently replied. "You said she met him on the internet, right?"

Wendy nodded.

"Then, we have no way of knowing for sure if this guy really is a paramedic. I want you to think of every detail that Tara told you about him."

Hannah cut in. "He had a girlfriend, maybe she was a fiancé, named Rosemary who killed herself."

"And, his dad was in the military. He told Tara that he moved around a lot as a kid."

The officer took careful notes. "Did he or she ever mention any certain places that he liked or spent time at?"

"I think Tara said that he spent the most time in Colorado and Utah as a youth."

"Anything else?" the officer questioned.

"Just the places around town. The Peachtree, Nightlife, and the Red Rose are all places he took Tara. I really don't know much about him," Wendy explained.

"What about her profile?" the officer asked. "Do you know what internet dating site she was using? Maybe we could access her profile and pull some information up about him through that."

Wendy shook her head. "I don't know. She used her laptop for all of that. Her room is cleaned out. The laptop is gone. And, they broke mine – not that she ever used mine anyway."

"What about pictures of him and Tara?"

"I have pictures of Tara, but I don't have any of Stewart." Wendy looked at her friends. "Do any of you? Did you happen to snap any pictures of him?"

They shook their heads.

"I just don't have much to go on," the officer explained. "It seems likely that it was the two of them who ransacked your apartment. I can dust for fingerprints and put out a warrant for Tara, but we don't even know for sure if Stewart is this guy's actual name or not."

Hannah spoke the question they had all been thinking. "Do you feel that she might be in trouble?" she asked. "Not for this, but do you feel that she might not be safe with him?"

The officer hesitated and stared at his notepad. "Based on what you have told me, I do. You have described a very manipulative person. If it was indeed Stewart who ransacked this place, that proves that he is definitely capable of violence. Combine that with a potential drinking problem plus the matter that we aren't sure if he even is a paramedic as he claimed. It doesn't seem like a safe situation for Tara to be in. If we can't get a match on his fingerprints, the best we can hope for is that she gets arrested or that she feels guilty and contacts you. If she does, do your best to assure her that it's okay to come home. I would rather her be safe in prison than be in this guy's hands from the sounds of it."

Wendy and her friends nodded in agreement and thanked the officer as he left. They stared silently at the mess until Hannah broke the ice.

"I am so angry right now that I can't think straight, and to be honest, forgiveness if the furthest thought from my mind. I just don't understand how Tara could do this. But, the officer was right. We need to have an attitude of forgiveness because one day if Tara does contact us, we need to have forgiveness in our hearts to reassure her of our love for her. What she did to us and to Wendy is absolutely inexcusable. And, she definitely doesn't deserve our forgiveness. I don't feel very forgiving right now, and I'm sure none of you do either. Yet, I am also worried about her because no matter what she has done, I care about her. Somehow, I am sure that you can make a sermon out of this, Jonathan. All I know is that we need to decide right now that we forgive her and let our hearts be convinced along the way."

"We'll keep forgiving her until it no longer hurts," Wendy softly said. "Because that is what God has done for each of us. He showed us grace, and we are to do so to others – even when it hurts and we just can't understand."

"Yes," Jonathan commented. "Matthew 6:14-15: 'If you forgive those who sin against you, your heavenly Father will forgive you. But if you refuse to forgive others, your Father will not forgive your sins.' Jesus is pretty clear in those verses on how He feels about forgiveness. We can verbally agree to forgive her and wait for our hearts to catch up. One way that I've personally found that helps with forgiveness is to pray for that person regularly. Somehow while praying for that person, God removes the anger you have toward him or her and replaces it with love. It's healing to pray."

"Let's pray for her now," Travis voiced, "because I sure am having angry thoughts about her and Stewart."

Jonathan smiled. "I'll lead. Father, we come to You again this evening because we are hurt and confused. We just don't understand how our sister Tara either did this or allowed Stewart to do this to Wendy's stuff. We are hurt, Lord. I thank You that You lived as a man upon this earth and experienced the same feelings that we do. You are a God who understands. You know the hurt and betrayal we are feeling because You too were hurt and betrayed by one of Your friends, Judas. Your other disciples let You down too as You were arrested and beaten.

"I agree with my friends here. I too don't feel very forgiving right now. But, we ask that You will open our eyes and let us see Tara and even Stewart through Your eyes. Give us Your love and compassion for them. As we make a pact before You to forgive Tara, and even Stewart, we ask that You will quickly let us feel forgiveness in our hearts.

"Let it not just be words that we are mouthing. Let forgiveness flow from us just like it does from You. We thank You for the grace You have shown us by Your sacrifice on the cross. You have shown us mercy when we didn't deserve it. Help us to show that same kind of grace to others and especially to Tara and Stewart right now. Wherever Tara is tonight, we pray that You will keep her safe. Let her know that she can call on any of us at any time and that we will come get her. Help us to make love an action verb and to put our faith into action. We praise You and thank You. In Jesus's name, Amen."

PART 3

SIX MONTHS LATER

~CHAPTER 48~

(Thursday)

Tara sighed as she tiptoed past Stewart who lay passed out on the lumpy couch. She didn't want to accidentally wake him and endure the brunt of his anger. The last six months had been a blur, and not in a good way. She cringed as she remembered how she had stood back and allowed him to destroy Wendy's belongings the night she moved out. Stewart had wanted to make sure that the bridges between Wendy and her were completely burned. He frequently reminded her that Wendy would be unable to forgive her for the destruction of her property despite her professed Christian beliefs. He had also made it clear that the only full name that Wendy and her friends knew was Tara's and not his. She had lived in fear for months of being arrested for vandalism. She was afraid to live with Stewart, but she was also afraid to live without him.

She had quickly realized upon moving in with him that most of what he had told her was a lie. There was no stressful paramedic job where Stewart worked long hours saving lives. Maybe there had been at some point, but Stewart spent most of his time drinking. When she asked him when he was going to work, he simply got angry and hit her. He always apologized, but she had come to learn that his apologies meant nothing. There was never true repentance.

Instead of the glorious apartment with an indoor pool and workout room that he had promised her, they lived in a dingy, run-down motel room that had been converted into a one room studio. He made her quit school and her job. He didn't allow her to go anywhere without him, not that she really wanted to. She didn't know anyone in this neighborhood and didn't have any friends left.

At first, she thought that she could just love him enough to change him, but that didn't work. He seemed to thrive off of controlling her, yet no matter how far she bent over backwards to please him, it was never enough. He stripped her of her dignity and made her wear flimsy outfits when he took her to dinner or to a bar. She had tried refusing to wear those, but that only resulted in a black eye or a swollen jaw. Tara was beginning to wonder what had really happened to Rosemary. Had she killed herself because she just couldn't take Stewart's abuse anymore? Or, did Stewart go too far with a beating? She shook in fear at the thought.

She carefully opened up the dresser drawer and felt underneath her underwear and socks for the cell phone that she kept hidden there. Stewart had thrown it against the wall the night she moved in with him in an effort to make her totally let go of her past. He wanted to be number one in her life and didn't want her to have any contact with her former friends. Later that evening after he had passed out, she had retrieved the phone and found to her surprise that, although cracked, it still worked.

Tara turned the phone on and scrolled through her short contact list which consisted mainly of names of former co-workers and her four friends: Wendy, Hannah, Travis, and Jonathan. She wiped away the tears that came to her eyes as fond memories swept over her. Tara sighed again. *Not that I would contact them anyway. I'm sure they hate me for how I treated them.*

She had often thought of calling them, especially Wendy, but the threat of going to jail for Stewart's vandalism made the beatings more bearable to endure. She smiled as she thought about Wendy who made God's love as real as the sunshine that warms her. *I know Wendy loves me a sister, but even she couldn't forgive me for what I have done.*

Tara wiped her eyes once more as she turned the cell phone off and returned it to its hiding place. Then, she reached to the back of the drawer and pulled out her Bible that she also kept hidden there. She made her way in the dark to the bathroom, quietly closed the door, turned on the light, and sat on the floor to read. She hadn't opened her Bible in several months. If Stewart caught her, a beating was inevitable, but lately she was realizing that it was worth the risk. She felt so alone like she was stuck in the bottom of a pit with no way out. Wendy and her friends had introduced her to God's love, and they had shown her the human love and acceptance she had craved for all of her life as well. Yet, she had pushed them aside for Stewart and treated them horribly in return. Guilt over her actions gnawed at her as tears flooded her eyes once more.

She sniffed as she began to read Psalm 139:7-12.

"I can never escape from Your Spirit! I can never get away from Your presence! If I go up to heaven, You are there; if I go down to the grave, You are there. If I ride the wings of the morning, if I dwell by the farthest oceans, even there Your hand will guide me; and Your strength will support me. I could ask the darkness to hide me and the light around me to become night – but even in darkness I cannot hide from You. To You the night shines as bright as day. Darkness and light are the same to You."

Tara buried her face in her hands as she began to pray. "Father, is this true? Are you really with me right now in this nightmare that I'm living in because of my own poor choices? It is my fault that I am here, but I never imagined what this life I chose with Stewart would be like. I thought I

~ 233 ~

would live a fairy tale dream life, and instead I'm barely surviving day to day in this dingy apartment that is roach infested. We barely have enough food to eat, and I don't even want to know where Stewart finds the money for that. I am hiding here in the bathroom reading Your Word afraid of what Stewart would do to me if he found out, yet, according to these verses, I am not hiding from You. Even in the darkness of my world, in this pit I am living in now, You are with me! You see my circumstances as bad they are, but you haven't abandoned me. You are still here! I believe it! I have to believe it because right now You are my only hope!"

Tara continued to read Psalm 139 and paused at verses 17 and 18.

"How precious are Your thoughts about me, O God. They cannot be numbered! I can't even count them; they outnumber the grains of sand! And when I wake up, You are still with me!"

Tara smiled as she prayed once more. "You think about me, God? For real?"

Her smile turned to a frown. "But, what precious thoughts could you have about me? I took Your gift of friendship and threw it away for Stewart. I haven't lived a lifestyle honoring You. Instead, I have lived these past six months to honor Stewart. I haven't treated my body as a temple. I haven't shown love to anyone. How could You think anything precious about me much less have so many precious thoughts that they outnumber the grains of sand? Why are You still with me? Why haven't You abandoned me as I deserve?"

Tara stared at the words on the page. One thing that she remembered from Unplugged was that God never lies. If He says it in His Word, then it is true. As she contemplated on what precious thoughts God might have about her, a folded piece of paper fell out of her Bible. She opened it up and stared at it in wonder. It was a list that Wendy had given her of who she was in Christ.

She quietly sobbed in joy as she read in Jeremiah 31:3 that she is beloved. "I have loved you with an everlasting love." Tears streamed down her face as the words in 1 John 3:1 and Romans 8:15 reminded her that she is a child of God. She stared in wonder at 2 Corinthians 5:17 which promised her that she is a new creation and mediated over the words.

"Anyone who belongs to Christ has become a new person. The old life is gone; a new life has begun!"

But, God already made me a new creation, and I blew it. She thought sadly then smiled as she came to 1 Peter 2:24-25 that stated that she was forgiven.

"He personally carried our sins in His body on the cross so that we can be dead to sin and live what is right. By His wounds you are healed. Once you were like sheep who wandered away. But now you have turned to your Shepherd, the Guardian of your souls."

Tara began to pray once more. "Father, now I see what precious thoughts You have about me. I am beloved by You. I have been adopted into Your family, and You call me Your child. I am a new creation because You have forgiven me and paid the price on the cross. You are my Shepherd, and I am your sheep who has wandered away.

"Please forgive me for deserting You. I am no better than Your disciples were the night the soldiers came for You. They too turned their backs – only they turned theirs out of fear. I turned my back on You because I made Stewart my top priority when I should have kept You at the top. I let Stewart's will dictate my life instead of Your will. Thank You for forgiving me and reminding of who I am. I have been living with such shame and regret.

"I don't know what to do to fix this situation. If I leave Stewart, I don't know where I would go. I have no money and no friends left to call on. Yet, I know I am not alone for You are still with me. Even though I walk in darkness right now, I trust in You. Shine Your light in me and for me. Let me be a light to Stewart. He is so lost and angry. He thinks he will find happiness by being in control of everything in his life, but what he really needs is to give his control to You to find the peace that he has searched so hard to find. Draw him close to You, and please protect me for am I becoming more scared of him with every passing day. In Jesus's name, Amen."

Tara sat in silence and felt God's peace wash over her. She may have abandoned God, but He had never abandoned her. She thought of something that Wendy often had said. "Even when we are faithless, God is always faithful." Tara was sure that was from the Bible although she couldn't remember where. "Thank You for reminding me tonight that I am not alone," she whispered as she quietly opened the door and hid her Bible once more before crawling into bed.

~CHAPTER 49~

(Friday)

Jonathan smiled at Wendy as she arrived at Unplugged. He admired her unwavering faith in God. Tara and Stewart's vandalism had really hurt her not just emotionally but also financially. Her dream of being a photographer was put on hold as she had to take a part-time job again to pay the bills. She didn't have renter's insurance to cover her losses, so she was forced to save up for another professional camera. She also made the decision to drop one class so that she could pick up extra shifts to cover Tara's portion of the rent. She refused to get another roommate in hopes that Tara might one day return. Despite the unforeseen and unfair circumstances, Wendy hadn't lost her joy in the Lord. She still bounced around and praised Him as loudly and as often as she could.

Hannah had suggested that he look at Wendy as more than a friend, but he knew the truth of where his heart lay. His eyes glistened as the memory of a broken woman whose trust in people had been consistently shattered came to mind. Tara was searching for a trust and a love that would never be shattered, not realizing that only God could fulfill that desire in her. Jonathan smiled to himself. He knew exactly who had his heart, and he was willing to wait until God worked out the timing. No other woman would do! He felt that God had spoken to him directly and said, "This is the one! Wait on Me!"

Wendy loved Tara as a friend, and he loved Tara as his future bride. He chuckled to himself as he pondered what Tara's reaction would be if he ever told her that. If she was truly the woman that God had planned for him to marry, He would prepare her heart too. As the months went by with no word from Tara, there were days where he doubted that he had heard God correctly.

Only Wendy knew his true feelings. After the first week went by with no word from Tara, Wendy had an idea to start advertising in the classifieds of the local newspaper. He had been against doing that because not many people read a newspaper anymore with the advancement of technology. He had felt that an online advertisement would be better. But, Wendy had insisted, and the two of them shared the price for a daily ad that simply said, "Tara, we love you. Wendy and Jonathan."

There were days that he felt the advertisements were just a waste of money. After all, they had no idea Tara was even still in the area. For all they knew, she could be in another state. Yet, Wendy kept insisting that she felt that God wanted them to advertise specifically in the local newspaper, and so they did. As month after month went by, Jonathan was losing hope, but Wendy remained hopeful.

"This might be the day," she said in greeting. He smiled once more at her faith. She absolutely believed that God would send Tara back to them and was ready to welcome her with open arms despite the hardships she had caused. So was he for that matter.

~CHAPTER 50~

Saturday

Tara cringed and dodged a beer bottle that Stewart threw at her.

"You're so lazy," he snarled. "I asked you to walk to the liquor store and buy me some more an hour ago."

Tara bit back the retort that he had only asked her fifteen minutes ago. Instead she replied, "I'm sorry. I'll go now."

His lips curled as she put on her sneakers and began to tie the laces. "Hurry it up! Do I need to teach you a lesson?"

Tara quickly finished lacing them and stood up. "No, I'm on my way."

"Don't you dare talk to anyone while you are out!" he demanded. "Remember that I am your top priority."

Tara sighed and whispered to herself as she stepped out of the dark, dingy apartment into the glorious sunshine, "No, God is my top priority from now on."

She hurried to the store knowing that Stewart would be impatiently waiting for her to return. As she stood in line to check-out, she noticed a stack of newspapers by the register. She picked the top one up and glanced at it.

"Want it?" asked the clerk. "It's yesterday's news. Go ahead and take it."

Tara nodded a thank you and hurried out the door. Stewart liked to stay current on events. Maybe the gift of the paper would appease his mood today.

Stewart glanced up from the television as she entered and grunted a thank you for the beer. She handed him the newspaper as well.

"Where did you get this?" he asked belligerently.

"The liquor store gave it to me. It's yesterday's news, but it's news to us," she smiled. "I thought you would like it."

Stewart smiled too. "That's what it's all about," he declared. "You thought of me. That's all I have ever asked for is for you to show your love for me. Even in such a small thing as this silly newspaper."

He glanced at the front page. It depicted a story about some hikers on Blood Mountain which was located on the Appalachian Trail near Blairsville, Georgia.

"How far away do you think this is?" he asked.

"I don't know. I've never heard of Blairsville," she replied.

"Why don't you look it up on the map on my phone?" he suggested.

Tara was confused at Stewart's sudden interest as he handed her the phone. "Looks like the trailhead is about five hours away," she replied.

Stewart placed a hand on her shoulder. She tensed and then relaxed at his words. "Want to go there Monday?"

She stared at him in surprise. The last time they had gone hiking was when they visited the island the day she agreed to move out of Wendy's apartment. "Sure," she responded as she thought to herself, *Maybe God is working on his heart. This is the nicest he has been to me in months.*

Stewart smiled and stood up. "I'll run to the grocery store and buy us some steaks to grill for tonight at the park nearby. It will be a romantic evening just like when we first met."

As Stewart practically ran out the door in excitement, Tara sat on the couch and began flipping through the newspaper totally confused. *Who knew that God would use a story about hiking some mountain to change Stewart's attitude?* She had been beaten too many times to believe it would last, but she also knew that God could make the impossible possible.

Tara began to glance through the classifieds while she was waiting for Stewart to return. Reading the personal ads was always interesting to her. She paused in shock as her eyes ran over an ad that read, "Tara, we love you. Wendy and Jonathan." How many Wendy, Jonathan's, and Tara's could there be in the Savannah area? What were the chances that it wasn't meant for her but was meant for someone else?

She read it once more. "Tara, we love you. Wendy and Jonathan." *That has to be my friends! Could they really have forgiven me?* The cynical side of her took over. *Or, is this just an attempt to draw me out and throw me in jail?*

She pondered showing it to Stewart but didn't want to ruin his good mood. He had too few of those. Instead, she folded it and placed it in her Bible to look over again that evening after Stewart fell asleep.

Stewart returned in a jovial mood carrying a bag that contained a bottle of white wine and two filet mignons. She thought of asking him how they could afford such an expensive dinner when neither of them was working but hesitated. She had her suspicions on where Stewart got money, but she was afraid to confront him about it. He left at odd hours and came back with a wad of cash. She was terrified to confront him afraid that he might incriminate her in his actions somehow. He definitely was manipulative enough. She had learned to see right through him.

"You look beautiful tonight," Stewart drawled.

Tara knew that he was lying. She had lost a significant amount of weight the past few months. She looked half starved, but the truth was that she had just lost her appetite. The constant beatings had done that for her. Stewart was looking at her thoughtfully.

"Thank you," she responded. "You always look handsome."

He smiled again as she reached in the cupboard for some wine glasses and plates to take to the nearby picnic tables. "This is real nice. We haven't done this in a while. I like having you all to myself."

Tara bit back a response that he always had her to himself. There was a such thing as giving a person space. After all, absence was supposed to make the heart grow fonder. She felt suffocated by his constant need to have her by his side.

As the two sat down for dinner on the faded picnic table, Stewart reached for her hand. "I'm so happy that you agreed to go hiking with me at Blood Mountain on Monday."

Trying to please him, Tara responded, "We can go tomorrow if you want."

"Nah, it's the weekend. There will be too many people on the trails. All of the weekend warriors got to get out ya know. Monday is the better day to go. The trail should be empty. We should have the place to ourselves, and I will have you to myself."

Tara felt chills crawl up her spine at his words. It always creeped her out when he talked about having her to himself. Even with his new attitude, she was still afraid of him. She forced herself to smile in response and cut a piece of steak that was dripping in blood. Stewart knew that she didn't like her steaks rare and that the blood bothered her. She glanced at him. He was watching her intensely to see if he could get a reaction out of her. She refused to let him and ate it anyway.

After Stewart fell asleep, she once again crept toward the dresser and silently made her way into the bathroom to read the Bible some more. She decided to read Psalm 140 to see if it too spoke of God's thoughts for her. Her mouth gaped at the words in the first four verses.

"O Lord, rescue me from evil people. Protect me from those who are violent, those who plot evil in their hearts and stir up trouble all day long. Their tongues sting like a snake; the venom of a viper drips from their lips. O Lord, keep me out of the hands of the wicked. Protect me from those who are violent, for they are plotting against me."

Tara's thoughts immediately turned to Stewart. *Is God trying to warn me? Is he plotting evil against me? What is the real reason behind his change of attitude?*

The newspaper came to mind, and she pulled it out and reread the ad. "Tara, we love you. Wendy and Jonathan." *What are the chances that this could be meant for someone else?*

She carefully pondered the words in the ad. As cynical as she knew she could be, she did know without a doubt that Wendy and Jonathan were both people of integrity. If this was truly from them, it wasn't a trap to get her arrested. It was totally sincere. The question was what was she going to do about it.

She knew she owed them an apology and that she owed Wendy restitution. But, how could she face them after what she had done? How could she ask them for help to get away from Stewart after she had pushed them away? Shame paralyzed her as she began to weep. *Even if they have forgiven me, how can I face them? I know I don't deserve their forgiveness.*

~CHAPTER 51~

11 p.m. Sunday

Tara wrapped some ice cubes in a washcloth and carefully placed it on her arm as she settled on the bathroom floor of the run-down motel in Blairsville to read. She had known better than to question Stewart, but his request for her to wear the infamous red dress while hiking in the morning was ridiculous. She frowned. *Who hikes up a mountain in a dress – much less one like that?*

Stewart's eyes had gleamed with anticipation when he placed his request although she knew by now that his *requests* were actually demands. She slowly rubbed her aching arm with the cold washcloth as she stared at her cell phone she had hid in her duffel bag of clothes along with her Bible. By now, she knew the ad by heart and was curious as to if Wendy and Jonathan were a couple now. For some strange reason, the thought left her unsettled although she knew that they would be perfect for one another.

Her hand tensed around the phone. *Just do it! Make the call!* She turned the bathroom fan on to drown out the noise and finally pushed the send button on Wendy's number. As it rang, she began to pray. "Let her not answer. Please let it go to voicemail. I can't face her. I don't think I can handle it if she rejects me."

The phone continued to ring as the seconds ticked by. Tara's pounding heart eased up as Wendy's voicemail answered. "Hey, you have reached Wendy. I'm busy living life right now, but I will call you back as soon as I can. Have a wonderful day and remember Jesus loves you!" Tara smiled at Wendy's voice as she began to haltingly leave a message.

"Wendy, it's Tara. I saw an ad in the paper and thought maybe it was you. Umm, if it wasn't, then I guess this may sound weird. I, well, I miss you, and umm I'm really sorry. I don't expect you to forgive me; heck I can't even forgive myself. But, I really miss our friendship, and I would give anything to have it back. I'm scared Wendy. Stewart isn't the person I thought he was. I can't please him, and he hits me frequently. He wants to take me up Blood Mountain to go hiking tomorrow, and I don't know, he just scares me anymore. I wish you would have answered. I really miss you. Maybe you didn't want to talk to me. I totally understand. I just saw that ad and really hoped it was you." Her voice broke completely. "I'm so sorry, Wendy. I'm so sorry." Her hand trembled as she hung up the phone.

She flipped through her Bible to the Psalms and settled on Psalm 40.

"I waited patiently for the Lord to help me, and He turned to me and heard my cry. He lifted me out of the pit of despair, out of the mud and the mire. He set my feet on solid ground and steadied me as I walked along. He has given me a new song to sing, a hymn of praise to our God. Many will see what He has done and be amazed. They will put their trust in the Lord."

Tara sighed as she began to pray. "Father, I feel so alone. I know I was praying that Wendy wouldn't answer her phone, but I wish she had. Even if she had yelled at me like I deserve, I know that she would never purposefully hurt me. I am stuck deep in a pit – one I willingly set my feet into. Please rescue me somehow. I don't know what to do or where to go. Please give me a new song to sing. Maybe I should just leave Stewart after hiking tomorrow and turn myself in. Being in prison would be better than the life I live now which is basically a prison of my own making. Direct me. Be my light and show me which direction to take. I praise You in advance for getting me out of this pit and giving me a new life. Amen."

~CHAPTER 52~

6 a.m. Monday

Wendy's heart leaped when she noticed that she had a missed call from Tara who must have called after she fell asleep. She sipped on her morning coffee as she quickly connected to her voicemail to hear the message. She then joyously texted Jonathan, Travis, and Hannah who had all been praying unceasingly for Tara. Her fingers flew over the tiny keyboard as she typed out:

"I heard from Tara. Come over quick!"

The friends gathered in Wendy's apartment as she played Tara's message over the speaker phone. Tears filled Hannah's eyes.

"This is worth being late for class over! I'm so glad she called, but I wish she had told you where she was in the message."

Travis looked pointedly at Wendy. "Have you called her back yet?"

Wendy's hand flew to her mouth. "Oh no!" she exclaimed. "I was so excited to hear from her and wanted to share that with you. I didn't even think about it." She quickly reached for her phone and dialed Tara's number. She knew that the line was active because the bill for it still came to her apartment every month. She had been paying for it in hopes that Tara would one day call. To her disappointment, it went straight to a recording. "I'm sorry. You have reached a number that has requested not to accept your call." The tinny recorded voice hung up with a resounding click.

Wendy stared at her friends in dismay. "I can't contact her. She still has me blocked!"

Travis pulled his phone out. "Let me try," he said as he dialed her number with the same result.

Jonathan and Hannah tried as well. Disappointment showed on their faces. They were back to square one with no way of knowing where Tara was and no way of reaching her. Wendy began to sniff. "We were so close."

"We have to put this in God's hands," Jonathan said as he ran his fingers nervously through his hair. "There is nothing we can physically do. We know that God is working. She saw our ad and responded! That's a start!"

Travis stood up. "Why does Blood Mountain sound so familiar?"

"I don't know," said Hannah. "Where do you think it's at? I've never heard of it."

Travis hurried over to Wendy's computer and typed the words "Blood Mountain" into the search engine. Two locations showed up. One was in Blairsville, Georgia, about five hours away from Savannah while the other was in a remote area of Colorado in the San Juan Mountain Range.

"Maybe it sounded familiar to me because it's located on the Appalachian Trail," Travis said as he quickly scanned the search engine's results. Suddenly, several news articles caught his eyes that contained the title of "Murder on Blood Mountain."

"Hey guys, listen to this," Travis said as he began to read.

"The body of a young college student was found Tuesday by a small group of hikers who were looking for a geocache on Blood Mountain. The victim, Rosemary Miller, appeared to be strangled to death and suffered many contusions on her body which appear to be the result of physical abuse. Rosemary Miller, a student at Mountain High University near Silverton, Colorado, has no immediate family and was on a full scholarship at the university.

Her closest friends said that she was active at her church until she met a man named Vince on the internet who seemed to suddenly occupy all of her time. After only knowing him a short period, she withdrew from school, church, and her friends. Nobody heard from her since then until her body was found late Tuesday morning. It is believed that she died on Monday from strangulation. If anyone has any information as to the whereabouts of this man named Vince or if anyone saw her on Blood Mountain on Sunday or Monday, please call the Silverton Sheriff's office."

Chills ran up Travis's spine as he read. "That was three years ago. When did Stewart tell Tara that Rosemary died?"

Wendy's eyes were round in shock. "About three years ago! You don't think Stewart is Vince, do you?" she asked quietly. "Did they ever catch the killer?"

Travis felt tears come to his eyes as he scrolled through the search engine results and finally replied. "No, it doesn't appear so. It seems to be an unsolved murder." Travis picked up his phone. "It lists a number for the Silverton Sheriff's Office. I'm going to give them a call and see if maybe they have a picture of this Vince guy that they can email me."

As Travis made the call, Wendy grasped Hannah's hand tightly. "It can't be. I mean we knew Stewart was manipulative, but a killer? Surely, we are jumping to conclusions."

Jonathan solemnly replied, "We all heard Tara's message. He is beating her just like this Vince guy beat Rosemary. I think Vince and Stewart are the same person." His heart skipped a beat. "And, he is taking Tara to Blood Mountain today. He is going to try to kill her just like he killed Rosemary – on a Monday on Blood Mountain."

"Which Blood Mountain?" Wendy asked incredulously. "The one here in Georgia, or the one all the way out in Colorado."

"My bet would be the one here in Georgia if they are still living here," Jonathan said. "We have to find a way to stop him!" He reached for the phone that Travis held to his ear and motioned that he wanted to talk as well. Travis passed him the phone, and Jonathan began to share his fears with the Silverton Sheriff's Office as Travis hurried back to the computer.

"They emailed me a composite of Vince," he explained as he quickly typed in his password. The friends gathered around as the picture downloaded and stared in horror. Stewart was Vince!

Jonathan confirmed the connection with the Silverton Sheriff's Office and assured them that the composite they sent was indeed the man known to them as Stewart. Since there were two Blood Mountains in the United States, they would have to get an agency from Colorado and one in Georgia on the lookout. Jonathan described Stewart's bright red Mustang to the officials knowing that there was no guarantee that he was still driving it. A man as manipulative as Stewart would probably have ditched the vehicle by now.

Heart pounding, the friends sat down on Wendy's couch and began to pray. "Father, we are scared and worried for our friend Tara. We pray Your words in Psalm 91 over her. We ask that You will be her refuge and her place of safety. Rescue her from Stewart's trap, and let evil not touch her. Protect her wherever she is. Let her know and feel Your love. If Stewart's intentions on taking her to Blood Mountain are evil as we suspect, we pray that You will somehow protect her from all harm and lead the officials to her in time. Amen."

As Jonathan finished praying, he jumped to his feet and ran to the computer. "I'm not waiting around. I have to do something. I'm looking up how to get to Blood Mountain – the one here in Georgia. If she is there, I want to be too!"

Wendy nodded in agreement. "I'm coming with you!" she exclaimed.

"Me too," Travis and Hannah said in unison.

In a matter of minutes, the friends jumped in Travis's SUV and hit the road for the five hour drive to the Blood Mountain Trailhead.

~CHAPTER 53~

7 a.m. Monday

Shivering from the morning chill as she stood with Stewart at Blood Mountain's trailhead, Tara was thankful that he had relented about the red dress. Since they were getting an early start to beat the crowd, he agreed to let her dress in sweats and change into the dress at the summit.

"I want everyone to know you are a sophisticated lady," Stewart proudly declared as she carefully folded the hated dress and placed it in her backpack. If it kept the peace with him, then it was worth it. She had decided after a long, sleepless night in the dingy motel room, that this was the last day she would spend with Stewart. As soon as they got back to their home, she would leave him and take her chances with Wendy. If Wendy didn't want anything to do with her or turned her in to the authorities, that was okay. Anything was better than the constant abuse she endured.

The two of them quietly read the historical marker that described the history of Blood Mountain. There was a huge battle between the Creeks and the Cherokees over control of the territory. The conflict was so major that it was said that the water literally ran red with blood. Thus, the highest peak on the Georgia section of the Appalachian Trail, standing at a lofty 4,458 feet in elevation, was named Blood Mountain in memory of the fateful battle.

Tara stared in horror at the marker while Stewart seemed to smile in glee. She frowned at him as she tried to understand how he could think a battle that horrible was funny. She felt sorry for those brave warriors who fought so hard for the territory only to be forced out years later by the white men along the infamous Trail of Tears.

Tara shivered again as Stewart placed his arm around her shoulder and nudged her to start walking up the steep, rugged path towards the summit a few miles away.

~CHAPTER 54~

11:45 a.m. Monday

Travis whipped his SUV into the parking lot of the Blood Mountain trailhead which was filled with police vehicles. Wendy hopped out and ran over to the nearest officer.

"Did you find her?" she quickly asked.

The officer stared at her as Jonathan stepped to the side of Wendy.

"That's our friend you are looking for," he exclaimed. "We are the ones who called in that she might be here. We came as quick as we could."

The officer's hardened expression softened. "We haven't heard anything yet. There is no vehicle here that matches the description. We sent a crew up on the trail with a picture of Tara and a composite sketch of the man you know as Stewart and are waiting to hear back. They haven't been spotted on the trail, but they could be hiking somewhere off-trail. In that case, it will be a lot harder to find them, if they are even here. There's not any real proof that they are at our Blood Mountain. They could very well be at the one in Colorado."

Travis bit his lip in frustration. "What about a helicopter search?"

The officer shook his head. "Since we aren't sure if they are even here at this location, we can't justify that. If we knew what in particular she is wearing today, we would at least have something to go on. But, out of the hikers that we have met, not a single one remembers a couple that answers their description. A helicopter search at this point would be useless. We simply have nothing to go on."

Wendy looked sadly at the officer. "Are you sure you have asked everyone on the trail?"

He nodded. "Yes, we haven't closed the trail because once again we aren't even sure that she is here. However, we are on the lookout and have asked every hiker that we have come across to notify us if they see a couple matching their descriptions. We are taking this seriously, however. We have about twenty police officers interspersed around the mountain right now searching for them."

Travis clenched his fist. "I think they are here. Colorado is too far away. Stewart could have changed vehicles. Is it okay if we look around as well?"

The officer nodded once more and stepped aside to allow them to pass.

~CHAPTER 55~

1 p.m. Monday

Tara stumbled over a rock as she begged Stewart once more to slow down. They had been walking off-trail for almost three hours after reaching the summit of the 2.5 mile trail. To Tara's surprise, there was a two-room stone shelter at the top of the mountain that allowed her some privacy to change into the dress. After stuffing her sweats in her pack, she had expected to eat lunch while enjoying the view. Instead, Stewart had insisted that they find a more secluded place to eat because he heard nearby voices coming up the trail to the top.

Instead of going down the trail, Stewart began making his own way over the boulders until he found a small shelter cave that smelled as if an animal had recently took refuge in it. There, Stewart finally declared it was lunch time.

He looked at her fondly as she removed the peanut butter and jelly sandwiches she had made for the trek from her backpack along with some peanut butter crackers. He ran his finger over her arm and smiled in appreciation.

"Thank you for wearing the dress for me. I know it would have been more comfortable to have had lunch up on the summit, but this way, I get you all by myself. I want to remember every moment."

Tara looked at him quizzically. "Remember every moment? Are you going somewhere?"

Stewart smiled again. "No," he replied. "Not me."

Tara was beginning to feel creeped out by Stewart. "Good," she said as she patted his hand. "I wouldn't want you to go anywhere."

Stewart slowly and methodically took a few bites of his sandwich then turned to her.

"You wouldn't be thinking of going anywhere? Would you?"

"Of course not!" Tara sputtered.

He grinned again as his eyes took on the crazy look she knew so well. She scooted back to block the blow but didn't move quickly enough. His fist connected with her ribs and knocked her backwards.

Cringing from the pain, she looked warily at him as he reached into his pocket and pulled out a folded piece of paper. He slowly opened it knowing that he had her full attention as he mockingly read:

"Who I Am In Christ. I am beloved. I am a child of God. I am a new creation." He ripped the paper into shreds as Tara stared in fear.

"I told you that I must come first at all times. I will not come second in your life to your friends, your family if you had one, or even to God. I come first!" he screamed. "I always come first! This is from Wendy, isn't it?" he spit her name. "I found it on the floor in the bathroom Friday morning. When did you contact her?"

"I didn't," protested Tara. "She gave me that a long time ago. It must have fallen out of my Bible."

"Your Bible," Stewart spewed. "I told you to get rid of that a long time ago. Have you been hiding it from me?"

Tara nodded as she thoughtfully replied. "What do you have against God, Stewart? I thought you told me that you were a Christian when we met. Don't you know that Christ always has to come first? Not us! In fact..." She stopped herself and stood up as she backed away from Stewart once more. His eyes were open wide, and she could see the rage in them. Caught in fear, she began to run.

~CHAPTER 56~

1:30 p.m. Monday

Travis smiled at Hannah despite the seriousness of the situation. She looked totally at ease as she carefully studied the terrain from atop the tree that she had climbed. Hannah was the most experienced in the outdoors and had presumed that they should skirt the mountainside in their search since the officials had already checked the normal route. The group had readily agreed since the news article stated that Rosemary's body was found in a remote area off-trail. Two deputies accompanied them presumably to keep them from getting lost although it was quite evident who was disoriented and who was not. Hannah's skills in the outdoors were exceptional.

"I see something," Hannah shouted as she carefully shimmied down the tree. "There's something bright red hanging from a bush below us to the right. Travis quickly turned but didn't see anything. Then again, he didn't have the viewpoint that she had from high in the tree. The group quickly followed her lead as the deputies began questioning them.

"Does Tara own anything bright red?"

Wendy paused as her eyes lit up. "Yes, sort of. Stewart bought her a ridiculous red dress. It was so short and skin tight on her. I can't see her hiking in it though unless Stewart made her wear it. You don't think..." Her words trailed off at the thought as they pushed past an overgrowth of kudzu and thorn bushes. Hannah paused every few minutes to check the bearings on her compass then suddenly squealed in excitement. A large strip of red material clung to some thorns on a bush.

Wendy stared at the deputies as they examined it.

"It looks like someone ran through here and got snagged up on the thorns some. There are little droplets of blood on the leaves and on the ground. I'm going to call this in." The deputy reached for his walkie talkie as his partner continued to study the ground for clues.

"It looks like she went this way," he pointed. "I can't see much ahead of me because of all this dense overgrowth. What did the terrain look like past this?" he asked Hannah.

"This is just a small patch. It will open up in just a minute to a more rocky area."

The deputy sighed in relief as he carefully made his way through the overgrown bushes. This looked like prime snake terrain. It was easy to spot the route because of the blood droplets. Whoever had ran through here must have been cut up pretty good.

~CHAPTER 57 ~

1:45 p.m. Monday

After thrashing through thorn bushes and stumbling over rocks, Tara panted for breath as she hid among the boulders. She stared in fascination at the droplets of blood dripping from the ragged cuts in her skin. The thorn bushes she had frantically ran through sliced her like knives. As she sought to regain her breath, she gripped her throbbing side. The vicious punch was sure to leave a nasty bruise. She trembled as she heard Stewart's angry voice and heavy footsteps come closer. Heart pounding, she begged God to make her invisible. "Hide me among the clefts of these rocks," she prayed in desperation as she realized that she no longer had the strength to run. Catching sight of Stewart's leering face nearby, she curled herself into a ball and waited for the beating to come as she thought to herself: *Why is my trust always shattered?*

Stewart's eyes gleamed as he spotted a smear of blood on a boulder. He had been searching for Tara for quite a while and was getting tired of the hunt. Finally, his persistence would pay off. He carefully looked around for more evidence of blood. She must have run right through a thorn thicket. He paused as he tauntingly called, "You can run, but you can't hide. I will find you. I will always find you!" He spotted some more blood and took a step forward smiling as he saw Tara pressed into a gap in a boulder cowering in fear.

He stretched his foot out and kicked her head hard as he roughly pulled her out of the stone shelter by her arm. He smiled as he heard her gasp in pain. She deserved it for making him search so long for her. He rolled her over so that he could see her eyes open wide in terror as he roared.

"All I ever wanted was to be your number one. I wanted to be your top priority, but you just didn't love me enough. Rosemary didn't either. Nobody ever has. I grew up being second rate. The military was more important to my family than I was. It didn't matter to them that I didn't want to constantly move and that it was hard to make friends. All they cared about was my dad's job. Nobody cared about me!" He kicked her again in the side as she moaned in pain.

"I just wanted to be first. Is that so hard to ask? Was it too much to ask you to sacrifice your friends and your religion for me? Was it? Why couldn't you just love me like I deserve? I know the Bible. I grew up in a church. I can quote verse after verse to you. But, you know what, none of it matters. If there is a God, He sure doesn't care about me. You think you had it so bad growing up. You don't know what I went through. My old man knocked me around all the time until I finally ran away. I was never good enough. I couldn't do things right enough for him. I could never please him. So, he beat me in the name of God. Spare the rod, spoil the child! That's in your Bible you know! And, God just stood by and let it happen over and over again. I wanted to take you from God just like I tried to take Rosemary. I thought if I could convince you to put me first that you would forsake the God that you claim to love. He doesn't deserve your allegiance; I do." Stewart began to angrily weep.

Stewart put his hands around Tara's neck and began to squeeze. "I'm sorry, Tara. I liked you. I did. All I asked was for you to put me first." Tara's eyes began to bulge as he pressed harder on her neck. Her hands frantically tried to pull his off of her to no avail.

~CHAPTER 58~

1:50 p.m. Monday

Jonathan stared in horror at the figure in the distance in front of him. It looked like Stewart was bent over squeezing someone. "Tara!" he screamed. The deputies began to run. "Stop!" they demanded as they withdrew their handguns from the holsters.

Stewart whirled and released his grip on Tara as he faced the deputies. He tackled the one closest to him and grabbed the deputy's gun after punching him in the face. Stewart pointed the gun at the deputy's forehead as he sat on top of him. The other deputy froze, unsure of what to do. He didn't want to jeopardize his partner further.

Deputy Smith closed his eyes feeling that this was the end and decided to make an effort to fight. He lifted an arm and punched Stewart hard in the stomach. Startled, Stewart loosened his grip on the gun just enough for Deputy Smith to wrestle him onto the ground. As Deputy Smith fought for control of the gun, Stewart turned the gun on himself and fired. His body slumped as a momentary silence reigned.

Wendy and Jonathan ran to Tara who lay motionless on the ground breathing rapidly. Wendy stroked her head while Jonathan stood awkwardly to the side. Tara looked at the two of them in amazement. "You came," she gasped wonderingly.

Travis and Hannah approached holding hands. "We all did," they declared as they looked down at their outstretched hands. In the heat of the moment, he had grabbed hers, and neither had let go.

EPILOGUE

~CHAPTER 59~

(FRIDAY, 4 P.M.)

Tara lay in the hospital bed and counted her blessings. Her head injury, bruised neck, and broken ribs had needed time to heal. Heavily medicated for the pain, she hadn't been awake much in the past few days. Several policemen had come in and out trying to ask her questions, but she had trouble focusing. The last few days seemed a blur. She had sensed Wendy in the room a few times stroking her hair and praying over her. And, someone else had been there too. A man who sounded a lot like Jonathan begging God over and over to let her live so that he could marry her. She laughed at the thought. *Jonathan sure wouldn't want me for a wife. I'm definitely not a pastor's wife material.* She shook her head. *I must be imagining things, besides Wendy and Jonathan are clearly an item.*

There was a light knock on the door as Wendy quickly entered. She was followed by Travis and Hannah who looked surprisingly like a couple. Travis had his arm around Hannah's shoulders. Jonathan, carrying a vase of flowers, closed the door behind them.

"How are you feeling?" Wendy asked as she lightly touched Tara on her bruised forehead.

"I'm okay," Tara said as tears spilled from her eyes. "I just can't believe y'all are here. If it wasn't for you, I don't think I would be alive."

Wendy's eyes glistened. "It was a God thing! He orchestrated the details. I felt God's urging to advertise in the personals of the local newspaper, and Jonathan helped me with the costs. God led you to our ad in the newspaper and convicted you to call me. If you hadn't mentioned in your message that you were going to Blood Mountain..." Wendy's voice trailed off. "It was all God, Tara. He worked out all of the details because He loves you."

Travis spoke up as he looked lovingly at Hannah. "And, God blessed Hannah with the outdoor skills she needed. It was she who insisted that we skirt the mountainside off-trail. She led the way – with God's guidance."

Jonathan stood solemnly next to the bed. He had interceded in prayer over Tara by her bedside the past few days for her recovery and confessed his love for her to God. He didn't think that Tara would remember it though as out of it as she had been. He still felt that Tara was the woman that God had in store for him, but he also felt that it wasn't time yet. He wanted to make sure of where her heart was with God before he admitted his love to her. He didn't want to be a stumbling block for her Christian growth. She needed to put God first in her life, not him. He smiled fondly at her as he said,

"The doctors said that you can leave – as long as you agree to stay in a wheelchair. They don't want you walking yet. We would like to take you to Unplugged with us – that is, if you would like to come."

Tara looked at the group in astonishment. Not a single person had mentioned the elephant in the room. She decided to get it out in the open. If she was going to jail, then she wanted to get it over with.

"What happens after Unplugged?" she asked quietly.

Wendy stared at her quizzically. "What do you mean?"

Tears filled Tara's eyes again. "Nobody is mentioning what I did. I treated all of you horribly, especially you Wendy. I deserve to go to jail for what I have done. I stood by and let Stewart vandalize your stuff knowing how much it meant to you. I even helped him at his urging. I don't deserve your kindness. I don't deserve normalcy like going to Unplugged with you. And, I sure don't deserve your friendship. Y'all dropped everything to look for me on Blood Mountain. I appreciate it, and I don't think I would be alive if you hadn't. But, I don't deserve it."

Tears streamed down Tara's face as Wendy handed her a tissue. The room was quiet for a moment, then Wendy grasped her hand. "Tara, it's true. You don't deserve it. You were horrible, and you don't deserve grace. None of us do. Yet, that is what God has done for each and every one of us, so how can we not show it to you? You are our friend, and we love you. Love covers all wrong. Love forgives. You aren't going to go to jail. I dropped the charges. I only wanted the police to find you so that you could be safe. There is no more warrant out for you."

"But, what about the damage that I've done?"

Wendy sniffed as she replied. "It's only things, Tara. We have you back. That is what is important."

Travis, never one to mince words, quickly added. "Although, I do think that you should make restitution to Wendy for everything that was destroyed. It really set her back financially. These last few months have been really hard on her."

Wendy looked at Travis as if to shush him, but he continued. "Forgiveness doesn't wipe away the damage that was done, Tara. You need to make it right. We estimated the damage to be around nine hundred dollars. I know that you can't pay that all at once, but maybe you can give Wendy a certain amount each week until it's paid."

Tara immediately agreed as Wendy added. "The money is not important, Tara. Having you back is what is important. I have missed you. We all have. I am not going to legally demand for you to make restitution. I want that to come from your heart."

Tara continued to sob. "I will, Wendy. I will pay you back for everything – not just the damage. I have taken advantage of you since I met you. I won't anymore. I promise. I'm not sure why you are still my friend, but I am so thankful to God that you are. I deserve jail, but you have given me freedom, forgiveness, and love. I will never forget that. When I was hiding from Stewart on that mountain, my first thought to myself was *"Why is my trust always shattered?"*

But, it's not always shattered. You have never shattered my trust. You have been there for me and loved me when I wasn't loveable or easy to be around. You have shown me God's love by your actions. You don't just spout the words; you live it. All of you do! I have spent all of my life being a victim and feeling sorry for myself. Sure, I had a lot of things to feel sorry for. Life was unfair to me. But, it's been unfair to you too, yet you have responded differently. I don't see you, Wendy, living in bitterness over the death of your fiancé or over your past with your grandfather. You embrace each day with thankfulness and praise. I have been a victim, but you have been a survivor. You led me to

God when I didn't want to be led. You showed me His love. I'm so thankful for you! I thought about calling you so much in the past six months, but I was so afraid that you hated me for what I've done."

Wendy smiled at Tara. "I could never hate you. I love you as a sister." She wrinkled her nose. "Now, let's get you dressed and ready to leave this place. The smell of disinfectant that lingers here is getting to me. Will you go to Unplugged, please?"

Tara agreed as the tears flowed down her face once more.

~CHAPTER 60~

10 p.m. Friday

Tara smiled as her friends helped her into Travis's SUV as they left New Life. The message at Unplugged was based on the love chapter in 1 Corinthians 13. Jonathan had spoken on what love is, and what love isn't.

"Love is not selfish," he had said in opening. "Love does not demand its own way. Love is not manipulative. Love is not abuse. If someone is abusing you verbally or physically, that is not love no matter what they say. This past week, I watched a man kill himself rather than face the consequences from what he had done. I know many of you have read about this in the headlines or seen this on the news. I don't want to go into the details. What I will say is that this man had a mixed up concept of love. I don't think this man was shown love as a child. As a result, he wanted to be worshipped. He wanted to be loved above everything else, including God.

"Well, we read in the Bible about a certain fallen angel who wanted to be worshipped as well. Turn with me to Isaiah 14 verses 12-15." He waited until the rustling of the pages stopped, then he began to read."

"How you are fallen from heaven, O shining star, son of the morning! You have been thrown down to the earth, you who destroyed the nations of the world. For you said to yourself, I will ascend to heaven and set my throne above God's stars. I will preside on the mountain of the gods far away in the north. I will climb to the highest heavens and be like the Most High. Instead, you will be brought down the place of the dead, down to its lowest depths."

Jonathan paused as he took a sip of water. "You see, Satan wanted to be God. Satan's position according to Ezekiel 28:14 was to guard the throne of God . He had the highest of all positions. Yet, he didn't want to settle for being God's servant. He wanted to be served. Even though he was the created, he wanted to be number one instead of God. Just like us, Satan was created with free will. He had a choice. Instead of being joyful in his assignment, he chose to rebel. He couldn't stand it that God received all the love and glory instead of him. Pride and jealousy were the reasons for Satan's fall.

"The same goes for us. When we let pride and jealousy consume our thoughts, we have taken our focus off of God and turned it upon ourselves. There is nothing inherently wrong with wanting to be loved. The problem comes when we demand it above everything else. As Christians, God needs to be at the top. He deserves all praise, honor, and glory. Not us! Sadly, this man didn't understand that. To him, God was just words on a page. He didn't understand the truth of God's love. This man had a mixed-up concept of what love really is. He thought love was manipulation and games. He thought love was abuse. He thought love was putting yourself first and others second. He is not the only one to think that way. There are many in the world today who don't truly understand the concept of what love really is. The Bible explains it in 1 Corinthians 13. Turn with me there."

Jonathan began to read. "If I could speak all the languages of earth and of angels, but didn't love others, I would only be a noisy gong or a clanging cymbal. If I had the gift of prophecy, and I understood all of God's secret plans and possessed all knowledge, and if I had such faith that I could move mountains, but didn't love others, I would be nothing. If I gave everything I have to the poor and even sacrificed my body, I could boast about it; but if I didn't love others, I would have gained nothing.

"Love is patient and kind. Love is not jealous or boastful or proud or rude. It does not demand its own way. It is not irritable, and it keeps no record of being wronged. It does not rejoice about injustice but rejoices whenever the truth wins out. Love never gives up, never loses faith, is always hopeful, and endures through every circumstance.

"Prophecy and speaking in unknown languages and special knowledge will become useless. But love will last forever! Now our knowledge is partial and incomplete, and even the gift of prophecy reveals only one part of the whole picture! But when full understanding comes, these partial things will become useless.

"When I was a child, I spoke and thought and reasoned as a child. But when I grew up, I put away childish things. Now we see things imperfectly as in a cloudy mirror, but then we will see everything with perfect clarity. All that I know now is partial and incomplete, but then I will know everything completely, just as God now knows me completely.

"Three things will last forever – faith, hope, and love – and the greatest of these is love."

Jonathan glanced slowly around the room as he made his final point. "Jesus loved with a perfect love. If you want to understand what love is, look to the example of Jesus. Pray for a heart that loves God and his people more. If you are looking for a trust that will never be shattered, you won't find that in people. No matter how good their intentions, people will let you down even if they didn't mean to. Yet, Jesus will never let you down. He will never shatter your trust because He is the epitome of love. He is the creator of love! He is love!"

His face grew solemn as he closed. "If you are wondering if a relationship is right for you, ask yourself these questions. Is she patient with me? Is he kind to me? Is he constantly jealous? Is she rude to me on a regular basis? Does he demand his own way? Is he manipulative? Is she constantly irritated at me? Does he keep a record of wrongs that he is ready to recite?"

Tara smiled as she remembered the discussion that followed during group time on the question of "what is love?" She wished that she had truly understood that before she met Stewart. She had been desperate for what she had thought was love not realizing that the Bible was very clear on its true meaning and that her friends were positive examples of it. Stewart didn't love her. He loved the power he had over her. The power she had given him. She was sad that his life had ended the way it did. He would have to answer to God for his actions. But, she knew that she had never really loved him either. She had been in love with the idea of being loved and being prized.

She smiled as Wendy buckled her seatbelt for her and reminded herself, "I am the apple of God's eyes!"

Tara wasn't sure where her friends were taking her and was surprised when they pulled up to the apartment that she used to share with Wendy. Maybe Wendy was going to let her crash there for the night. She hoped her new roommate wouldn't mind the intrusion.

Jonathan carefully pushed her wheelchair up the handicap accessible ramp to Wendy's floor as Travis held the door open for them. She looked questioningly at Wendy as she noticed the room was filled with flowers and balloons that read "Welcome Home!"

Wendy took Tara's hand as she said, "Welcome home, Tara. I'm so glad you're back!"

Tara shook her head in confusion. "But, your roommate?"

"Is right here." Wendy finished as she patted Tara's shoulder. "I didn't get another roommate. I kept the room for you in hopes that you would one day come back."

Tara's eyes filled with tears once more. "Love never gives up," she cried as she stretched her arms out to embrace Wendy.

Wendy added, "And, loves forgives all debts. Welcome home!"

Jonathan smiled as tears threatened to fall from his eyes as well. *"And, love is always hopeful,"* he thought.

~AFTERWORD~

This book is a work of fiction. However, the issues in this book are unfortunately all too real. Below is some information about sexual abuse, domestic abuse, and suicide prevention. Please visit the websites listed for further details. Break the silence! Speak up!

Sexual abuse:

Sexual abuse is not often spoken about in our society. Victims shoulder guilt and shame while tending to blame themselves for the actions of the perpetrator. It is common for victims to struggle with low self-esteem, eating disorders, depression, and have trouble maintaining healthy relationships.

If you have been a victim of sexual assault or abuse, I urge you to speak out as loudly and as often as possible. The more you share your story the less power it will have over you. Break the silence! Find a person you can trust and tell them your story. It will initially be the hardest thing that you have ever done. However, you will find that God not only uses your willingness to be vulnerable to bring healing in your life but also in the lives of others.

If someone shares with you that she has been sexually victimized, reassure that person that you can be trusted and that knowing her story doesn't change the way you think of her. Let her know that she is not alone and be willing to listen to her story as often as she needs to share. Most importantly, show support by conveying that it's not her fault and that you believe her. It takes a lot of courage to break the silence.

RAINN (Rape, Abuse, and Incest National Network) operates the National Sexual Assault Hotline and has programs dedicated to helping survivors of sexual assault. Visit www.rainn.org for more information.

Domestic Abuse:

The following information comes directly from the National Domestic Violence Hotline (www.thehotline.org). Visit their website for more resources and to get help.

"It's not always easy to tell at the beginning of a relationship if it will become abusive.

In fact, many abusive partners may seem absolutely perfect in the early stages of a relationship. Possessive and controlling behaviors don't always appear overnight, but rather emerge and intensify as the relationship grows.

Domestic violence doesn't look the same in every relationship because every relationship is different. But one thing most abusive relationships have in common is that the abusive partner does many different kinds of things to have more power and control over their partners.

Domestic violence can happen to anyone of any race, age, sexual orientation, religion or gender.

It can happen to couples who are married, living together or who are dating. Domestic violence affects people of all socioeconomic backgrounds and education levels.

Abuse is a repetitive pattern of behaviors to maintain power and control over an intimate partner. These are behaviors that physically harm, arouse fear, prevent a partner from doing what they wish or force them to behave in ways they do not want. Abuse includes the use of physical and sexual violence, threats and intimidation, emotional abuse and economic deprivation. Many of these different forms of abuse can be going on at any one time."

Suicide Prevention:

According to the National Institute of Mental Health, over 41,000 people commit suicide each year which makes it the 10th leading cause of death overall. There is a National Suicide Prevention Lifeline at 1-800-273-TALK with trained crisis workers standing by willing to listen and offer help. Visit www.suicidepreventionlifeline.org for more information regarding risk factors and warning signs. If someone you know is talking about suicide, be direct, be ready to listen, and most importantly be available to show support. The above website offers more tips on how to help someone contemplating suicide.

Made in the USA
San Bernardino, CA
27 February 2018